Kingdom Rattus

Kingdom Rattus

The Rodent Chronicles

A Novel By Michael A. Novelli

iUniverse, Inc.
New York   Bloomington

Kingdom Rattus
The Rodent Chronicles

This is a work of fiction. All of the characters, names, incidents, organizations, and dialogue in this novel are either the products of the author's imagination or are used fictitiously.

iUniverse books may be ordered through booksellers or by contacting:

iUniverse
1663 Liberty Drive
Bloomington, IN 47403
www.iuniverse.com
1-800-Authors (1-800-288-4677)

ISBN: 978-1-4401-5759-2 (sc)
ISBN: 978-1-4401-5757-8 (dj)
ISBN: 978-1-4401-5758-5 (ebk)

Library of Congress Control Number: 2009932636

Printed in the United States of America

iUniverse rev. date: 09/10/2009

There was no point in fighting-on our side or theirs. We all had a beautiful momentum; we were riding the crest of a high and beautiful wave.... So now, less than five years later, you can go up on a steep hill in Las Vegas and look west, and with the right kind of eyes you can almost see the high-water mark-that place where the wave finally broke, and rolled back.

Dr. Hunter S. Thompson, "Fear And Loathing In Las Vegas"

For Katie & Amanda

Introduction:

||||||||||||||||||||||||||||||||||||||||||||||||||||||||||||||||||||||||||||||||||||||||||||||||||||||||||||||||||

In a windswept metropolis just south of Richmond, in the great park that is the hallmark of the city, is a large lake. Two main tribes, the Marrow-Vinjians and the Least-Rogonians, live on opposite sides of the lake. Seldom visited by humans anymore, the park is almost entirely the domain of the rats. The Marrow-Vinjians, named for their current king, are a "civilized" tribe, who mimic the humans and seek to force the other tribes in their empire to follow suit. The Least-Rogonians are a mystic society, more rural, but whose power and wealth was built on the back of slavery. All throughout the city and underground, beneath the lake, the war between them for dominance is felt in every corner and every shadow.

During the great historical nothingness that predates our story, there was an era when the inhabitants of the underground were ruled by a race of god hares with hawk-like talons, known collectively as the Warren. From their home in what is now known as the Land of the Blind—but was then known as Warren's Burrow—they lived in seclusion and rarely ventured among the rats who paid them homage. On those rare occasions that the hares left their burrow, they'd traditionally assume the form of a mortal rodent and pass themselves off as beggars and such–not unlike the human gods. Since many generations passed without verified sightings, many rats ceased to believe in them.

Without believers, gods, omnipotent as they are, eventually lose strength and fade away – particularly ones who are not immortal, as hares were not. Realizing this, they convened and decided that a grand and noble gesture would restore the faith of the rodents who lived beneath the lake. According to legend, it was their chieftain, Hurucan, who had the perfect solution.

In the millennium that rodents had lived beneath the lake, they had dug hundreds of miles of labyrinthine tunnels almost a mile beneath the earth's surface. Finally it became apparent that, for all the work the pioneers had done to reinforce them, the lack of dirt would eventually cause the bottom of the lake to cave in and would bring down an epic flood that would most likely drown the majority of the inhabitants before they could swim the three days' travel to the surface for air.

Summoning his most powerful mystics, Tepeu and Gukumatz, Hurucan ventured down to the deepest territory of all: Metnal, a cavern so far below the ground that it was believed anyone who dared to seek it would never come back. Sinking his talons into the cold dirt, Hurucan sent his power seeping into the mud and clay and drew from it a mighty Ionic column that shot up through the many layers of soil, straight to the highest tunnel beneath the direct center of the lake. There the Romanesque structure began to emit a strange green glow, and as the glow expanded like a titanic umbrella, the earth around it shifted and changed, and all of the many miles the rats had dug were bathed in its power. That column came to be known as the Citadel.

Halfway up from the base, the column had passed through the keep of a small, insignificant tribe known as the Strega. Never large to begin with, they were dying out with each passing year and were considered worthless by all the other tribes. But having been closest to the Citadel when it soared upward, the entire tribe was transformed by both the column and the aftershock into a new race of rats the likes of which no one had ever seen. They shriveled almost to skeletons, and their eyes grew large and cat-like, their spines bent, and their bodies contorted so badly they looked more like insects than rats. Tepeu and Gukumatz wanted nothing to do with the pitiful wretches, but Hurucan took pity on them. The creation had taxed most of his powers, and to keep the magic flowing he charged them with the care of the great thing. The two mystics were assigned to teach them the secrets of the gods so that the awesome spectacle of the Citadel, more than any other feat in memory, would bring glory to the hares and their offspring.

But the Strega's hearts were filled with treachery. Armed with the forbidden knowledge of the ancient hares, they looked to dominate all who came in patronage. Their plan worked, and soon the Strega, who were once unfit to lick the feet of the old guard, were now the most feared of all rats in the park.

The Warren caught wind of this deception and raced to put the ambitious vermin in their place, but with the powers of Hurucan and the teachings of Tepeu and Gukumatz the Strega quickly overpowered and destroyed the weakened hares. The only one left alive was one the hares scorned many years earlier, a drunken lout named Sivad.

With no one to turn to and the Strega firmly established as the leaders of all rats in the park, Sivad retreated to Warren's Burrow. The Strega began their three-hundred year reign while

Sivad, driven slightly mad, took to capturing the random souls of waylaid travelers. One such soul was a frog named Main Scout, whom he traded to a mysterious ferret for an opportunity that no one who'd fallen so low would ever turn down. All he had to do was play a small part in a grand and clever scheme.

The only odd part about it was that as the ferret walked off into the tunnels leading away from the Land of the Blind, Sivad heard him, talking much louder than necessary, cheering, "Now I have all the pieces I need!"

Day One

Least-Rogonians, Chapter One: Astran

||||||||||||||||||||||||||||||||||||||||||||||||||||||||||||||||||||||||||||||||||||||||||||||||||||||||||||||||||||||||||||||||||||||||||||||||||||||||||||||

He crouched in his burrow among the nesting-material, idly grooming the fur on his chest with rough, methodical strokes of his tongue. He nibbled at the tangles, reordering the hairs until they lay flat and clean against his skin. Satisfied, he lifted his head and yawned widely, showing his long incisors and the tiny, sharp molars beyond. A moment later a scent caught in his nostrils and he looked up, whiskers quivering. He saw the shape pausing uncertainly in the entrance to his home, and a satisfied smile settled over his face.

"Mystic…"

Astran stood up at the sound of the voice. "Come," he rumbled. "Do not be afraid."

She smelled of fear and uncertainty as she ventured toward him, but as soon as she came closer, he could sense the hot lust growing inside her as well.

His smile widened. "You are the one I sent for?"

She paused, lowering her snout to him. "Yes, Mystic. My name is Sequis."

Astran bent and nibbled at the fur on her head. "A beautiful name. Raise your snout, female. I want to see your face."

She obeyed, and he stepped back to examine her. She was young and soft–her gray fur still downy with youth. Most likely she had never mated before. Astran thought of that, and his lust instantly strengthened. A fresh female was better than any other. He eyed her fine, delicate snout and black eyes–bulging slightly with fright. Yes, she would do very nicely.

"Come here," he said. "Relax, and let me touch you."

She obeyed, and he began to groom her. His motions were firm and assured, and he soon felt her muscles loosen under his snout and paws. She had been withdrawing from him, shying away, but before long, as she relaxed under his skillful tongue, she began to press herself against him, wanting more. Astran was happy to oblige her. He led her to his nest and bade her crouch down with him while he groomed her back–slowly working his way down toward her rump.

When he reached her tail, she shuddered and went rigid, her snout thrust forward and her ears quivering. He continued to work at her tail until she let out a little cry and suddenly turned and thrust her snout into the spot where his neck met his shoulder, nuzzling frantically. He let her groom him, all over his broad back and shoulders and his belly, relishing every moment of it until, finally, she reached his tail and the great bulge at its base–and hesitated.

"Do it," he said softly.

To encourage her, he nibbled at the back of her neck until she had satisfied him. After that, growing bored with this play, he gently but firmly turned her around and coupled with her, from behind.

It was over in moments, as it always was with rodents. Astran nuzzled her ears as he made the one, quick thrust that was all their lovemaking amounted to, and then let her go.

She lay very still among the nesting material for a few moments, after he had done. "Is that…?"

"Yes. Did you like it?"

She raised herself and nodded shyly.

"Good."

She paused. "Would… would you do it again?"

He reached out for her again, in reply.

They mated several more times that night, and when they were finally done they curled up together in the nest and slept, buried in each others' fur. Astran slept deeply, faint snores rumbling in his chest, untroubled by dreams.

✳   ✳   ✳

When he woke up the next morning, Sequis had gone. He rolled over and yawned. As he lay on his back, idly scratching his flank, his nose suddenly twitched. There was an unfamiliar scent in the burrow.

Astran started to growl. He sat up, ears aggressively flat against his skull. And then, a split second later, he was under attack. A pair of shadowy figures darted forward and seized his arms, wrenching them behind his back. Astran snarled and lurched forward, teeth bared, but he froze as a knife pricked his throat.

"Don't struggle," said a harsh voice. "We've orders not to hurt you."

Astran spat. "Give me one good reason not to hurt *you* and maybe I won't tear you apart."

The speaker's response was to press the knife into his throat until a trickle of blood started to soak his fur. Astran moved away from it, and furiously allowed the two holding his arms to tie his wrists together.

"Get up," ordered the one with the knife. "You're coming with us."

Astran strode out of the burrow, his powerful tail lashing. She was going to suffer for this, he vowed.

Least-Rogonians, Chapter Two: Ophiuchus

S he too was grooming, in an idle manner that served as a severe insult for her guest. Two mouse slaves opened the door leading into the great burrow where she sat, but she acted as if she hadn't noticed and continued to nip at an imaginary patch of dirt as Astran was led into the room. Astran noticed, as he often had before, that for someone who disapproved of humans she certainly did act like one from time to time.

The trio of powerfully built rats who had brought him stopped in front of the throne and bowed low. They were all large and heavily muscled, but next to their prisoner they looked much smaller. The mystic all but towered over them, radiating aggression. His sandy-gold fur bristled, and his big, ragged ears were laid flat. In a straight fight, Astran could probably have taken them, but his anger had a way of clouding his perspective; had he not been so enraged by his treatment he might have convinced them to allow him to walk in with his head held up.

"Mistress," one of the guards intoned. "We have brought him."

She finally looked up, and her single eye gleamed slyly. "Welcome, Astran."

He glared at her. "Ophiuchus, if you do not have an excellent excuse for this, I'll have no choice but to kill you and toss your carcass into the streets as a souvenir for the mice."

She yawned. "Menudo, untie him and be gone. We shall talk alone."

"Yes, Mistress."

The three rats removed Astran's bonds, and hastily left the burrow. Astran ignored them and rubbed his wrists as he stepped closer to the throne.

"Explain yourself."

It was his custom, when he confronted her, to stand slightly to the side, so that in the extremely unlikely event she got physical with him his punch would have more momentum. He wasn't certain why, but it had become habit by then.

Ophiuchus rested her paws on her bulging white belly. "Well-mannered as always. I am pleased to see your month of binge drinking and whore chasing hasn't changed you for the worse."

Astran rolled his paw and bowed in the manner of the imperial court of Marrow-Vinjia, causing her great consternation, then promptly spat. "Spare me the pleasantries and get to the point."

She watched him for a moment. "You know," she said, "once I wished you would give me grandchildren. Now you give me nothing else. Have you nothing better to do with your time than take every female you find into your nest? You'll run out of rats and be forced to start bedding the mice before long."

"It will be a miracle if I get to bed at all if you plan on making this a habit, dragging me in so early in the morning."

"It's the only time off the day I know for certain you're not drunk."

Astran feigned shock and slapped his cheek. "Well, I'll be," he sang in a mock-genteel voice, "if that just doesn't justify everything. Although, if I may say so, you might have done better to wait. I'm more likely to listen to your tripe with a good brace of wine in me."

"I swear you get more like your father every day…"

Astran bristled. "Don't insult me. You may be mistress of my tribe, but I won't hesitate to bite you if you do not show me the proper respect."

Ophiuchus sighed. "You are a mystic, Astran, and a powerful one, whether you value it or not. Surely you could spend your days in study? There are so many things you could learn to do." Now, there was an insult of the highest order. All Least-Rogonians knew a little magic, Astran far more than most, but to suggest that one, especially a male, might need to *learn* magic?

"Well, I'm so very very sorry if my choice in self-destructive habits doesn't mirror your own. I happen to like being drunk, just as much as you like to delude yourself about life in general."

"You have the gift, Astran…" she remarked, stopping just short of adding "for asinine comments".

"Yes, I do, and I do not need to study, as you put it," Astran sneered. "I have better things to do."

"Such as fighting and drinking and fathering an entire tribe's worth of pups," she observed, and sighed again. "Ach! What were the gods thinking, to put so much power into the body of a jackass?"

"I'm sure you would know better than I would, Mother," Astran said sourly, "about 'jackasses' especially."

She froze, "You know I don't like talking about that."

"We can't ignore it forever."

"Well," she said. "Perhaps we can ask the gods later. In the meantime, we have more important matters to discuss."

Astran resigned himself. It never failed to impress him, the way he and his mother could have conversations and never actually say anything to each other. He leaned forward. "Important enough to have me dragged here like a criminal?"

"Yes."

Her bluntness surprised him. "Do not hesitate to enthrall me with your news," he said, hiding it behind sarcasm. "If it happens to be something important I'll buy you drink!"

Ophiuchus shifted on her flame-shaped throne. "I have received word that Marrow is planning something. It is time for us to make our move. We must win the Citadel before he does. Therefore, I am going to send my own emissary to barter with the Strega–you."

"Oh, dammit, not this again."

"It is a solid plan, and as long as we get there first, the Vinjian threat will be forever neutralized."

"Yeah, and the Least-Rogonians will never forget that it happened on YOUR watch."

"Deceiving the Strega would bring a fair share of glory your way, too."

Astran sneered. "And what makes you think you could possibly win their interest? They have all the power they could want."

"But they have desires, as all rodents do," she said simply. "I plan to offer them their own most powerful."

"And what would that be?"

She rose from her throne–the transition making her look much smaller.

"You will offer them immortality," she said. "they will know it is within your power, Astran."

Yes, Astran thought, if I was willing to kill myself doing it. "I would have thought they lived long enough already," he said.

"But it is not true immortality, is it?" she said. "They suffer by time's paw, they grow old and blind and decrepit. Your power could give them youth and vitality."

"I see. And what would prevent them from turning on us once I had granted them their wish?" As if I don't already know, he thought.

"Oh, it would be simple enough," she said, waving a paw. "Kill them all once you have gained their trust. I know that is well within your power."

Astran scratched at a torn ear, while he thought. "And what would there be in this for me?"

"Gods curse you, Astran, are you simple?" she snapped, suddenly losing her temper. "What would be in it for you would be the defeat of the Marrow-Vinjians! The power of the Citadel would be ours–our territories would increase a hundred-fold, and we would have slaves and gold beyond our greatest imaginations! That is what would be in it for you, and if you had stopped antagonizing me for one moment, you would have realized that already."

Astran grunted by way of an answer. He knew that none of that was what this was really about, but it was enough of a reason to go on. "I see. And assuming I accept?"

"You will leave immediately," she said, ignoring him. "I will send others with you; they will be at your command. Do not fail me, Astran."

Least-Rogonians, Chapter Three: Tranah

||||||||||||||||||||||||||||||||||||||||||||||||||||||||||||||||||||||||||||||||||||||||||||||||||||||||||||||||||||||||||||||

As a rule, Astran was not a religious rat; he felt that a true warrior, so much as he could be called one, did best without seeking the blessings of some nonexistent entity—and even if they were real, why would you do any better if you had to worry about them suddenly turning against you over some minor incident you didn't even know about? Nevertheless, upon leaving his mother's den, he proceeded begrudgingly to the Least-Rogonians' "Shrine of The Four Gods". It was a large den; some said it had belonged to a badger before the One-Eyed Witch's two-eyed mother had slain it with a single glance. Ophiuchus's mother was subject to a lot of ridiculous urban legends among their tribe. Supposedly, the statues of the four gods were carved by a human that she shrank down to a mouse's size, whom she then devoured. Or, to quote another story, that they were fashioned by two Capra-Vinjians she'd captured while disguised as a pigeon, whom she then devoured. Personally, Astran was of the mind that they'd been carved by a human for his own amusement, and were then stolen by her subjects, who built a religion around them...

A sandy female, a half inch or so shorter than Astran himself but with much wider shoulders, was crouched outside the doorway, posed something like those that the humans called "cowboys": her head tilted low as if there were a hat that covered her eyes. Astran would have ignored her immediately had she not finally spoken.

"So, what did Mom want?"

It was the sickening sappiness of her voice that irritated him most, he decided. His sister was the only rat, save Ophiuchus, whom he desperately wanted to kill with his bare paws. If he was less inclined to kill Tranah, it was only because his mother was more likely to intrude on his love-life.

"The hateful bitch who spawned us has a mission for me..."

"Quest."

"What?"

"We mystic types call them quests. Humans call them missions."

"Are we really having this conversation or is there something you want?"

"That depends. Who're you fighting this time?"

"Aside from various bums around the watering hole?"

"Which will come after your quest, hopefully."

"Gods, but you're annoying..."

"You still haven't answered my question."

"King Marrow."

"Who?"

"Ruler of the Marrow-Vinjians."

"The ones with the pretty uniforms?" Her eyes were bulging with excitement.

"You know, the One-Eyed Witch would have you hanged for treason if she heard you say that."

"Mom's asked you not to call her that."

He ignored her and proceeded inside. Right beside the doorway was a yellowish figure of a rat with paws that were supposed to look like a mole's, but really looked more like an anteater's. His claws and hands were raised to the sky, as if he was trying to dig out of Hell. This was Chigu, God of the Earth. Astran bowed politely, scooped up a pile of dust off the ground, and ritualistically sprinkled it over Chigu's feet, which were considerably dirtier than the rest of him.

Across from Chigu was a dancing rat covered in flames; this one was Astran's favorite, as he often fantasized about turning Tranah into a replica of it. This was Pul, The Flame God. Before Pul's dancing feet was a ceremonial flame, which was actually a run-down candle–one of few human extravagances Ophiuchus allowed these days. He reached behind his ear and pulled out an ingrown fur which had been bothering him for days, and watched as it fluttered slowly into the fire. To Pul's left was Mul, Goddess of Water, which looked like an ordinary statue of a rat, except that it had webbed paws, one of which was extended outward like a beggar's. Mul only accepted offerings of blood, the water of the body. Astran demurred at the thought of cutting himself, especially since he had no knife, but a quick scan of his body revealed a forgotten scab on his elbow, which he picked at and held over her paw as a single glob of blood eked out.

The final god was a three headed monstrosity: one male, one female, and the final a mouse of indeterminable gender; each one's neck at an odd angle, as if the heads were chasing each other. This was Param, the God of Wind. Some argued that since Param had a mouse as one of its heads, it was a sign that the slaves should be treated less cruelly, perhaps even freed. Others argued that the mouse merely represented the south winds, which were normally the most mild, or that there had simply been an error when the statue was constructed. Whatever it all signified, Astran breathed heavily on it, and bowed a fourth time.

Stuff and nonsense, he thought. They might as well have worshiped those hares the under-grounders were said to revere in the days before the Strega. Astran squatted down, grumbling at his mother and wondering how his day could have been so bollixed up. Tranah came up behind him and, upon making her presence known, presented Astran with his mystic staff, which Ophiuchus had seized from him after he'd turned a member of the visiting emissary of frogs into a butterfly and nearly sparked a war until Tranah, with help from her friend Syrinx, managed to convince them that he was merely some random drunkard with no say in the tribe's affairs.

"Why are you here?" he said.

"I want to come with you."

"No."

"Come on, if you're going to assassinate someone…"

"It's not an assassination."

"Then why would she pick you? The only thing you're good for is killing."

"I have the urge to prove you right."

"Oh? So you've got to find something?"

"I already know where it is."

"Well, knowing you, you'll have a devil of a time retrieving it."

"Probably."

"Why is that?"

"'Lack of caring' comes to mind."

"Well, if you are going on a quest, our law says that you need to travel in a group of five, and who better for your first pick than your adorable sister, Tranah?"

"I have a sister?" he said, taking his staff from her.

"Oh, come on, Astran. You know Mom doesn't think too highly of me."

"Can't imagine why."

"Oh now, brother, you know I never ask you for anything. Just give me this one chance to curry to her favor." Her voice was too sincere for even Astran's cynicism. And besides, it would save him the trouble of having to find a fifth.

"Fine. What time is it?"

Tranah backed toward the door and looked up at the sun, squinting momentarily. "About noon, I'd say."

"Good. I'm gonna go drink for a few hours. You round up three of your friends and meet me about an hour after sunset."

Without looking at her, he left the temple and scurried off between the subtly distinguished mounds of dirt that marked the various burrows. Tranah knew without watching where he was going: a large burrow just along the edge of the gigantic lake which gave the park its fame and provided the greatest barrier against the Marrow-Vinjians. That mound was where every undesirable character in the Least-Rogonians' territory gathered around to drink the finest wines in the park (some from as far away as the Fountainhead, at the other side of the lake) and beat each other senseless, having gotten too drunk to kill each other properly with magic. She sighed and lowered her head. Even she couldn't find any point in it.

But, still, he had said that she could come, and with that thought she became more excited. Ophiuchus had never let her leave the territory; no one knew why exactly. But that didn't matter now, her big brother was letting her come on a real live adventure! Dashing over to the lake, she daintily soaked her paw and dampened various unruly bits of fur around her body. She knew she was pretty, but no one ever commented about it–except her friend Syrinx, who was a female, and a lizard–and it helped to remind herself every once in a while.

So, she thought, they're the Marrow-Vinjians now. Wonder what they're like?

Marrow-Vinjians, Chapter Four: A Night At The Opera

The stage is completely dark, no lights, no music, nothing at all to set the scene until the actor speaks: "All I ever wanted was to not exist. I think I've achieved that now…"

I don't know if he's supposed to be me or not. I mean, I know, because the play is about me, and as impressive a physical specimen as the actor is, he certainly wouldn't be playing anyone else. I'm uncertain because I don't remember ever saying that. Come to think of it, I don't think I've ever heard any Marrow-Vinjian speak so philosophically; I almost wonder where the playwright stole that from. Certainly one of my fellow countrymen wrote this–other tribes don't have the theater, unwashed vermin that they are–though perhaps they heard some human say it, and felt it would sound wonderfully coming from the ominous baritone onstage that sounds nothing like my infamous falsetto. But still, imagine: me, sounding like an honest-to-god HUMAN BEING!

I glance over to the pocket-watch hanging over the grand-archway near the door, with which we replaced the more visible, but uglier, factory clock. Technically, my men and I are only killing time until our mission kicks off in ten minutes, but now that I'm here I regret it. Think of how disheartening it would be for my fellow rats to see the subject of what promises to be a most complimentary drama walk out so early in the proceedings. Hopefully, something more theatrical will happen; I could slip out much more easily then…

I glance around the theater. Back when the humans still controlled this building it was a factory, but they've since abandoned it and King Marrow determined that we should have a grand rodent opera like they have in Europe It hasn't been easy. The other tribes—most of them, anyway—still scamper about in minimal clothing and huddle like greasy rabbits in dirt heaps by the park which is just down the road. The house is packed; it must've been hard forcing the inferiors to come. I would hardly think that brutes like the Farris-Ianists or the Farj have the mental capacity to appreciate the finer arts humanity has given us. They all look immensely silly, scratching at the starched collars we've donated to them, dirt and sweat stains on their sleeves, their paws wringing in agony, straining against the urge to claw their way past their vestments and escape back into the urban jungle to eke out a beggar's life in the squall. But no, they know they need to get in with their coming masters, and quickly. It will not be long before the king completely conquers the park and turns his attention to the streets where we earned our greatest early triumphs.

Sneering at them, I'm filled with a colonialist's pride at their folly, their minstrel-like attempts to mimic their superiors. They don't want to be here, but they come because they know that Marrow-Vinjians might respect them more if they did civilized things like attend plays. And they also come because the play is about me. Me, they've heard of. The story they're watching isn't much, some insignificant battle I was a part of, but many of them have heard the story, and it was as good as any to introduce me to the world of drama. It's one of the first of its kind in Vinjian history. Soon we'll have monuments and literature and everything else this bayou of urban refuse will never truly appreciate during my lifetime but will play along with anyway.

On either side of me are my men, Spoolnicker and Astairelike. Astairelike is a smallish white mouse, between three and four inches tall with piercing red eyes, heavily scarred around the mouth, with a curiously long curled mustache he's dyed black with shoe polish. I've often wondered whether he intends to grow a goatee to complete the affect, but I don't especially care. It's his skill with an ax that I'm mostly concerned with; that and his odd habit of mispronouncing my name as "Bedford". Spoolnicker, the hulking six inch black rat to the other side, can pronounce Bloodford perfectly, but for a fellow his size he seems ill at ease with conventional weapons. He is nondescript despite his enormity; in fact, were he not so large, I would never be able to pick him out of a crowd. Fortunately, he has an aptitude for the bow and arrow that suits me just fine.

I turn to the watch again. Six minutes left. Astairelike is getting antsy, and with the remaining members of the cast filling onto the stage it seems as good a time as any to scurry away…

The Royal Guard are quick to meet us outside. They wear our bright-red uniforms at all times, which in the army are mercifully not burdened with. Not to sound unpatriotic, but if

I'm to commit wanton acts of murder, mayhem, and occasionally rape, I'm dead-certain it's best if I don't find myself burdened with an overly-fancy wardrobe that I would be constantly obsessing over in terms of cleanliness.

Armed and ready, the three of us turn away from the theater and scamper down the road toward the park where the majority of our empire—as well as that of our hated enemies, the godless Least-Rogonians—lies. Just before we reach the main gate near the chestnut tree where the few remaining rebel squirrels reside, we bank left and head across the street to a small, family-owned restaurant. We have an appointment with the tribe there…

We've made good time, but in the interest of intimidation we're walking slowly now. A sense of drama is never a bad thing, especially in cases such as this. A cockroach scuttles across the pavement. I draw reflexively and impale it. The damn bug doesn't come off the blade right away, it just hangs there like a wad of chewing gum; a terrible nuisance that completely ruins our image.

The night is dark, and the wind is gathering strength. Standing in front of the doorway like the world's skinniest cat is a long, graying ferret, decked in a stiffly-starched, copper-tinted vest and pantaloons over a silver tunic with a dark gray cape hanging over his shoulders. One doesn't normally see ferrets in our part of the world; I wonder if our host sprung him from some pet shop or another. That could be a problem, as pets are often blindly loyal to their liberators. For the first time in I don't know how long, I feel uneasy. He stands double my height, and resembles nothing less than a great hangman's tree, and his eyes, those horrible, dead things…

I glance left to Astairelike, his small but sharp ax affixed to a long chain that connects to his belt. He has a slight limp—it doesn't slow him down, but it prevents him from standing still.

He always seems to have a hot foot. He looks back at me with his imposing eyes and ridiculous mustache; he is surprised like I am, but outwardly unafraid. I don't need to look at Spoolnicker, he will go wherever I go.

The ferret is surveying us scornfully, as a mongoose stares down a cobra before the battle begins; he has his arms crossed across his chest, as if that will do anything to stop us. I don't know his name, or if ferrets even have names, but there's a marked detachment in his glare. I feel as if he were an entomologist, looking down at me through a microscope as I lie pinned against the glass slide.

"You," it croaks. "You've come seeking Chumsa?"

Nobody replies. Speaking has suddenly given him the same power over my companions as he has over me.

"Come," he intones flatly…

✵   ✵   ✵

He leads us around back into the alley, pointing his gnarled snout toward an overturned garbage can with light emanating from the "top". So, this is the site that Chumsa has chosen. Lovely.

"He's in there?" Spoolnicker finally speaks, but gets no answer. We turn, and the ferret is gone. He's left no footprints or scent. It is as if he was never there at all.

"What the hell?" Astairelike mutters. I share the sentiment, but instead lock my jaw in thought. Chumsa has gone to a lot of trouble, obviously. If he's planned this much we might be walking into an ambush. Spoolnicker reads my mind and nods slightly. He tightens his grip around his bow and turns determinedly toward the meeting place with Astairelike half a step behind.

"Spoolnicker," I whisper, upon reaching the entrance, "keep

watch." He grunts complacently. Astairelike and I step onto the rusting metal and walk toward our host. Chumsa, decked in what might be a mock-up of the Ancient Greek togas made out of a neckerchief and, sitting on his haunches behind what might have been intended to resemble a desk, is surrounded on three sides by naked sewer rats with splotches of gunk in their fur. They have a criminal hardness about them, a certain deadness behind the eyes that says they've seen as much death as I have, but were not in a position to enjoy it. The smell is awful.

"Welcome, my friends!" Chumsa says, rolling his tongue on every other letter. "It has been so long since we've had such distinguished guests. Tell me, Bloodford, what brings Octave-Vinjia to my doorstep?"

"Marrow-Vinjia," I correct him.

"Eh?"

"Queen Octavia died three years ago." I narrow my gaze just far enough to be intimidating. "Surely you knew that?"

"Err, Marrow is in control, now?"

"Yes."

He looks uneasy. Clearly, the stupidity he's unveiled upsets his plans.

"Well, we have been preoccupied, daily survival, you know… Marrow is in control? Yes, yes, yes yes yes… How did she die?"

"Who?"

"Octavia."

"Asking too many questions," Astairelike deadpans. It lacks subtlety, but the color drains from Chumsa's face nicely.

"Yes, well, daily survival, you know…"

"You've mentioned that," I bark, "and it seems a damned nuisance that you should be so preoccupied that you miss out on so much history even as it's happening all around you."

"Urm…"

"Of course, you must realize how embarrassing it is being so busy scrounging for crumbs that you don't even know what's happening across the street."

He can't stall for time much longer; he's fighting to get his composure back. I don't look at his underlings, that's what Astairelike is here for, but the room is getting tenser especially near them.

"What is it you want, Bloodford?" he says, finally.

"I want? I want nothing, sir, for I live to serve others, just as you should."

"I don't understand…"

"As is to be expected."

"Humph."

"Don't interrupt. We know your people have been friendly with the Least-Rogonians…"

"In the past, yes, but it's been years…"

"Quiet. It is not my concern whether the Wahid tribe consorts with trash. What does concern us is whether or not you've ever been involved with a certain other tribe."

He looks confused, but I'm sure it's an act. "Who?"

I lean forward, my paws perched pointedly at the edge of his "desk". "The Strega."

The rats behind him shrink back. Chumsa himself has gone white as a ghost. "What do you want with them?"

I grin, perhaps too leeringly, and draw my sword from its sheath slowly, so as not to provoke his guards. I hold it at an angle and twist back and forth, reflecting the candlelight directly back into his eyes. "The reign of the Strega is nearing its end. What few of them remain are several centuries old, if not more, and once they're out of the way…"

He sprints up, knocking over his makeshift table and nearly toppling his candle. "You'll not take The Citadel!"

"Sit down!" Astairelike pounces, soaring over Chumsa's head and landing on his shoulders, bringing the ax's handle down on Chumsa's forehead; not hard enough to knock him out, but enough to paralyze him. His guard leaps into action. The one behind him jumps for Astairelike, but the mouse dodges! I lean backward, turn my sword and slash with all my might in a wide arc, catching the guard right in the skin between the jaw and the skull. Ducking his hulking frame, I turn my attention back to Astairelike. He flings his ax toward the guard to the right and hits him in the forehead, blood spurting from it like oil. A flick of the wrist, and the blade exits his head and flies left, implanting itself in the last rat's neck. He isn't dead, so Astairelike lassos the rest of his chain around the poor fellow's head and jerks, killing him instantly.

A moan from behind me! The rat who leaped at me is back on his feet, his claws bared. I raise my blade…and he falls, courtesy of an arrow from Spoolnicker. Astairelike glares at him.

"Couldn't have done that sooner?"

"Didn't need to."

"Of course," I gloat, turning back to our toga-clad friend, "that means that I'm the only one here who hasn't killed anyone tonight." I kick him in the shoulder, and level the tip of my blade squarely against his windpipe. "Now, Chumsa, my dear friend, you were just about to tell us everything you know about the Strega, the Citadel, and everything else you and you tribe are going to do to help us take control of the entire park and banish the heathen Least-Rogonians once and for all. Now, where were you?"

He wheezes pitifully. "You cannot defeat them. Octavia tried, and even she…"

"She, benevolent though she was, led an army of rodents. Marrow, on the other paw, leads an army of soldiers…"

"I don't care how human he's made you think you are," he spits, "the Strega will never let you take control of the Citadel. You are impure."

I'm beginning to lose my patience. "Oh, I see. So, what you're saying is that because we wear respectable clothing and don't walk on all fours and don't do everything else that would prevent us from becoming the greatest empire that rats have ever seen–*that* is why we'll never take the Citadel? Is that it?"

"…"

"Chumsa," I mutter as I compose myself. "You disappoint me. Even you couldn't be superstitious enough to believe that a modern military can't defeat a pack of xenophobic old Mummies who want us all to return to the Dark Ages, could you?"

"…"

"What you and the rest of you primitive vermin don't realize is that you're simply delaying the inevitable. The park WILL be united under our king, and once it is the city will be ours for the taking. The handwriting is on the wall, sir, and unless you want yourself, your family, and everyone you've ever met to go the way of the Ottomans simply because you don't think a proper military has a chance against a handful of old rats…"

"It is not that you cannot fight them!" he cries childishly.

"What?"

"There are too many other tribes in the park. You will never get there in time. Once they die some minor tribe will take control and the madman you serve will fall. Any pact with you is useless." He's weeping uncontrollably now. I'd reproach him harshly, but he does have a point. I must remember to bring it up with the king next time I see him.

I stand upright once more and kick him viciously. I kick him again, and don't stop until I'm sure my next one will launch a barrage of candy out of his stomach. Astairelike and Spoolnicker prepare to finish him off but I motion for them to leave. They follow dutifully, but grudgingly.

"Well," Spoolnicker pipes, sounding oddly cheerful for someone so morose looking, "that wasn't so difficult."

"Our mission failed," Astairelike mutters.

"No," I say, "our mission was to find out whether they would join us or not. Having gotten the definite answer, our task is successfully over and done with."

"I was talking about the fight, actually. Totally useless, all of them."

"Especially that ferret," Astairelike blurts. "Bloody coward didn't even show up."

A battle cry erupts behind us! The rat Spoolnicker shot–he's still alive! He's limping from the arrow in his back, but he's gripping a spiked club as if it were the only thing keeping him from falling. He raises it up and charges us full bore with a fiery rage. Brushing the other two back before Spoolnicker can raise his bow, I sprint, my sheath at eye level, building up enough propulsion to launch my special attack. When he and I are close enough I fall to my knees and power slide past him, undressing my weapon and removing him from his legs. He pumps forward, not even writhing in agony, but numb from the sudden loss of limb. I lift him up by the tail, exposing his genitals, and place the harsher edge of my steel against them. THAT gets his attention.

"Did Chumsa send you?" I ask with no emotion at all.

"Noooooooooooooooooo," he wheezes in fear of complete uselessness.

"Good." I penetrate his stomach so far that the tip of my

sword comes out by the arrow that wounded him earlier and pull it back out so quickly that he actually bends backward to almost complete uprightness. Not wanting to miss such an unexpected position, I slice through the back of his neck, not quite cutting his head off.

"Not bad," Spoolnicker marvels.

"It wouldn't have happened if you'd just shot him in the head," I mutter, grimly wiping the blood off the metal.

"I told you, it just doesn't feel right. Besides, the body is a much better target."

"Yes, and it's full of things that won't kill you if hit by an arrow."

"Lay off."

I feel a chill run up my spine. I turn toward the roof of the restaurant, and, speak of the devil, there is our friend from just a few minutes ago, staring down at us. For a moment, I'm almost convinced he's the Angel of Death.

"There he is," Spoolnicker remarks. "What do you think he's doing up there?"

"Watching us," I reply. "I'm beginning to doubt whether he's with the Wahid."

"Then who is he?" Astairelike spits, with far too much false bravado.

The ferret eyes us a split-second longer, then rotates noncommittally and scampers off.

"He might be going for reinforcements."

"How many did you say the Wahid have?" Spoolnicker asks me.

"At least three dozen," I whisper, not anxious to be outnumbered twelve to one so early in the evening.

"Chaps," says Astairelike, "let's get the hell out of here…"

✻　　✻　　✻

When we arrive back at the theater, the Royal Guard make haste to take our weaponry and re-attire us is a civilized fashion.

"Send word," I mumble to the Guard closest myself. "The Wahid will not co-operate."

"Yes sir. His Majesty will wish to know. What do you recommend?"

I smile. "Wipe them out. All of them…"

Least-Rogonians, Chapter Five: Menudo

||||||||||||||||||||||||||||||||||||||||||||||||||||||||||||||||||||||||||||||||||||||||||||||||||||||||||||||||||||||||||

stran finally stumbled out of the bar, reeking of wine, to be confronted by his sister wielding a tiny ax, and three bruisers he didn't recognize carrying spiked clubs and grinning insolently. Astran, his eyes drooping heavily, was in no mood to put up with any such nonsense, but just when he lunged forward to prove his point his left foot decided to attack his right and the mighty hero went crashing into the dirt. Tranah laughed heartily, her high-pitched squeaking doing inhumane things to his head. He cursed and slapped the air in front of her, sending a wave strong enough to knock her down.

The three bruisers' eyes illuminated all at once and from them an envelope of warmth surrounded him. His stupor was being lifted away against his will. As soon as his head had cleared up enough he screamed, "What the hell did you do that for?"

"You were drunk," the nearest rat mocked.

"I like being drunk."

"Well," the next rat purred, "now you're sober."

"I don't like being sober. It means I have to look at you. Wait, aren't you the same gorillas who dragged me out of my bed earlier?"

"Yep," the final thug nodded.

"…Which one of you is Menudo?"

"We're all called Menudo."

"…Tranah!"

His sister, still sitting on the ground, was giggling uncontrollably. "Well, they were convenient."

Astran rubbed his head, agonized over his rightfully deserved hangover being stolen from him. By everything that was holy, the last group of rodents he wanted to do this with was this one.

"Okay," he spat. "While I was in the pub, *drinking*," he shot Tranah a look, "one of the dumb bastards who steals food from the city for us mentioned that the Strega have a sister tribe called the Wahid. They have a settlement in the outermost portion of the city by the outline of the park, near the gate on the Marrow-Vinjian side. They may have useful information."

"About what?" the first Menudo asked.

"And what do the Strega have to do with this?" Tranah wondered.

"Don't you know? Everything has to do with them. Anyway, that sounds like as good a place as any to start. So, hop to it."

Nobody moved.

"Do we not speak English all of a sudden?"

"We don't know where that is," the third Menudo mumbled.

"And we've never been in the city, either," the second Menudo added.

"Ah. Well then, since none of us knows what we're doing, thank you Mom, we're gonna head for gate and hug the park wall until we get to the enemy's side, and find someone in the know."

"And how will we know when we find them?" the first Menudo spat.

"That I do know. Their leader is called Chumsa. Fat rat, wears a toga. Smells bad. And I know how we'll know we're getting close: there's a warehouse about halfway there that the Marrow-Vinjians turned into a theater."

"A what?"

"Can't say, but there'll be a lot of rats wearing clothes around, so keep a low profile."

"Why?" Tranah asked. "We could easily take them out." To emphasize her point, she stuck out her paw and pretended that a massive jet stream of flame surged from her fingertips.

"Well, if we were to just barge in, fingers blazing, to a crowd of uninvolved rats, that would be stupid. Besides, we're not planning on killing anyone just yet. This is straight reconnaissance, because that's exactly what will piss the Witch off, which means it's the right thing to do."

No one saw any point in arguing with him.

Astran and two of the Menudos squatted down low to plan their next move while Tranah, looking even younger than usual, stared at the abandoned warehouse with an earnest sense of wonder.

"Just think," she whispered to herself, "our enemies are just right there…." Her ax hung limply at her side. "Do you think it's true? That their mice are actually free?"

"Of course not," the standing Menudo scoffed. "How would they get anything done? They already don't use magic."

"True, but that actually makes all that they've done a little more impressive, don't you think?"

"If I didn't know any better, I'd think you were enamored with them," Astran smirked.

"Hardly, but it never hurts to have an appreciation of your enemy. I mean, then you won't underestimate them."

"She does have a point," one of the sitting Menudos said.

"Well, if she has a way to find the Wahid, I'll be impressed."

"I actually might be able to help you on that one," a strange voice purred.

They all sprung into position as, there came from over the wall a menacing ferret in a bottle green bronze buttoned vest and loincloth, weaving seductively. He left no scent, which disoriented them. They all felt a twinge of impending death with his presence.

"Name's Bathin." The ferret extended his paw. "I believe I may be able to help you."

The five looked at each other, confused. Who could this strange rodent be? They'd certainly never seen a ferret before, and were uneasy about just how much taller he was, and how strangely he was dressed, even by Least-Rogonian standards. The ferret sensed this and flashed a smile which actually made him more intimidating.

"How, exactly?" Astran finally spoke.

Bathin pointed toward the theater. "See them over there?"

They looked, and saw two rats–one brown, one black–and a small white mouse leaving the theater at a fast clip.

"They're heading to the same place you are. If you hold back and stay downwind, you should be able to follow them without being seen."

"What if they kill Chumsa before we get there?" Tranah said, ignoring, as they all were, the fact that this mysterious stranger knew exactly what their business was.

"I can assure you that won't happen. Wait until they're almost out of sight, then follow. I'm going ahead of you. I need to have a word with them before they reach the Wahid."

And, as quickly as he appeared, he was gone.

The five stood puzzled, which was fortunate, because when they snapped out of it the Marrow-Vinjians were a safe enough distance away, and the five set out after them. From what little Astran could make of them, the leader of this party was none other than the famous Lord Bloodford. Astran knew his face all too well and was not too fond of the idea of confronting him. Bloodford and his small party veered too close to their home territory for Astran's comfort, but fortunately they soon turned and headed away from the park, toward a restaurant.

Bathin…no, it couldn't have been him; this ferret was dressed more similarly to the Marrow-Vinjians. Whoever he was, he was perched out in front of the eatery, and Bloodford's party stopped to speak with him. Astran and his party held back a block or so, crossing the street quickly so as not to stand out.

The three Menudos flattened themselves against the edge of the building while Astran and his sister crouched low.

"What's he saying to them?" Tranah whispered.

"I don't know, but I wonder. You think that ferret has anything to do with ours?"

"They look alike."

"I'd imagine all ferrets look alike when you get right down to it. It is kind of strange, though. I'd don't think I've ever seen a ferret before and now we've seen two in one night. This promises to be…" he shuddered, "…interesting…"

"Afraid you won't get back to your drinking in time?"

"That possibility is disconcerting, yes…"

The ferret led the three rodents into an adjoining alley; Astran and Tranah darted ahead to where Bathin had been standing a few seconds prior. Still no scent. They paused to give their enemies sufficient distance, but when Astran went to look around the corner he was snatched from behind as Bathin, seemingly coming from nowhere, pulled him away.

"If they see you, they'll kill you," he barked.

Tranah, shocked by his sudden appearance, brandished her ax high. "What's going on, here?"

"Those Vinjians are meeting with Chumsa. I'm afraid they might kill him, and I know they will if they see you here." Before any of them could answer, Bathin jutted his paw upward. "Quickly, up on the roof!"

His speed double theirs by virtue of his size, the ferret was halfway up the building before the rats could contemplate what he'd said, but Astran and Tranah quickly caught up and the Menudos were just climbing over the edge by the time Bathin had led the siblings to a perch over looking the alley.

"There's not much time." Bathin shook his head sadly. "Chumsa will refuse his offer and his companions will die horribly, but he must not…"

"Where do you stand in all this?" said Astran.

"My only interest is making sure that your feud is conducted fairly," he tossed off enigmatically.

"Why?"

"Shh." His paw sliced the air as the sound of a struggle erupted from an overturned trashcan below. The blood of the males was set ablaze. There was a battle to be had! But their giant companion held them back, not seeming to care so much about the fate of the Wahid below as long as their presence remained a secret. In no time at all the noise had stopped, and once more the ferret motioned for them to crouch low while he himself remained upright. There was further noise from below–another fight had broken out, but that too was over quickly. Tranah strained her ears to make it all out, but the most she could catch was the Marrow-Vinjians making very subdued conversation:

"Not bad," said a deep voice that could only come from a rat the Menudos' size.

"It wouldn't have happened if you'd just shot him in the head," said a ridiculously high-pitched voice.

"I told you, it just doesn't feel right. Besides, the body is a much better target."

"Yes, and it's full of things that won't kill you if hit by an arrow."

"Lay off."

She unfocused her ears and put her paws over them. Something about the casual way they were speaking made this all not quite so fun anymore.

Astran had been listening too, but what he noticed most was that they mentioned the ferret and then left very quickly. Perhaps the enormous rodent had threatened them beforehand, and now they feared his vengeance. That was comforting. With them gone, the party returned to their feet. Tranah, guessing astutely that they needed to get down as quickly as possible, pressed her palms together, and, upon opening them, conjured a long rope dangling from nowhere that was long enough to reach all the way down to the ground. Without taking time to roll his eyes, Astran leaped first for the rope.

When they reached the trashcan, they were confronted by the stench of death and the sight of a rotund old rodent hunched over himself crying. That must be Chumsa, they all thought.

Tranah approached him first, knowing Chumsa could have no idea who she was, but hopefully he would notice that she wore no clothing and could therefore only be an ally.

"They'll come back," he wheezed at her. "They'll return and all of my tribe will be killed. I just know it!"

"Chumsa," said the ferret, "it is of utmost importance that I get you to safety."

"My tribe will die," he continued, taking no heed of what Bathin had said.

"Chumsa, listen to me! Without you, there is no chance of the Marrow-Vinjians being overthrown. If you die, there will be no one to rally their enemies against them!"

Astran grimaced. What did the ferret mean, exactly, about making sure that their feud was conducted fairly?

The ferret continued to barter with the old rat, finally convincing him to come along, and before Astran could press him for any useful information the two were gone.

"Well," the third Menudo spat, "that was a waste of time."

"Well, what else is new?" said Astran, scratching his chest noncommittally. Still, he thought, it was a shame, things were just starting to get interesting.

"MEOW!"

A jolt ran down everyone's spine as a long black cat sprang suddenly up the wall from the other end of the alley and started slowly toward them. Instinctively, the three Menudos pushed the two royals back and made a phalanx against it. The situation was dire, as black cats were one of the few animals magic had no affect on. Thinking fast, Astran and Tranah looked toward the park, wondering if it was worth the risk to sneak unprotected into Marrow-Vinjian territory. A pink sparkle of light, barely distinguishable in the moonlight to the inexperienced eye, caught

Tranah's attention. Syrinx was there! She turned and nodded to her brother, who faced the three bruisers in front of them. Deciding they wouldn't be much help any longer, he channeled the same spell he'd used to trip Tranah earlier, and released it, much amplified, into the backs of the three Menudos. They were catapulted toward the slinking feline, who pounced heartily on them and gave the siblings ample time to escape in the park on the Marrow-Vinjian side.

Least-Rogonians and Marrow-Vinjians: Chapter Six

||||||||||||||||||||||||||||||||||||||||||||||||||||||||||||||||||||||||||||||||||||||||||||||||||||||||||||||||||||||||||||||||||||||

The Royal Palace, and indeed the whole Marrow-Vinjian stronghold, is a sight to see, I've always said. It was built decades ago as a dollhouse village for human children. Each intricately detailed, four foot tall dollhouse based on a world famous building. The village, located more than a mile from the park entrance, is shaded by oak and sycamore trees and borders the lake under which the Citadel lies. A massive wooden fence surrounds the village; apparently the humans had to pay to get in. The walls, to which we've added cheap shoebox housing, have the added attraction of creating an impenetrable defense system-save from above-but the squirrels know better than to attempt such an attack. It was in the reign of King Capra IX, Octavia's predecessor, that we assumed control of this long-forgotten nook by the simple addition of a "Keep Out" sign on the wooden doorway. Great as the humans are, even we sometimes outsmart them.

I had barely sat back down in the warehouse when I was summoned for an immediate audience with His Majesty. It was breaking with routine–not him summoning me, of course; he always wants to hear about my missions from me personally–but he usually waits until I've returned to Marrow-Vinjia. It might have been a propaganda loss to have the rodent's champion walk out twice on his biography, but the king's messenger was thoughtful enough to bring the entire play to a stop so he could catch my attention.

Leaving my cohorts behind, I was whisked outside and greeted by the royal limousine, a remote-controlled toy car we'd liberated from a neglectful hobbyist. Speeding away, I gripped at my powdered wig to keep it from flying off. Taking a smug glance back to the theater in case some peasant should be praying I'd grace him with eye contact, I caught a glimpse of the ferret we'd encountered earlier standing directly where the Royal Guard had been and looking menacingly in my direction. I don't know what it is about that fellow but he makes my stomach turn…

We reach the stronghold at last, having detoured in case that radical squirrel contingent I've mentioned decided to be uppity tonight, but I still spy a group of three or four, staring menacingly at our party. Along the way we pass the collection of shoe boxes that line the inside of the fence on the east side. These will, at some point in the future, become housing for rodents of other tribes who opt to pledge complete loyalty to Marrow-Vinjia. We circle around some of the other structures, mainly buildings modeled after landmarks I don't recognize. The streets are largely empty this time of night, except for a few soldiers carting human objects toward the palace. A few stop to salute me, but I take no real notice of them, save two - carrying vials of what looks like broken chalk.. Can't imagine what those are used for.

The centerpiece of this village, modeled after the legendary 10 Downing Street, had once been the center of our own Parliament, but, since that had been dismantled by His Majesty, it serves as a fitting home to the center of our universe. It fills me with warmth to see it, though I've been here many a time before. Indeed, my own estate, modeled after the Taj Mahal, is nearby.

The dress uniform of the Marrow-Vinjian army, like the British army before it, consists of a red tuxedo jacket, white vest, pants, black tri-corner cap, and silvery powdered wigs as opposed to the talc powdered wigs we wear day to day. Unlike the other vermin, who dummy-up human clothing from scraps, we've long since mastered the art of tailoring our own clothes, even before Capra's time. Of my party, only Astairelike wears a tri-corner, though. Spoolnicker, being an archer, is given what you might call a deerstalker cap, while I, being an officer, have the right to wear a stovepipe hat if I so chose, which I do.

So dressed, I'm escorted through the hallways toward what in real-life would be the House of Lords, which had been extensively renovated into the king's bedroom. My escorts straighten what little of my outfit needs it and scamper away. King Marrow does not like to have servants in his chambers unless he calls for them.

Almost immediately upon entry the stench of stagnant water is overpowering. I have to close my eyes to keep from going blind. My uniform prevents me from completely doubling over, but I find myself in a most undignified pose.

"Ah, Bloodford, old boy…"

My Liege saunters toward me, I can hear his steps as they waddle back and forward; I still can't quite open my eyes, but there is a distinct squishing noise following him. Sticking my nose into my sleeve, I snort as much fresh air as there is still trapped in the fabric and will myself into a standing position, eyes slitting back open gradually. I only hope that my look seems more like concentration. I bow my head respectfully. "Sire, I pray the evening finds you well." I struggle not to wheeze.

"Well enough, my friend. I was just discussing business with our Maharajah friend."

Maharajah? Good Lord, he hasn't brought FROGS into the palace, has he?

"Yes," an unmistakable croak belches from His side. "We were enraptured with His Majesty's ideas for modernizing the park. Very interesting, indeed…"

I could vomit, I honestly could. "Yes, well, I hope his grace will support My Lord in his endeavors…"

"Oh, yes, of course…That is…if he agrees to assist us in OUR endeavors…"

My Lord lolls his head appreciably. "Naturally, my aquatic friend. Now tell me, when will I receive word of…"

"As soon as it becomes official, Sir. Now, if you'll excuse me, I must return home."

He hops out, taking a majority of his stench with him, but I'm still uncomfortable about the squishing sounds echoing down the hallway outside. I look back to My Liege. His squat frame is practically hugging itself in triumph, and his pugnacious eyes are beaming all the more brightly that someone else was here to witness his victory, whatever it was. I repress a shudder; rats, and, to a lesser extent, mice, are usually above consorting with such riff-raff.

My Liege likes me, which is why I can get away with forgetting my manners in front of him. "Dealing with animals now, are we?"

My callous remark amuses him. "A most novel turn, wouldn't you agree?"

"I don't see why…"

"Bloodford, Bloodford, please. Everything I do has at least one purpose. Now." He motions me over to a cigarette carton that's almost taller than he is and heaves one out for himself, searching diligently for wherever he last left his matches. "What became of your meeting with Chumsa?"

"Aside from getting to kill a few sewer dwellers, my men thought it was a tremendous waste of time."

"And yourself?"

"I am honest by proxy, not in person."

He guffaws heartily. Whatever the pestilential amphibian did for him has certainly left him in a good mood. "I trust the good Wahid did not turn out to be valuable to us?"

"I should hope not. I've ordered the entire tribe to be executed."

"Humph, most decisive. My congratulations, sir. Ah, there's the matchbook…"

He waddles toward his massive bed, which I'd gamble is large enough to fit a badger comfortably, and pulls up the edge of the bed sheet to reveal a tattered book of matches that one of my most recent expeditions took from a nightclub nearby. I take it from him, select a match and strike it. He props his cigarette up with both paws and reclines onto his haunches, looking oddly similar to Chumsa. My Lord isn't as tall as you would imagine him. By my reckoning, he should be about my height, but for whatever reason he's closer to Astairelike's. I suspect he hunches.

"Now, you're positive that nothing of value was gained by your venture?'

"Most… Sire, what was the other purpose of my mission tonight?"

He draws long and exhales slowly, debating whether he wants

to dignify me with an answer. Just because I can be frank with him does not mean he doesn't know that I'm beneath him. "An Old Wives' Tale, mostly."

"I'm sorry?"

"As you know, the Wahid were, at one time, very close to the Strega, the ones who control the Citadel…"

I know damn well who the Strega are, but I also know enough not to say this.

"…Some say they might be related, or were at one point…" He puffs on his cigarette. "That's not important. What 'they' say, I mean. But if the Strega and Wahid were related, then the Wahid might know something about the Strega–and by extension, the Citadel, which might be invaluable. I do not doubt the force of the army my empire has raised, but when dealing with such things it helps to know absolutely everything…"

I'm struck with regret. "Good Lord, they might still know something. I must delay their execution at once!" I turn to leave.

"Do not go." He doesn't shout, but his voice pins me to the spot. "By now they will all be dead, and besides, they knew nothing."

"My Liege , are you certain?"

"If Chumsa knew anything important he would have used it to bargain for his life. As he did not, he had nothing that could help us."

"He seemed awfully concerned that we wouldn't be able to take the Citadel, now that I think about it. Something about…"

"A pathetic attempt. I remember a conversation I had with my son, shortly before he left for his Grand Tour. The one he's on now, I mean…"

What ho? His Majesty almost never discusses his son with me. Marrow II has been abroad almost his entire life. Were his existence not required for My Liege to keep his throne, most Vinjians would have forgotten him by now. Those who do remember him have affectionately dubbed him "The Phantom Prince".

"We were discussing music, or perhaps just musicians, but what I remember most was saying, 'My son, integrity is what you have when you don't have talent.' Integrity and loyalty are the same thing, Bloodford. Chumsa had nothing, so he was loyal. And look what it got him."

I'm not following him. "Sire?"

He looks at me sharply. "Your errand was to find whether any good would be done through the Wahid. You have proved it would not. Your mission is an unqualified success. Do not think of it any longer…"

He snorts hard, then inhales with all his might, as if he's trying to bring the flame completely back to the filter in one foul blow. He nearly succeeds. "Now, are you not curious why I had the filthy toad in my chambers?"

I can hear the twinkle in his tone. He seems to find my disgust amusing. "I did give it pause, yes."

"Ha! Our friend the Maharajah has it in mind to unite all the frogs together into a single culture, with himself in charge, naturally. I've agreed to supply him with military muscle in exchange for various services his subjects can provide us…"

"Military, My Lord?"

"Yes, it seems the stupid brutes want to take that lagoon by the southern gate back from the ducks who expelled them years ago. Like all birds, they have no intelligence, but are still a formidable adversary. But once we get our paws on them, we'll have the beginnings of our own navy!"

"I thought we were building boats for that?"

"The process is too slow. Besides, if the humans should see

fleets of ships just mysteriously appearing, they might become suspicious, and make mischief. Besides, there's a certain poetic quality toward using avians for such purposes, just like those pigeons we've captured."

Ah yes, the Airborne Cavalry. I've always thought that was an incredibly stupid idea.

"But, the hour grows late, and I've no more mind for business. Besides, I've something to show you!"

He has that familiar tone in his voice that he gets whenever he wants to show me something else he's gotten from the humans. He grabs my wrist and sits me down on the edge of his bed. Then, squatting beside me, he claps his paws sharply, and pulleys begin squeaking above us. As I've said, he chooses not to have servants in his chambers, but the room he had built above this one is fully staffed.

A small, velvet-covered cylinder is lowered down in front of us as sleek, seductive music pipes down from the hole in the ceiling. The King chooses not to disgrace the Royal Chamber with electrical devices, but he does enjoy having assorted gadgets nearby, should he want to listen to music. I remember, a few months back, he was actually in talks with some nomads to move a television into the Palace! Thank merciful God he abandoned it.

The cylinder has clunked against the floor, shaken the velvet off to unveil a wire-framed chair. Two females, a white mouse and a white rat, skimpily clad in negligee with large chartreuse bows where the cusps of their bosoms would be, if they were human shaped, and pompous, Voltaire-esque wigs–orange and lavender, respectively–glued to their heads, uncurl themselves from their narrow seat and step slowly onto the floor. They sway back and forth but remain in constant contact, swerving their arms and contorting their hips to the music, their smiling faces and pouting eyes never leaving us.

I'm not certain what to make of them.

"Bet you've never seen anything like that, eh, Bloodford?"

"His Majesty would be right…"

"The humans call it 'lesbians'. It took ages to train them how to dance like that, but I suppose it's worth it, eh?"

"I don't follow, Sire…" I can't take my eyes off them. It's a strange sensation. On the surface I can't see what's so special about this. I share my domicile with at least a hundred other rats, and one can't sleep anywhere in my home–or do much else, for that matter–without frequently touching another rat in a similar fashion. I can't say why this transfixes me.

He chuckles. "You still think like a rodent in so many ways. The reason humans wear clothes is to gain greater appreciation of them not being there, which is why they're so uncomfortable…"

I can certainly agree with that.

"To the human eye, the woman in her underclothes is poetic and sensual. I fear only you and I are advanced enough to see it as they are."

He purrs slightly, but I'm too busy committing them to memory to care what the dirty old pervert says. "What do they call them, again?"

He nudges me in the stomach far too hard. "The mouse is Idi, the rat is Amin. Your men liberated them from that village the Least-Rogonians tried to capture last Spring…"

Amin cranes her neck seductively in my direction as Idi strokes her chin.

"Really?" I say.

"Yes. Heheheh, they know first hand my kindness. Under

the One-Eyed Witch, they would be slaves. Under King Marrow, they are free."

"Freedom truly is a beautiful sight, My Liege …"

"Yes, and these two are my gift to you, Bloodford, for all your many services to the empire. After I've had my way, of course…"

I tear myself away from the females; it isn't like him to reward me like this. Come to think of it, he's never rewarded me at all, save one or two titles here and there. He's up to something.

Astran and Tranah had run almost an entire mile before stopping, hoping against hope that all the grass and other creatures would be enough to confuse the cat's nostrils so it could follow them no farther. Tranah kept checking the air for a sign of her friend, but Syrinx had yet to appear. Astran knew nothing of what his sister might be up to, but he was tired of running, so he gestured her toward the wooden fence that circled Marrow-Vinjia. There was a tree nearby they could hide behind.

"That was embarrassing," huffed Astran, desperate for breath.

"I dunno," a raspy voice hissed from behind them, "I think you looked exceptionally heroic."

"Hello, Syrinx," Astran spat.

Syrinx Silvereye was a lizard of some as yet unknown species who possessed no feminine qualities save the babushka she wore over her head. She carried a pouch of wine with her at all times, slung over her shoulder, but she never seemed to drink from it. Astran had only met her two or three times before, and didn't think more or less of her then than he thought of Tranah.

"How'd you get across the lake so fast?" Tranah piped excitedly.

"Oh, King What's-His-Face is meeting with those frogs we met that one time. I hitched a ride on their raft. Unseen, of course."

"Why?"

"Well, I figured if there was to be any kind of messing around with the Stuffed Shirts I wanted in on it, particularly if there's to be a reward for my services, maybe?"

"Do you think they'll let us come back with them?"

"Well, not being a paying customer myself, I can't say; but they should be finishing up at the palace right about now, though they said they wanted to have a look around before they left, so I couldn't say how much time we have…"

"Well," Tranah's ears perked up mischievously. "There's only one way to find out!"

Syrinx's eyes bulged in response. "Sneak into Marrow's palace and see if they're still there?"

"Whoa!" Astran screamed, perhaps more loudly than he should have, given how deep they were in enemy territory. "Do you really think we're about to just barge into Marrow-Vinjia on a whim to ask a favor from someone we barely know, who's most likely here to betray us in the first place?"

"You're not scared, are you?" Syrinx teased.

"No, but I'm not dumb enough to go against the Marrow-Vinjians when their entire army is there to greet us."

"Oh please," Tranah rolled her eyes. "They're bugs. They don't even use magic."

"Well, I don't know what you heard, but the last time a handful of mystics went against the whole lot of them, those 'bugs' fucked them up so badly they only ever found pieces of them, and that was in about seventeen different places."

"Oh, Astran…"

"Trust me, these are not rats you just fuck with on a whim. If you could, do you really think they would have lasted this long with us just across the lake?"

The thought had honestly never occurred to either of them, but even as he said it, Astran could see a twisted logic in going along with the gag anyway. He had his own reasons for staying away from Marrow-Vinjia, ones which didn't involve Tranah or her worthless friends, but he was slightly curious. Though it would serve no real purpose, it was perversely intriguing to sneak back to their home turf by crossing their enemy's. It would require more stealth than the others realized, but…

"Of course, they would never find out just how badly they'd slipped up, letting three Least-Rogonians (well, two, actually) sneak past them unnoticed. THAT might be worth a few free drinks down at the pub." He motioned for Syrinx to toss him her wine pouch. Syrinx grinned triumphantly and handed it over.

I excuse myself while His Majesty "breaks in" his gifts for me. All in all, this has been a strange evening. It comes with being in the military, certainly, but I'm starting to wonder if I wouldn't have been better off simply staying in the theater and learning what other lies are being told about me. That one line is the only thing I can remember: "All I ever wanted was to not exist. I think I've achieved that now…" I wonder who came up with that…

Bah, forget all that nonsense. I just need a good night's sleep, that's all. Still, I can't imagine I'll get any tonight. My Lord hasn't dismissed me, so I must wait out here in the hallway until his lust is satisfied. Looking around, I spy two butlers carrying a painting toward the now vacant spot where the painting of my great-grandfather leading the charge during the Battle of Warren's Burrow once hung. Well, maybe they're replacing him with a picture of me.

No…

Mother of God, it's Ophiuchus! The One-Eyed Witch!

Why the devil would His Majesty want a portrait of that hateful peasant? And where my great-grandfather's glorious charge should be? I step toward them, but they catch me in the corner of their eyes and scarper off, painting and all.

The Witch in question had retreated from her throne to her private den, which none of the other Least-Rogonians seemed to know about. Before her lay the quartered entrails of an chickadee, spread in the manner of a pagan ceremonies. The fortune telling portion was really just for laughs, as the bird was intended to be her dinner, but after a brief once over she stopped and stared hard at the pattern which said she would receive a mysterious visitor in her throne room, and that he would be a great mystic of questionable loyalties. Curious, she dipped her fingers in the blood to tide her appetite over and made her way back into the chamber where her three late henchmen had dragged her worthless sperm bank of a son earlier that morning. In a flowing burgundy cloak with a pleated hood stood someone she hadn't seen since before her husband had killed himself.

"Yes?" She mustered as much self-assurance as possible.

"Come now, is that any way to greet your old friend, Rommel?" the ferret began.

"What business do you have here?" she asked.

"It seemed the right thing to do. As per the signs, you may have need of my assistance."

"Hardly, old weasel. If anything, we're in a position to brag."

"A little early in your son's quest to be so chipper about how it's going, wouldn't you say?

"How did…never mind. Either way, I'm not worried. I've steered Astran on a path so perfect and delicate he couldn't fail if he tried."

"My, aren't we modest? Of course, there is always the possibility that the *little prince* is smarter than you give him credit for, and might want to shake things up a little."

"I'm afraid that hard drinking and fast females have robbed him of that flash of brilliance, Rommel. But, given the nature of his venture, I don't see how he could veer too far off course."

"I just love the way you're delicately avoiding telling me what he's doing when we both know that I already know."

"As you wish…"

"Couldn't veer too far off course, eh? Would leaving the park, and entering the city, leaving it and standing presently within the territory of your hated enemies be 'too far off course?'"

"What? How can… That stupid vermin! I give him one simple task and he…"

"Gets drunk and decides to infiltrate the most dangerous portion of the park on a whim with his sister in tow?"

"How did… Tranah is with him?"

"Indeed, as well as the lizard Syrinx Silvereye. It seems the lizard tempted the both of them with bragging rights, and they've secreted themselves into Marrow-Vinjia…"

"Damn that hellcat son of mine! What is he even doing on that side of the park?"

"The stars have told me that Astran was seeking the council

of the Wahid, close cousins of your intended 'allies' the Strega. Alas, he arrived too late, as Lord Bloodford had already ordered the army to exterminate the entire tribe."

"My word!"

"Indeed, the rats of Marrow are whipped into a blood lust tonight..."

"What is happening now?"

Rommel tilted his head back, his eyes closed, and hummed ominously. "While in the guise of peasants, they've encountered a drunken free mouse, Astairelike, Bloodford's second in command..."

"A mouse! Second in command?"

"Indeed, the Marrow-Vinjians are a backward race. Anyway, Tranah has convinced Astran to use his magic to blank Astairelike's mind, leaving the mouse incoherent and readying the dominoes of fate for a duel the mouse will soon fight. But that is not important. Tranah's caught sight of Marrow's palace. Tranah wishes a closer look. She actually thinks Astran will let her get close enough to Marrow to assassinate him, misunderstanding the greater subtlety of your true plan..."

"Humph, that sounds like her."

"At present, Marrow is speaking with Bloodford about his former wife, Queen Octavia..."

Ophiuchus smirked knowingly. "Oh, I know ALL about her."

"When he is finished, Bloodford will leave and Tranah will attempt to sneak into his palace. This itself is unchangeable, but unless you act all three of them will die, and your plans of the Citadel will be laid to waste forever!"

Resisting the urge to ask just what business any of this was of his, she just managed to choke out, "What does he need of me?"

"Summon your raft, the one the Maharajah gave you as a

goodwill gift. Use all your power to speed as quickly as you can to the center of the lake, and launch your most powerful spells against Marrow-Vinjia. Marrow will think the Strega have used the Citadel against him, and will send his greatest warriors against them, clearing a path for Astran and Tranah who will arrive just in time to rescue the Strega from the evil rats of Marrow…"

And with that, he left without another word. Ophiuchus was stricken numb with confusion. Ugh! What horrid wastes of rat-hood her children were! If she'd wanted them to march straight into Marrow's camp and lay the lot to waste she would have told them to! HER plan was so simple, so elegant, so SUBTLE!

She summoned another flank of guards and made orders to ready her craft. Oh, she was going to kill Astran and Tranah!

✳   ✳   ✳

At long last King Marrow summons me back in, grinning like the cat who caught the canary. He lifts another cigarette up to his mouth and I oblige with the match; he doesn't care. His eyes follow the cylinder as it rises back into the ceiling.

"You up there!" he screams. "Get out! I am done with you for tonight!"

The patter of servants fleeing echoes a moment, then we are truly alone. He inhales deeply, his eyes bloodshot and his head slinking low. "I think I can trust you, Bloodford…"

Hmm?

"I think, of all the rats in my army, you are most loyal to me…" He doesn't wait for me to answer. "The hallway… have they hung the new portrait yet?"

"No."

"I'm having a portrait of our enemy put up. Following her

destruction, she shall become quite a novelty indeed. But that is not the point. I believe I can trust you, Bloodford…"

I'm not at all certain where he's going with this. His tone is far too conversational. He's speaking to me as an equal.

"The people: they do not talk about my reign, how it happened?"

It takes me a second before I realize that was a question, "No, Sire. I don't see why they would. You married our Queen, and she died. Cut and dry, really…" I'm feeling uneasy, but I'm doing my best not to show it. I shouldn't bother; he's ignoring me.

"Octavia was a formidable wife, but I bent her to my will, and then I bent her further, and further still until she broke, and still I bent…"

"I don't follow, Your Majesty…"

He gets up, and motions for me to help him move the bed.

"Tell me, Bloodford, what did you think of Octavia? I know many said she was a great beauty…"

Oh, how to be tactful… "Hers was the face that launched a thousand soldiers."

We set the bed back down on the floor, he reclines back on his haunches again. "Did you ever lust for her?"

What?

"It is all right, my friend, we are both males. Get the door, will you?"

He points to the floor. Huh, a trap door. Already I love this. "Sire?"

"You'll see… It is the symbol of my power…"

The space beneath the Royal Bedroom is cramped and dusty, and I have problems breathing. My Liege seems better suited. I imagine he comes down here often. My eyes are only just adjusting to the darkness when:

"Master?"

That voice! It's wheezing and bent, like an old beggar woman's, but I've heard it before! It spoke to me the day I was made an officer in the Octave-Vinjian army!

"Master!" The poor wretch bounds toward us. "Master, Whore has waited long for you. She has no more food, but Whore is pleased. Master is merciful to Old Whore, he is!" Stroking his face with her knobby fingers, it seems unthinkable that this female was once my Queen. Her once plump face is now narrow, with the leftover skin hanging neglected off the bone. Matted and clumped with dirt, grime, and the remains of insects she's no doubt resorted to in His Majesty's absence, her robes, once elegant and ostentatious hang ripped and clawed-at, as if she means to look like a scarecrow. It can't be…

"My Queen?"

She doubles over in horror. "Not Queen, Whore! Queens are clean, Whore is filthy with her Master's love!" She weeps emphatically as she paws at him. "Master, the rat has called Whore clean, but Whore is filthy and knows her place. Master, my Master, please, if he has any mercy won't he throw dirt at me?"

Sire, looking indifferent toward this whole affair, backhands her right across the jaw with a force that seems impossible from a rodent so small. She practically sails over and lands with a tremendous thud into a pile of dust to His Majesty's right.

"Oh, oh thank you, Master. Whore could never be called Queen now. Nothing clean about Whore because she knows her place and Master has shown her!"

"Go," he says at long last. She trips majestically and runs on all fours in the opposite direction.

I stare stunned at her. "She…"

"Soon," he continues, as if I hadn't said anything, "The One-

Eyed Witch will tremble before as she does, for this my power. To that skeleton of a regent I am as the owl… I wanted you to see this, because of all my men only you would be loyal enough to understand." His voice sounds far away. "Ophiuchus will one day cower beneath my floor, calling me Master, begging me to hit her and have my way. Feh. I wouldn't touch her with a pointed stick, but she will beg me to, for this is my power. You will make this happen for me…"

I still can't believe this is happening. "My Queen…"

"Will make a fine nurse for the children you bear with Idi and Amin, once I have scarred her face beyond recognition. I grow weary of her. Come, we have planning to do."

Before I know it I'm back in his chambers, his bed re-affixed over the door, another cigarette perched in his mouth, being lit by my match.

"The Strega," he begins, "control the single most powerful entity we've ever known. The Citadel has the power to keep the lake from crashing down into the miles and miles of burrows and warrens the ignorant Under-Grounders dug so precariously close to the water. With a flick of the wrist, any Strega could drown the entire populace of the Lower Park. Such a gem does not rightfully belong to anyone but myself. Our scholars have suggested that the Citadel in and of itself may have sentience, but there is no proof, or else the Strega have told no one of it. Given the Wahid's extinction, in seems unlikely. Therefore, it must be the ground the Strega rule that gives them the power; control by virtue of occupation. That's a military concept if I ever heard of one, and truly, who has a finer military than I?" He gloats as well he can as he takes another long draw.

I try to interrupt, but he resumes, "The Strega know we are coming. Not officially, but their days are numbered, and no other tribe could logically take their place. You and your team will leave tomorrow on a diplomatic envoy to the Strega's burrow, officially. We've already dispatched a messenger to their ruler. As the route we plotted for him takes him the longest and most hazardous way, he should not arrive until you've already scouted the best sites for our artillery, which will be not far behind you."

"Artillery?"

"Yes, one of our contacts in the human research brigade has come across a small cache of revolvers. My own personal scientists are working on mounting them; they should make crackerjack cannons, I think."

This all so surreal; his strategy makes sense, but what just happened…and before that it was…I can't think…

"Go now," he yawns. "You leave at dawn…"

It was almost midnight. Bloodford had left 10 Downing Street and turned toward his own estate. Astairelike had dug well into his spirits and moved on to some mysterious wood all the poorer mice were gnawing on, a vice he often engaged in but could not name. Syrinx's wine was long gone, as was the lizard herself, who'd fled to see if the craft that had been carting the Maharajah had left yet.

Astran was perched on his haunches, stone drunk and deaf to the world. Tranah was livid, swearing and digging her ax into the ground, all the while staring at Marrow-Vinjia's pristine wooden border.

"What do you mean you can't think of a way in?"

Day Two

Marrow-Vinjians, Chapter Seven: A Duel Among Friends

||||||||||||||||||||||||||||||||||||||||||||||||||||||||||||||||||||||||||||||||||||||||||||||||||||||||||||||||||||||||

My estate is modeled after the Taj Mahal. Somehow or another I've gotten back, walked the entire fifteen yards without noticing. I venture around back, where my birdcage is. The attempts of My Liege to build an Airborne Cavalry were fruitless. Most of them escaped before we could train them, and what few we've kept have been rendered flightless. One of them was given to me, so they could paint pictures of me like the humans who ride horses. The cage has its curtain drawn, and my pet is dead to the world. I am alone with my thoughts.

I prop myself against the wall, no longer able to stand, my stovepipe slipping over my eyes. This night has been most…I can't even finish…

My head lolls stupidly to the left, and in my mind's eye I see an image of myself standing next to me, his expression grim and serious. I'm not surprised, really. This sort of thing happens now and then.

"It seems the king…" he says.

"Don't call him that!" I scream.

"I beg your pardon?"

"Octavia is still alive, Marrow is only her regent…"

"You don't seriously think that was Octavia, do you?"

"Of course she was. I know what my queen looks like."

"She didn't look like much of a queen to me."

"How can you…"

"Look! I'm not saying she wasn't Queen Octavia at one point, but whatever that pitiful wretch was she certainly wasn't the ruler of a civilized society. You saw her. She smelled so awful I could have sworn she was a male. The Octavia you knew would never have ripped up her clothes, beg to be muddied, and refer to herself in the third person as 'Whore'! No, my friend, whatever that disgusting lump of rodent was, Octavia is dead, and Marrow, right or wrong, is her murderer and rightful successor. Put it out of your mind and be at peace."

"I can't. My Liege is just…he's changed! Don't you see? The Marrow who came to power three years ago would never…"

"You say that, and yet it's been at least three years that he's kept her prisoner."

"What are you saying?"

"Think! In all your exploits, you never witnessed one rat do to another anything like what you saw back there with Her Majesty?"

"Never!"

"Well…?"

"But, if that were true, and His Majesty is…"

"Afraid so."

"What should I do?"

"Nothing."

"Nothing?"

"Nothing."

"Nothing? NOTHING? How can you just stand there and…"

"You swore an oath to that rat, Bloodford! And anything you do that breaks proves you nothing more than a traitor and damned coward! So what if he is a madman? It wouldn't matter an ounce if he became Caligula reincarnate! He is your King, and God will strike you down with the fury he loosed on Satan himself if you betray him."

"I…"

"Be at peace, old rat. The evils he brings with him are but the foul swamp that a great capital will grow from. From his insanity will bring an empire of culture and advancement to a million uneducated vermin all across the city! You'd turn you back on that? Over some paltry thing like your conscience?"

"But…shouldn't my loyalty be to the greater good?"

"Through your king, it is."

"But the others–the further into the abyss he goes, the more of them he endangers!"

"Since when do you care?" He starts to fade away.

He's gone.

I wander over to the cage, maliciously pulling back the curtain. The bird chirps violently, battering his wings in vain attempt to fly away. His futility soothes me.

My mind is edging back into proper alignment, but there are portions that seem too large to fit back into place. Ugh, thank goodness it's almost morning. My head is about to split open at the seams. Chumsa, Octavia, Idi and Amin…and that ferret. I don't even want to know how that beast factors into all this…

"Bedford!"

Astairelike's voice couldn't be more out of place, but I welcome it just the same… He looks far too chipper for so early in the morning, and he's still wearing his ax belt.

"So. What did the Imperial Head-Case want?"

He's been chewing wormwood again. I can smell it on his breath, and his limp is much more pronounced. Instinctively, I grasp the bars of my pigeon's cage and squeeze with all of my might, lest I should rush him and tan the insolence out of him. I don't need to hear that sort of thing just now. I've started to feel a little better when the stupid beast pecks at the bar, nicking my finger!

"Gah! Dammit!"

Astairelike starts laughing his head off. I don't see what's particularly funny…

"What are you blathering about?" I shout.

"The king gave you that, didn't he?"

"Of course…"

"Well, it is sort of funny, now that I've noticed it…"

"What?"

"The cuckoo gave you a cuckoo!" He's tripping over himself with tittering.

Without a second thought I've drawn my sword, flipped it around to the dull side and charged him, whipping the devil out him as if he were a Least-Rogonian slave. In seconds he has a fresh set of scars on his face, but in my fury I let my guard down. After closing his eyes and bracing his jaw, he tucks himself into a ball and reverse mule-kicks me hard in the chest, hard enough to push me back.

He's back his feet, the one paw on his weapon, his other babying the wounds on his face.

"Motherfucker!" he whines. He's paying more attention to

his injuries than me, which means he'll continue to fight. I'm not thinking it in words just now, but I know Astairelike. He's usually quite fearless until he gets injured. Then he becomes completely irrational, and much more dangerous.

I attack first. I lean forward on my toes and the tension in my muscles pushes me forward, effortlessly. With the grace of a boxer he hops backward, causing my attack to miss him entirely. He catches the dull edge of my blade with his foot and back-flips, kicking me in the face.

The pathetic wretch finally takes his paw off his face long enough to aim his weapon at me; he takes too long and loses some of his propulsion as he hurls his ax. With a bunt, I catch the chain and catapult it horizontally. Astairelike, still in mid-fall, is caught by the yank of his chain and accompanies his ax toward the cage. I'm not sure how, but he manages to catch the stupid thing before he collides with the bars.

I might clock our scuffle at just over two seconds, if that.

He struggles to stand back up, reaching for the bar I was holding earlier, but the stupid bird repeats his attack on me and severely damages his finger.

"FUCKER!" He flails in vain attempt to defend himself, but his axe misses my bird's head by a mile. Even in my rage, the sight is by far too comical.

As he finally manages to get on both feet, I've relaxed my stance a little. He himself is still rigid, but I doubt he wishes to continue. "You know," he spits, "I think you might really have been trying to kill me this time."

"No comment."

"Let me guess… His Majesty either showed you something incredibly disturbing he picked up from the humans, or we've been given yet another insane and completely unethical task?"

"Both, actually."

"Ah."

My heart rate is back to normal now. This wasn't the first time Astairelike and I have come to blows after I've met with the king. The thing about Astairelike is that, while he may have many rat-like qualities, he will always be a mouse, and will always let his stimulants get the best of him…

"Well?" He rolls his uninjured paw impatiently before recalling that his other paw's in pain.

I face the opposite direction. "Our Lord has dispatched a message to the Strega, requesting diplomatic talks. By the time it gets there, you, Spoolnicker and I will have already arrived and scouted artillery positions, if not carried the attack out ourselves."

"Oh, good. For a moment I thought we were going to do something unethical…"

I spin back around but he cuts me off. "You know, you shouldn't fake moral quandaries like that. You'll give yourself ulcers."

He sighs. "Perhaps you're right."

"Of course I'm right. Besides, if we weren't always out doing horrible, hell-worthy things in the name of our country, we'd be stuck doing stupid things, like sitting through that play."

"That play was not stupid. What little we saw of it was compelling drama at its finest."

"Please, it was poorly written and the guy it's about is an inane jackass."

"A deep and poetic jackass, if you please."

"'All I ever wanted was to not exist. I think I've achieved that now…'? Who talks like that?"

"Philistine."

"Yeah, well, if I knew what that meant I'd…err…lost my train of thought."

I chuckle. "Imbecile."

"Now THAT I understood…"

The air goes cold. Almost as if we've been caught in a fog, there are swirling breezes from every direction, and everything… blinks. It's as if one second the world is there and the next it isn't. It does it again. And again. And…

" Bedford ?"

"You too? Huh." My voice seems to echo slightly. A cursory glance, everything looks unusual. Not in anyway I can describe, but…

"LOOK OUT!"

He knocks me to the ground just as an explosion with no visible source erupts nearby, incinerating the bird and its cage. Its cries of dying anguish ring out, but are silenced quickly by another burst of air in the vicinity, possibly across the road.

"We're under attack!" I yell.

"No shit!"

The army has been raised and scrambled all along the fence, balancing furtively atop the ancient wooden barrier as behind and below our fellow Marrow-Vinjians are caught in the furor. Fires rage all through the village (save the replica of 10 Downing Street, which our brave and unrelenting troops have valiantly kept in one piece.) Their purpose is clear, but for the rest of us… well, one can't defend against an enemy they can't see, can they?

"They have to be projectiles," one of our captains squeaks, his eyes glued to a mock-up of binoculars His Majesty's scientists have been experimenting with. "The patterns of the explosions… They have to be using some kind of catapult!"

"If they were, we'd see them coming!" Spoolnicker shouts him down, but it doesn't change the captain's mind or solve anything. The chaos and carnage continues to run unchecked, a deafening roar erupting every few minutes, sometimes seconds.

A terrifying possibility dawns on me. "You don't suppose there is no attack?"

They all stare at me. "What sort of nonsense is that?"

"What if those bombs aren't being hurled at us? What if they were already there?"

Without even freezing in disbelief we hurl ourselves back toward the interior, studying the blows and bracing against the unbearable. We look closely, hoping…

"No," Astairelike says at last, "a lot of them are happening ABOVE the buildings…"

He breathes a slight sigh of relief, but the elimination of that grim possibility is ultimately meaningless. Somewhere, out beyond our heretofore-impenetrable barrier, someone is lobbing rounds at us and doing a damn good job concealing it!

"Look!" Spoolnicker points out into the lake. Knowing far too much about battle to question him, I immediately follow his finger into the epicenter of the water. A glow, perhaps too subtle to notice earlier but definitely visible by now; it's unearthly, a sort of orange blanket, spilling like oil across the night-blackened surface, and growing slowly, and, unless my eyes are deceiving me, solidifying!

"What is that?" Astairelike screams.

"Not a coincidence," I concede.

The solid glowing mass begins to sink. Nothing I've ever

encountered in my career prepared me for anything like this: it's sinking, and it's pulling the water down with it!

I can't hear anything, or feel the raging surge of wind, but that mass… Half the lake is gone now, and what remains…

A burst of air and the water it pulled down flashes upward and becomes solid, like the tail of a scorpion greater in size than a chestnut tree!

Everything slows to a crawl. Each inch of it forcing toward us appears as a still image, not movement. I can't even feel the pull of Spoolnicker's burly arms as he dead-lifts me into a fireman's carry, grabs Astairelike by the tail and bolts off the side of the fence!

I don't even feel the crash as Spoolnicker tucks and rolls, landing on top of me, knocking out what little breath remains. Just before blacking out, I manage to wheeze, "I guess they got our message…"

The Frogs In Question, Chapter Eight: Main Scout

The feasting was over. The males departed as the females swooped in to claim the leftovers, as was their custom, while the Maharajah himself secreted away into his private cavern below water on the isthmus that lay between the mainland and the peninsula where the frogs got all their mystical herbs. His aide, Main Scout, slipped quietly away from his master and crawled ashore to await the ferret. Main Scout, as his malefactor was constantly reminding him, was a small but important cog in a much larger machine of the ferret's design, but so far the brute had never bothered to explain to him what that was, exactly. Tonight, he had promised to do so.

The wind was dying, and as he waited his skin began to dry out. He ducked back into the water to facilitate the breathing process. Normally, when the frogs came ashore, they carried pitchers of water to keep themselves damp, but he'd forgotten. He was just settling in when a strange vibration coursed through the lake.

Opening his senses, he perceived a sort of orange blanket, spilling like oil across the night-blackened surface toward the middle of the water, but the after-wave had reached all the way to his remote corner. Whatever it was, it didn't care much about being subtle. The entire lake must have been able to feel it. He searched further and felt a tremendous thrust of force, like a blast of raw mystical energy that had erupted from the center of the lake. With minimal probing he focused and saw it all: the ferocious attack on Marrow-Vinjia, the carnage of the exploding air, the collapsing of their great wall, the deaths of all the innocent. It was madness.

"Saw that did you?" said the ferret. Main Scout eyed him with subtle suspicion; he was dressed immaculately in a fashion that the Marrow-Vinjians would have favored.

"There is nothing that happens in the lake that we are not aware of…Bathin, is it, or are you Rommel now?"

"Metatron, actually. In the human faith it means 'Voice of God'."

Main Scout, who had no idea what he was talking about, simply said "I get them confused."

"Well, don't worry, they're all me, anyway."

"…the Marrow-Vinjians have been attacked…"

"By the One-Eyed Witch, herself, no less."

"She struck from the center of the lake. They'll think it was the Strega!"

"That was the plan, yes."

"Exactly what you up to, old ghost?"

"Old ghost. That's funny, considering you're much the same thing, or were before that hare was willing to part with your soul."

"Now, why would you bring that up?" he said as he shuddered.

"Oh, you silly thing, I'd kick you in the ribs if you had any. Now, before you ask, yes, it was my idea to have the Least-Rogonians attack Marrow-Vinjia. It was also my plan to invoke images of the oh-so-sacred Strega in the minds of our more civilized rodents. With that much energy being thrown around up top, the actual Strega will more than likely be forced to get involved, and I'd like to think they'll work in my favor."

"Wait, slow down a minute…"

"It's quite simple, little frog. Both sides are making a play for the Citadel. It was the perfect moment to act, and now that everyone's done what I knew they would, they really have no choice but to fall with the dominoes. The Strega will be forced to protect themselves preemptively, which will put the emissaries from both sides so high on their guard that it will only take minimal prompting for me to set them against each other, and before you know it, the ultimate prize will be mine!"

"And that is?"

"Nothing that would seem quite so important to you, but I've always been a sentimentalist. Now, you will have a small part to play, since with all the variables I have to make absolutely sure things go according to plan. Nothing overt, mind you, but some subtle nudging here and there."

"And when it's all over?"

"Well, there will be some reward in it for your kind, I think. Granted, you might not get the Marrow-Vinjians' aid in fighting off those ducks, but with them and their friends out of the way there will be plenty of resources to go around. And if you don't mind rattling the saber a bit, I'm sure the rats in the city won't mind losing the park very much."

"And what's in it for me, personally?"

"Ever the pragmatist. Well, I won't have much need for you,

so you'll be getting your freedom back–which I'm sure you're clamoring for, since it's been about, what, a hundred years since Sivad captured you?"

"And what else?"

"You drive a hard bargain. Very well, I'll throw in a few virgins for you to sweeten the pot!"

"Very well."

"Good lad." He turned to leave, opening a portal with a gesture of his paw. "Unless I miss my guess, the Strega will probably attack using the squirrels on the Marrow-Vinjian side, so I'd advise you to keep away for a day or so. Oh, that reminds me: you know that vole, Reuel?"

"Sivad's rodent? Yes."

"Well, he'll be dead the next time you see him. Just a heads up…"

"Is that part of your plan?" he croaked, but the portal had already closed off, and as Main Scout crawled back onto the land he felt a shudder in his bones. In their folklore, the frogs spoke of a god they called Tade, who would turn his eyes away from those who acted on behalf of evil. Main Scout couldn't help but think that shuddering was Tade, turning his eyes away from him forever…

Least-Rogonians, Chapter Nine: Syrinx Silvereye

Narrowly avoiding the scrambling infantry around the perimeter, Astran and Tranah bolted toward a settlement nearby known as Berlinger Station. It was controlled by Marrow, but it was a well-known fact that the army almost never went there. They were just within spitting distance when the scorpion tail erupted from the center of the lake, making such an obscene spectacle they had no choice but to marvel at it.

"Mom's really gone all out." Astran shook his head.

"Mom?"

"Of course. Who else is that powerful?"

"Surely the Strega?"

"Nah, I've never heard of a big show of power from them like that, at least not one that didn't turn out to be us in the end."

"But Marrow will think so," whispered Tranah, catching on.

"That's just like her. Give me something quiet and messy to do, while she gets the grand display…"

"Jealous?"

"Unimpressed…"

"Oh really?" Ophiuchus' furious bellow erupted behind them.

"Oh, good," Astran sneered, "now I can tell you to your face just what…"

But just what she was exactly, Ophiuchus would never know. She snapped her wrists and telekinetically thrust the two siblings into each other. Unable to move, they were encased in clear yellow orb. Ophiuchus lifted it off the ground and catapulted it across the lake. Several days' worth of sailing passed under Astran and Tranah in forty-five hellish seconds. They landed head-first into their home territory with the force of a cannonball. Astran could barely see when his mother's mystical barge darted toward them. Upending topsoil, she leaped from her run-aground vessel and landed *just* beyond them. Shattering the orb, she bared her claws and mauled Tranah forty ways to breakfast before Astran, using his staff, stood up and sent enough of a tremor to startle Ophiuchus off his sister.

"You!" she barked angrily.

"Me," he sniffed defiantly.

"What the threepenny fuck do you think you were doing in Marrow-Vinjia?"

"In?" Tranah shouted, ready to give The One-Eyed Witch six types of Hell, but Astran, with tremendous subtlety, gave his staff a squeeze and closed off her throat before she could utter another word.

"What we do is our business!" Astran spat. "And anyway, just what do think you were doing?"

"I was saving your worthless mouse ass, is what I was doing, you ungrateful drunk! I gave you one job to do, and rather than do that you go gallivanting about in enemy territory just so some worthless barfly will pay to hear the story! So, Astran, what all did you do to alert them to our plans? Kill their soldiers? Rape their females? Oh, I'll bet you had no end of fun, polluting your member in their unholy bodies."

"Watch it, bitch…"

"You dare to speak to me like that! I'll teach you some manners if it's the last thing I do!" She raised her paw and launched a violet animation, shaped like a flying sword, straight for Astran's midsection. Dodging, he once more rammed his staff into the ground, summoning the ghost of a manticore, twice the size of a tiger with the angry face of a mustachioed man and a spiked mace tail of poisonous quills. The ghost roared threateningly with enough force to pin Ophiuchus to the ground. It glared down at the pudgy rodent, and retreated into the timbers of Astran's staff.

"Don't…fuck with me, old bag…"

Ophiuchus, shaken by her son's sudden decision to actually use his magical talents, cricked her neck angrily and brushed the dust off of her shoulders. "Nothing to be done now, is there, thanks to you? Marrow will surely be convinced that my attack was an act of the Strega. By noon he'll have launched his chief assassins against them. You shall follow them, and when they reach the Strega's keep you will kill them, thus ingratiating them to you."

"The Strega?" mouthed Tranah, shooting Astran a questioning glance which he may or may not have noticed. The lack of air was starting to get to her.

"Bit of a problem with that," Astran scoffed. "They're on the other side of the lake. We're not."

Ophiuchus, who had by now regained her composure and noticed just how far she had deviated from the ferret Rommel's instructions, clenched her fists bitterly and, flinging a sideways slap at nothing, locked the both of them up in separate yellow orbs.

"Dammit," she muttered under her breath, "how did you get over there so fast, anyway?"

"It's called running," Astran whispered mockingly. "You might try it sometime."

The One-Eyed Witch stormed off, leaving the two of them suspended for all of the Least-Rogonians to see. Astran didn't care; this might even get his mother to abandon her grand scheme, at least as far as it involved him. In fact, he took no notice of the orb at all until Tranah began tapping spastically at the walls of hers. Grinning paternally, Astran undid his spell, and Tranah gasped for air.

"Astran?"

"Hmm?"

"This is bigger than I thought, isn't it?"

"Matter of opinion, really…"

Back in her personal digs, Ophiuchus scowled at her chickadee, rotten almost to in-edibility in her absence. Swearing uncontrollably, she flicked her wrist and summoned a sword, not unlike Lord Bloodford's, and hacked the dead thing's head off. It helped a little, but the trickle of stagnant blood from the bird's neck formed yet another fortune-telling pattern, saying that a stranger would be waiting by the far chestnut tree where her father, Tristram, had been buried years earlier. Since teleportation was a spell far too complicated even for one as powerful as her, she instead cloaked herself with invisibility and darted out, almost levitating out of the mound and toward the majestic tree.

Rommel, chewing nonchalantly on a blade of grass, was leaning against the bark, standing directly on top of what would be considered the old rat's grave! Furious, and impatient, she raised her paw yet again, but Rommel froze her in her tracks with a single glance that despite her invisibility managed to hook her eye to eye.

"I wouldn't do that," he murmured matter-of-factly.

"You were right," she sighed, which wasn't the best way to start, but she was beginning to notice that keeping her off-balance was probably his entire strategy.

"But of course. I'm always right."

"Then what should we do now? Astran's no longer on the right side of the lake…"

"Because of your temper."

"Well…"

"I must say, you've desperately complicated the situation. However, no knot is so tangled that can't be undone."

"Then…"

"Clearly, you can no longer take advantage of Marrow's ego and short-sightedness. Certainly by now the Strega will have noticed the burst of power you unleashed, and when they investigate and see the expansionists in full seek-and-destroy mode, they'll do everything in their power to delay the Marrow-Vinjians as much as possible. The only thing you can count on, Ophiuchus, is that those delays will give you enough time to outfit your son and daughter properly, and get them underground as soon as possible."

"How much time do we have?"

"The future is unclear, but I can almost certainly guarantee they won't reach the underground anytime today. The Strega will undoubtedly seal all the tunnels off as a precaution, which means that you'll have to take advantage of one they don't know about."

"One they don't know about? How is that possible?"

"The Strega only have so much knowledge of the underground because it is the magic of the Citadel that keeps the lake from crashing through the over-dug earth and drowning the poor fools who live there. There is one entrance that is so structurally sound that they never gained influence over it, and subsequently forgot it existed. But it will take time to get there. It is not far from the center of the lake, and anymore magic used on the waters will only draw the Strega's attention."

"Very well, I'll gather my very best and send those two off at once. But tell me, what of this entrance? Where is it?"

"Firstly, I would suggest not sending anymore of your guards. Astran seems to not care about their safety much. Secondly, I know your laws require you to travel in fives, so I would suggest you include the lizard Silvereye in his party."

"What?"

"She knows of this entrance I speak of, and will leap at the chance for an adventure with your daughter…"

Ophiuchus closed her eyes in consent, as much as it pained her to think of a filthy lizard being part of the holy five in her son's quest! When she opened her eyes, the ferret Rommel was gone. Dropping her camouflage, the One-Eyed Witch sank to her knees. Why, she asked herself, why should I believe him? But what other choice did she have? He'd been right about everything else so far…

Astran, unlike his sibling, was not restless is his mystical cage. He had a nose for such things, and while Tranah was working herself into a lather, fidgeting and picking at her hairs, he sat and waited until…

"Astran?" she broke his concentration.

"Mmm?

"Earlier…why didn't…?"

"Would she have believed us?"

"I guess not." She shrugged. "So, how long do you think she's gonna keep us in here?"

The right moment had finally arrived. The magic holding them had weakened just enough. Astran balled his fist, and with all his strength, struck the weakest point of the orb and fractured it. He dropped into a low crouch while Tranah looked on, wide-eyed.

"How'd you do that?"

He eyed her with contempt. "Magic."

"Really?"

"No."

He rapped his staff against her bubble and dropped her onto her chest, knocking the air out of her.

"Oh," she snorted, "I see, this is that masculinity you're always blathering about."

"Masculinity? Astran?" Syrinx's exaggeratedly girlish voice floated over them from behind Astran's right shoulder.

"Syphilis, how wonderful for you show up finally."

"Ha. I would be glad to see me, if I were you, seeing as how we're going to be working together."

"Tempting, but I don't really have time to steal candy from an infant just now."

"The One-Eyed Witch will be employing me as a guide soon, at a steep fee, of course."

"Guide? To what, the gates of Hell?"

"Close."

Tranah brushed herself off finally, and stepped toward her friend. "Syrinx?"

"Well, all right. Since your mom blew her top last night, the Strega are gonna be on high alert. You'll never get underground discretely without my help, so I'm in a position to finagle old Ophiuchus for a significant portion of the royal treasury. Hurray for me!"

Astran looked askance at her, then looked at Tranah. "You know, maybe the gods do exist after all."

"Why?"

"Because they clearly hate me."

No sooner had Syrinx grinned suggestively at the thought of stealing his mother's money when the rat in question reappeared flanked by the three graying dormice whom Astran recognized as being in charge of the temple he visited yesterday. Without looking either him or Tranah in the eye, the One-Eyed Witch barked off her instructions: these church-mice should accompany them and carry their supplies, etc. Neither son nor daughter paid too much attention to her words; Tranah was waiting for her mother to give Syrinx a chance to proposition her while Astran simply fought off the temptation to transform her into a bedbug and declare himself ruler of Astra-Vinjia. Ophiuchus wound down eventually and ordered them to accompany her to breakfast.

"Already wasted so much time, you may as well leave on a full stomach," she sneered.

Tranah followed obediently, Syrinx a few steps behind. Astran, as usual, ambled slowly in the opposite direction, toward the lake. He dug his staff into the ground carefully and let it stand upright while he dipped his paws in the water and wiped off his face. He had hoped, somewhat foolishly, that having failed, Ophiuchus would have let him off the hook for this stupid little errand of hers. But, she didn't. If only I'd failed on purpose, thought Astran. THEN she'd let me go.

"You don't like your mother much, do you?" The unmistakable voice of Bathin took him off-guard as the great ferret slithered from behind a small mound to Astran's right which shouldn't have been large enough to conceal him.

"I dunno. Probably not."

"Then why are you helping her? Seems to me a rat like you wouldn't give in to someone he didn't respect unless they had something on him. Knowing that can't POSSIBLY be the case…"

"Well, you're in good spirits today."

"Chumsa is safe and the Marrow-Vinjians are not noticeably closer to taking the Citadel. Today is a good day."

"R-i-g-h-t, and… What's your stake in this, again?"

The ferret sighed. "My stake is to protect the futures of the tribes which have no part in your conflict."

"Oh." Astran was impressed. "Awfully decent of you."

"Yes, well, as stabilizing as a cold war is, we both know that sooner or later this will all come to a head, and if one of you has to come out on top it is to the benefit of everyone else for your side to win."

"Oh." Astran's guard went back up. "So you're here to help, then?"

"No."

"No?"

"If I help you, that means I have to take my eyes off those I look after. That wouldn't be very smart."

"True." Astran shrugged.

"Though, if I might give you a piece of advice?"

"I'm all ears."

The ferret took a second to note the chunk that was missing from one of Astran's ear, then moved on. "The lizard is going to lead you to a small isthmus between the mainland and the peninsula to the east in the marshy area of the lake. Since there are almost no tunnels underground in that area, the Citadel's power doesn't extend there. You'll be able to sneak in undetected, but as soon as the Strega get whiff of the Marrow-Vinjian soldiers they'll be moving in every direction looking for threats to their security, and even as powerful as you are I don't think you want to travel too long under those conditions."

"How long do you think that will take?"

"I don't think they'll manage to get underground anytime today, due to that attack, but if I were you I'd make as much progress by tonight as possible."

Bathin stretched to his full height, scratched under each arm, and made to leave. "By the way," he called over his shoulder, "this park is five miles across. How'd you get over there so fast?"

Astran smirked knowingly. Well, he thought, magic can have practical uses, if you're not too showy about it.

Marrow-Vinjians, Chapter Ten: Leaping Over The Edge

'''||||||||||||||||||||||||||||||||||||||||||||||||||||||||||||||||||||||||||||||||||||||||||||||||||||||||||||||||||||||||||||||||||||||||||||||||||||||||||||||||||||||||||||||||||||||

’ve been unconscious for several hours. Our wall has been completely destroyed. In every direction there is construction, disarray, and the citizenry moving at paces previously unforeseeable in polite society. The air feels as if there might be a fox nearby. In the epicenter of it all is our noble king, perched over a makeshift table in the center of the street, like an architect, and surrounded by officials and concerned rats willing to forget their place in the pandemonium. I can almost forget what I'd been thinking of him earlier. To see him like this is just inspiring. I don't think that in all the history of Vinjia has a king simply planted himself, in time of crisis, in the most vulnerable position possible, hard at work for the good of his people. I could almost imagine him changing right then and there into a god.

"Bloodford," he all but whispers, as if I'll just instinctively pick it out of the hubbub. "Come."

"My Liege …"

"I know what you wish to say, but there is nothing to it." He doesn't sound even slightly interested in what's happening all around him.

"But Sire," I protest, "that could only have been the Citadel; clearly the Strega have caught wind of our plans!"

"I said there was nothing to that, Bloodford. You," he turns to one of the captains, "fetch me a cigarette. No, Bloodford, I doubt very much that our messenger has arrived at their border yet. Had they reviewed and seen through our plan, as they undoubtedly will, their attack would have been much more devastating and involved more civilian casualties. As such, we have only lost our fence, an insignificant amount of rodents, and our image of invincibility. All cosmetic. Light it please." His captain had returned with a cigarette and a match. "This lashing out of theirs is undoubtedly retaliation for your attack on the Wahid. However, as minor as all this may sound, we've faced a potential credibility loss among the other tribes. Reports tell me that with an hour of the attack, the nearest tribe of squirrels launched a raid on Berlinger Station…

"The venture into the Strega's territory, while planned anyway, has now become even more important. If we do not commence our campaign soon, some other tribe might take it upon themselves to do it for us, if not attack Marrow-Vinjia itself…"

He breaks for a puff on his cigarette. I know that what he hasn't mentioned so far is begging to come out, so I make the first move:

"That attack last night…I didn't even know the Citadel was capable of such things…" I eye him nonchalantly, knowing he'll take my bait. I can't explain it; he's certainly not trying to hide it, but I need to hear it from his own lips.

"The Citadel is capable of many things, Bloodford, far

beyond the mere architectural uses the vermin have in mind. I do not think they can grasp what power the Strega have had at their disposal…"

He cuts off to inhale more smoke, and the catharsis I'd wanted hadn't done much for me. He abruptly changes the subject by shoving a map in my face. "Berlinger Station is, now more than ever, the safest entrance to the underground." His finger traces through a large circle that leads into a two-way divide. "Once you have gone through the Fountainhead," his finger follows the divide to the right, "you will make your way through the Eastern Tunnel. It will be the shortest route…"

"Sire," I gasp, pointing at the underground cavern the Eastern Tunnel leads into, "that path leads through the Land of the Blind." I don't belabor the point too much. His Majesty knows that I am not a coward, and knows exactly what happens to those who chance the Land of the Blind.

"At the end of that cavern there is a junction that connects with many other tunnels. The last one," he points to a narrow tunnel right next to a much larger one, "points directly into the Strega's territory, with only two tribes to worry about. Were you to take the Western Tunnel," he moves his finger back, "you would have to face the Lakova," he moves his fingers to the next open space, "the Shrii," he moves up to the tunnel that leads from the Shrii territory, "the Ocanom," he traces his finger back to the left, naming every tribe we'd face along the serpentine path into the Strega's keep. "And by the time you get there, our messenger will be dead, and the Citadel will have reduced Marrow-Vinjia to charcoal."

I thrust my finger towards another entrance to the underground, in the upper left corner of the map. "What about the entrance at Greenshire? It provides a straight-shot to the Strega without any tribes in between!"

"It is too far away. If we wish to preserve any propaganda value we must get underground without any further delay. Gather your men…" And with that he returns to whatever he was doing, as if I'd never been here in the first place.

I walk the short distance to where Astairelike and Spoolnicker are crouched, eavesdropping.

"Berlinger Station, eh?" Astairelike deadpans. "Nothing like First Class. They've got THE best wine there."

"Everything's ready?" I ask.

"Been ready since last night." Spoolnicker picks his teeth. "We were planning to do this anyway, you know."

I smirk. "A little more respect for your fearless leader, if you will?"

"He really wants us to go against Sivad?" Astairelike says.

"Come now, old boy." Spoolnicker picks up his normal tone again. "You know Sivad's just a legend…"

"Yes, well, I know that, and you know that, but we're three chaps who can keep a secret, right?"

Nothing more to say. I start walking toward the border. The other two follow, much more enthusiastically.

"Think they'll make a statue out us for this?" Astairelike queries.

"Only if we die," Spoolnicker responds.

"So, yes."

Berlinger Station has a certain kitsch quality a first. A hollow mound near the shore of the lake, with a train station facade made out of Lincoln logs. Most of the rat population lives in a hollowed-out tree nearby, but the mound itself sees constant ebb and flow of travelers from the underground. The Station itself had been established by King Capra as a trading post, but a war with another tribe had drawn attention elsewhere, and under Octavia it had been completely neglected after that disastrous campaign.

The earlier flux of savages were not as advanced as the current epoch to begin with, and they had had a devolutionary effect on our countrymen, who for the most part had dispensed with wigs and wore only the most minimum of clothing.

"What do you think?" Spoolnicker tosses out nonchalantly. I ignore him.

Astairelike pretends like a rodent possessed not to notice to intertwining tribes circling concentrically around each other between the lake and the hollow tree, even though this is hardly an unfamiliar sight when one has been in the city as often as we have. I think it's just the co-mixing of different rats outdoors is what gets to him. Spoolnicker pays much more attention, which I find unusual, but he must be looking for someone in particular.

"You know the fellow we're supposed meet, Spoolnicker?"

"I met him once, a few years ago."

"Didn't His Majesty tell you all this, Bedford ?"

"He was feeling a little too…show-offish to get into details…"

"Just as well. One of the captains filled me in a little."

"And of course," Astairelike grimaces as a pair of naked voles stroll by within striking distance, "we get rushed out the door with as little preparation as possible and have to do everything ourselves."

"Somehow, I think this is the easy part."

"This fellow," I mutter, fixing my eyes on someone I have a feeling about, "he wouldn't be the Provincial Governor, would he?"

The fellow of in the distance has spotted us and is moving toward us.

"Indeed; given the state of things he shouldn't be hard to find. He'll either be the best dressed rat here, or the worst."

Astairelike has noticed the chap coming toward us. "Probably both…"

Were it not for the wig he still had glued firmly to his head I might not have placed him for one of us, but once he grew closer I could tell from the inherent upturn of jaw and the fact that he carried himself as a sophisticated rodent, even if he had gone native.

"Ah! The great Lord Bloodford himself! Greetings and salutations, good sir."

We all feel it; his mood is too cheerful, given what's just happened. He makes more introductory small talk, but the wheels are turning too hard in all our heads to pay much attention, Astairelike especially.

"So, tell me." He grasps my paw firmly. I'm assuming he's already introduced himself, I don't really care who he is. "What brings you to our little port?"

What?

Years of serving together have left us perfectly in tune. Knowing that the wreckage of our border should be clearly visible from here, just about anyone in this this burg should be able to guess why we were here. Spoolnicker, furthest from our host, casts a glance back to our home, signals Astairelike, who in turn alerts me imperceptibly. Something's going on here. Out of all of us, Spoolnicker is best at hiding his reactions, even Astairelike can't pick them up from how he's acting, but something's askew, and I can guess what it is. A real stretch, but after what happened last night I'd believe the moon was made of sterling silver if it sparkled bright enough.

Deciding it wouldn't pay to be so subtle, I feign a yawn and exaggerate a stretch, just enough to look back where Spoolnicker saw whatever…my God! Marrow-Vinjia looks completely intact from here! Something's wrong. Re-screwing my expression, I look back at our host. "Did you see what happened last night?"

His look of confusion is genuine. "I'm sorry?"

"Never mind."

He completely disregards it and resumes effusing over the hometown heroes. We play along as he hurries us over toward the mound. I doubt we'll be going inside just yet, but from what little I remember hearing about Berlinger Station the custom is for the governor to entertain guest in front of the main entrance so everyone can see them. Pesky little braggart. We don't have time for this.

Spoolnicker, ever the diplomat, makes mention as he escorts us over that we'll be needing supplies for an upcoming mission. The governor practically trips over himself leaving us alone to fetch some. We retreat to a small corner just off the mound.

"They don't know what happened," Astairelike begins.

"To them it's like it never happened," Spoolnicker finishes.

I glance back at Marrow-Vinjia; it seems fine, but if you squint at it you can almost see through the image. I rub my chin. "I think the Strega might not be done with us. If they were going to make such a big show out of attacking us, why would they shield the other tribes from it?"

"Can they even do that?" Spoolnicker poses.

"Clearly," says Astairelike, completely lost in thought by now. "The question is, if they have the power to do what they did and keep it a secret, what else can they do?"

"It's not them," I mutter, "it's the Citadel."

"But what does all this mean?" Astairelike speaks a little louder than he intended to.

I go to continue, but the governor returns, acting as if his brain has finally turned back on.

"Lord Bloodford! Lord Bloodford!"

"Oh, Christ," mumbles Spoolnicker.

"Who's invading us now…" curses Astairelike.

"Lord Bloodford, there's been a complication… at least, it might become one, it all depends… Not that I would be so brash as to inquire about your mission, what with you being so important, old chap, but, well, there's something that's been brought to my attention, and even if it doesn't affect the task at hand I think the king should know…"

"Quit babbling…" I start, but Astairelike interrupts me:

"Do you have our supplies ready or not?"

"Supplies? Oh, yes, yes yes yes, of course." He claps his paws quickly and three wards manifest, clutching three rucksacks made from a cotton kerchief. Astairelike snatches his greedily and pulls back the top cover to reveal a Grade A hardboiled egg.

Spoolnicker is more restrained. "Well, it should get us through the Fountainhead, at least. Now, you were saying?"

"The…Fountainhead? Then I'm afraid the news will affect you, sir. Yes, yes, yes, this is most distressing…"

I hold up a finger. I don't look at him or make any other movement, but he catches my meaning immediately.

"The tunnel has been sealed off!"

"WHAT?" we all shout.

"Well, that is…there's this odd green glow around the entrance, like glass, and, well, the beastly thing is, that while no one seems to have any trouble coming OUT of it, nobody seems to be able to get back IN…"

Astairelike takes immediate action, darting off into the station; Spoolnicker leans closer to the governor, "When did this start?"

"Well, that is, we're not sure. There's been a glow all morning, but it hasn't affected anything, so we just assumed it was a trick of the light. But the strange thing is that in the mornings, everyone comes out of the underground to trade, but most don't try to go back until just around now – and from what I've been told, the first to turn back ran into a transparent barrier, and no one's been able to break it or get through…"

"And after only a few minutes you've declared it an emergency." He looks incredulous.

"How many have come in since this fellow ran into the barrier?" I ask.

"Err, none that I'm aware of…"

"So what's all this business about 'they can come out but not go in'? That's utter nonsense and you know it."

"Err, yes, well, I only reported what I've been told, you see…"

"Just go." I rub my eyes in frustration. He scampers off without another word.

"What is it about governors that makes them so jittery around rats who are actually important?" Spoolnicker queries.

"I just don't know…"

"Well, I'd better get over to the tunnel before these simpletons trip over their tails and kill themselves." I don't think he meant for me to hear that, but he makes his way after Astairelike while I hold back. There's an unusual scent in the air, nothing like the grocery store of rat smells affronting me here, but something else. Something like the savage scent of a hostile squirrel. It's coming from the trees just beyond the hollowed out trunk where most of these rats live. I instinctively move towards them when I'm stopped by a familiar voice:

"In Egypt 's sandy silence, all alone,
Stands a gigantic leg, which far off throws
The only shadow that the desert knows:"
I don't want to face him. I have enough problems.
But still, the ferret continues:
"'I am great OZYMANDIAS,' saith the stone,
'The King of Kings; this city shows
The wonders of my hand.' The City's gone,
Naught but the Leg remaining to disclose
The site of this forgotten Babylon .'"

"Heh," I grunt, "Horace Smith."

"You know human poetry?" He sounds surprised.

"I know how THAT one ends, if that's what you're asking…"

"You make me sound like an assassin. You should really learn to trust others."

Funny, I would never have pegged him for having a sense of humor. "What do you want?"

"Not to be rude, but I'd be more worried about them." I tell from his voice that he's turned toward the trees I was heading to. I look closely at them, working my way up slowly. At the top, crouched low behind the leaves, are two squirrels, at least one of which has a bow and arrow.

"Well?"

"Not that I think it has anything to do with what happened earlier this morning, but it seemed awfully unsporting not to tell you."

"What!"

"I said, I don't believe they're working for the Strega, but I know they plan to make trouble."

"How do you know all this? Who are you?"

"I'm not involved in any of your petty squabbles, Bloodford." He raises his voice slightly, then turns and walks away.

"You didn't answer my question," I shout after him.

"You can call me Metatron if you like." He doesn't look back.

"What kind of phony name is that?" I'm more angry than shaken by meeting him.

"Not mine, certainly…" He almost sounds pleasant. I'm so ripped up about him that I barely notice Spoolnicker coming up beside me.

"Him again?"

"He knows about the attack…"

"What?"

"And apparently those squirrels in that tree over there know, too…"

He gives it a quick glance and spots them, probably takes a breath to gage how best to shoot them down with his own bow. "What next, wolves?"

Least-Rogonians, Chapter Eleven:
The Eldest Dormouse, Barnabas

As the three mouse slaves were loaded with food and matches, Tranah lazed by the shore, humming happily and skimming her paw along the top of the cool water. Her mother had retreated into her throne room to stew in her quiet anger, while Astran, filling his pouch with as much wine as he could manage, racked his brains for a way of getting to this secret entrance Syrinx told them about. It was an isthmus, so if they wanted to get there quickly they'd have to go over water at some point, unless they wanted to walk. That would have been a fine idea to get anywhere else in the park, but as this isthmus was in the marshy section where snakes and owls were said to live, it would be dangerous to go there on foot. And they couldn't cross the lake because the Strega might sense their presence. No one was sure how, exactly, but that was the general consensus.

"An offering, master," the eldest dormouse wheezed to him.

"Hmm?"

"To the water goddess, Mul. Surely she would take pity on us, and allow us to cross the waters safely."

"I doubt that'll do any good. Nice try, though. Glad you made the effort."

"Shame we can't fly," Syrinx mused absentmindedly, who was at that moment feeling slightly defeated for not having already solved the difficulty in reaching their destination.

"Say!" Tranah jumped up. "That's an idea! We could snag a few birds and ride over in no time."

"No!" Astran spat, more angrily than he meant to.

Syrinx stared at him in relieved disbelief. "No?"

Astran immediately deflated. "Nah. Those little bastards are so uppity, you know. Can't teach 'em a damn thing."

"Well, we could hypnotize one…"

Astran chanced to look up at the nearest tree, where leaves were dancing softly in the breeze. "Wait! I've got a better idea…"

Gripping his staff in the very back of his mouth, he bared his claws and sprinted for the nearest tree, making a mad dash for the top before the decaying bark stopped him about halfway up. He made a pitiful effort to go farther, but his claws sliced through the bark like butter and he ended up sliding a considerable distance back down the tree.

"Fuck it," he mumbled a last. Carefully supporting his weight with one paw, he clutched his staff from out of his mouth and stiffened his arm and aimed for the thickest and leafiest branch on that side of the tree. Silently mouthing the proper spell, he shot a pulse of heat which cleanly burned through the thickest portion of the branch, which dropped down to the water below, just missing his companions. The massive branch ran aground just in front of Tranah. It was an impressive formation, close-up;

the thickness of the leaves and conical shape gave it the look of a small evergreen tree, only more edible.

Astran focused all his will and shot out a black tendril from his fist that engulfed the branch. The leaves all ran together and made a sort of emerald shell, while the aged wood underneath it contracted and pulsated and contorted into thousands of oblong shapes, the green shell conforming all the while, until a definite and unmistakable impression of a small, and very leafy, albatross, took shape.

Tranah, who had been centimeters away the whole time, couldn't take her eyes off of the silly thing. It was as beautiful and enchanting to her as an actual bird, and probably just as dangerous, if she knew Astran at all. The dormice were doubled over in awe, as was their custom, while Syrinx simply snorted inconclusively and shot Astran a "My, aren't WE high and mighty" look.

"A blessing from the wind god, Param!" Barnabas squeaked.

Ignoring him, Astran barked, "Well, get in!"

Tranah was confused, "What?"

"Those leaves? Just leaves. Push 'em aside and get in!"

"What about you?"

Ha, Astran thought, it was taking all his concentration to hold his contraption together. Climbing back down would be too engrossing, and he'd just have to do it all over again. "Never mind, just get in the damn bird!"

Tranah shrugged and brushed some of the leaves aside, exposing the hollow interior and ushering the three dormice inside before following herself, absentmindedly closing the entrance behind her. Syrinx balked, not at her friend's rudeness but the whole silly enterprise. How in the gods' green earth was she supposed to direct them from inside of a bird?

"Well?" Astran shouted, his forehead drenched in sweat.

"I'll walk, thanks," she replied cattily.

Not having the most patience for games at the moment, Astran concentrated harder and projected his mind on his false bird, lifting it onto the tips of its claws, rearing back its head, and pecking the shifty lizard, swallowing her in one gulp. That accomplished, he relaxed his grip on his staff. With the basic gist of his spell embedded in his creation, he simply whistled for it and it flew up to fetch him. He whooped excitedly as he jumped onto its back and aimed it toward the marshy portion of the lake.

Marrow-Vinjians, Chapter Twelve: An Uprising

||||||||||||||||||||||||||||||||||||||||||||||||||||||||||||||||||||||||||||||||||||||||||||||||||||||||||||||||||||

"Just think," I keep saying to myself, "less than twenty-four hours ago you were sitting in a theater, watching a pretentious play about yourself, and now look at you…."

Berlinger Station proper, as if to counter-balance the shabby grandeur of its exterior, is literally a hole in the ground. The interior of the mound is hollowed into a dumpy, uninteresting dome with an empty space where the floor should be, as those used to walking on all fours would have no trouble traversing the walls of the tunnel unaided. Only, it seems that now, there is a floor–one made out of bright green light, which mixes nauseatingly with the earthen walls to create a ghastly affect on the eyes. Huddled around it are assorted mice and voles in various states of undress, as well as the Provincial Governor and my team. Astairelike, who has been here longer than the rest of my party, is bent low, his nose almost touching the light, his paw wrapped around the right half of his mustache in concentration.

Not feeling particularly confident, I ask him, "Any luck?"

In lieu of a response, he merely holds up his ax. One blade has been completely broken off, leaving it more like a hatchet than a proper ax. The remaining blade is chipped toward the top.

While looking down on all this, I catch that feeling in my spine again. Sure enough, Metatron or whatever his name is has slunk in alongside us.

I'm in no mood to play games with him anymore, but before I can give him what for Spoolnicker turns to him. "Don't suppose you know anything about this?"

"About how this floor got here, I couldn't say," he purrs, almost mockingly disinterested. "But now that it is I pity the poor soul who gets caught in here next time it floods…"

Astairelike frowns. "Is there any reason you keep showing up?"

"Well, I just thought you might like to know…"

"What?" I resign.

"Well, those squirrels I showed you earlier? There's about nineteen of them now, and they're planning to launch several explosive devices into the lake. Just thought you should know…"

✵   ✵   ✵

The first thing I see is a small bomb, the sort that human children make for school projects, falling into the lake. It hits the water's surface and blows, flooding us. We're knocked back into the Station as the second bomb blasts more water into the sky. I reach the door again. I can just make them out. Pesky little creatures, heaving the explosives with godlike strength.

The entire facade of the Station tumbles down. Half a dozen explosions flood the area with mud and water and reeds. Two more bombs hit the square and the surface of the water, coating anyone near so thick with mud they can hardly breathe.

The Station has been flooded. I can't get good footing until the ferret, in his first sign of friendliness, grabs me by my coat and forces me with all his might out of the water! I gasp, then turn back to help Spoolnicker, Astairelike already being lifted out like myself as I act.

As if borne on silver ice-skates, the squirrels glide across the mud, hacking away at the poor fools who chose to live here. The four of us flank, eying our opponents. One of the squirrels, spotting us and stewing at the thought of killing a real Marrow-Vinjian, skates through the mud and aims his bow center mass at my chest! With well-rehearsed precision, Astairelike grabs my arm and yanks downward. He hurls his chain over my head and knocks the arrow out of the way; Spoolnicker quickly launches a controlled pair into the beast's stomach. He lands on his knees and skids toward our party, just in time to impale himself on my sword.

Each member of my party hurtles toward an insurgent and dispatches him brutally. Spoolnicker neglects his bow's intended purpose and bashes the brains out of his enemy's skull before returning his weapon to its practical use, killing the one nearest Astairelike, who is currently battling five at once.

The remaining thirteen squirrels are farther away, beyond an almost circular pile of the disemboweled civilians. Some of the braver survivors have taken to the fight themselves. I could almost applaud their spirit if I didn't know for a fact that every one of them was about to die.

Metatron and I dash; I get there first, taking the first of them square between the shoulder-blades. We turn to his closest companion, but before he can so much as glare at me, my anonymous second leaps and hooks his teeth around the vermin's trachea. Taking advantage, I dig my heel into Metatron's side and launch sideways into still a third brave, his chest cavity sinking nicely as my sword torpedoes into his solar plexus. The ferret mule-kicks another two squirrels toward me, I twirl my sword and stake the both of them in whatever squirrels have in place of a heart.

"Get down!" Metatron croaks.

I sink obediently, turning as I do, spying three of them! One moment they're coming on with sure footing, but then for no visible reason they jerk and collapse.

I'm confused; I look up at my enigma but there is nothing to suggest just what he's done. I certainly didn't see anything hit them… or did I?

"How did you do that?" Astairelike limps forward. I glance back to where he was fighting. His four opponents don't bear the usual marks of his carnage, but are otherwise suitably decapitated.

He doesn't answer. He merely directs our attention back toward the tree, where the remaining six are trying to escape. Metatron reaches into the other side of his cloak and, gripping whatever it was he used before, flings his arm. We watch as five of them drop dead instantly, spurts of blood blowing out the back of their heads.

"Only five?" Spoolnicker approaches, readying his bow.

"Always leave one alive to tell the story," he matter-of-factly grunts, as the last one standing begins his climb up the bark.

"Mind if he tells it to us?" Spoolnicker takes aim.

"Not especially…"

Hit in the shoulder, the brute thoughtfully plummets back down where we can get to him.

Marrow-Vinjians, Chapter Thirteen: An Interview

"Bombs," I mumble. "Where on God's green earth do they get bombs?"

"Well." Spoolnicker laughs while he picks his teeth. "They're not that hard to make."

"Yes," Astairelike chirps, "but you'd think we'd have noticed. They did have a lot of them."

"Still…"

The walk over to the roots where the squirrel fell is hindered by all the dead rodents we have to step around, but I must admit my mood has improved somewhat. Killing, as therapy, is hit or miss, depending on what you kill, but with squirrels I've never had that problem. Maybe it's just the basic lowness of the whole species, but decreasing their population just feels so damn good. Perhaps, I suppose, we'd all be much happier if we expanded further into their territory after this business with the Strega is settled. I mention this to Spoolnicker, who chuckles:

"Again? We'd be up to, what, Squirrel War III by now?"

We make our way around all the dead bodies and lower life forms attempting to set things in order once more. Between all the mud and the disarray, Berlinger Station looks more like Southeast Asia's famous Rann of Kutch than it did when we arrived. I have more pressing matters to attend to, but I make brief notice of the headcount: the majority of the fallen are actually mice, not rats. So, with all due respect to my compatriot, the losses are not so great.

"What?" says Spoolnicker, also gazing around. "No fanfare for the conquering heroes?"

"Who's conquering?" the little mouse replies. "There's still one left."

"Fair enough."

I don't bother to look back, but since even the stench of all this death can't mask the noticeable absence of our mysterious benefactor. I turn toward whichever of them is nearest. "He's not there, is he?"

"Nope," Spoolnicker accedes casually. "Surprised?"

"Not really…"

In all the time it's taken us to reach him, the squirrel hasn't moved much. Perhaps out of hunter's pride, Spoolnicker approaches him first, kneeling like a great sportsman before a massive stag.

"Hi," he chirps sarcastically.

The savage, finally taking notice of him, grins moronically with several teeth missing. "Saw your little playpen get blown up last night. Figured it was open season."

Between everything else, none of the civilians are paying enough attention to guess at the true weight of his words, but we three hide our own reactions without so much as a flinch.

"Anymore of your friends coming?" Astairelike sneers.

"Not yet…" He spies me. "Ah! The great Lord Bloodford. They're waiting for you, especially…"

I once more raise my blade…

"No," he spits, twirling the arrow he's pulled out of his shoulder like a conductor's baton. Then, snaring it with both paws, he rams it deep into his stomach!

The pathetic wretch convulses limply and begins vomiting, then coughs up a bit of blood, then vomits some more. He looks like he's choking on something, but it's coming from the wrong direction; his jaw is unhinging itself to force it out. It's…solid, whatever it is, and large. Too large for him to have swallowed it! At last, he coughs the horrendous whatsit out completely, and collapses, dead.

This thing, appearing lighter now, rolls toward our feet; we dodge backward, lest it might be another bomb he'd swallowed earlier, but it doesn't stop at our feet, or even reach them. It comes toward us, generally, but in very short order it rises off of the ground and floats toward us, as if descending from the very will-o-the-wisps themselves! It hovers in front of my nose, then lets out a sort of gas, which drifts away while the shell itself disintegrates; the sound it makes is horrible:

"You will never take the Citadel…"

"This," Spoolnicker coughs, "is a direct challenge, an affront to all our honor. Imagine, issuing us a challenge, then preventing us from facing it? I ask you!"

It's true; as a gentleman I can't help but be insulted by this. I move to say as much but Astairelike speaks first. "Bedford , are we honestly going to…"

"Yes, we are."

"That's not what I was asking you."

"Doesn't matter. What we have here is a matter of principle, which, compounded with our duty…"

"I was going to ask if we shouldn't head for Greenshire. With the passage sealed off here there's not much else we can do. And why would you think…"

"We're not going to Greenshire," Spoolnicker interrupts.

"That's more my decision, wouldn't you say?" I mumble.

"Yes, but I have a sneaking suspicion that now that they've attacked us openly, they might be ready to stop playing games." He huffs ahead of us, leaving us puzzled by his resolve.

✻   ✻   ✻

Spoolnicker's wrong. The entrance is still sealed off. It's getting late, and considering how little sleep we've gotten in the last two days and how long it will take to get to Greenshire, there's really nothing we can do but rest now. I mull things over briefly as I doze off, wondering why the Strega would strike so fiercely against us, and then use their mystic abilities to prevent anyone else from seeing the damage they'd caused. That simply isn't a good strategy; if you behead a king, you put his head on a pike so the whole kingdom see it, you don't hide it under rock and tell everyone he's still alive.

Strange rats, these Strega…

Least-Rogonians, Chapter Fourteen:
The Middle Dormouse, Trismegistus

Ophiuchus paced back and forth, unable to sit still, and despite the best efforts of the many Menudos she kept around her mood kept swinging violently. Ever since Astran and Tranah left she'd had an unshakable but mysterious sense of dread, as if everything was about to go horrendously wrong somehow. Of course, between her two idiot children, it wasn't a very far-fetched possibility…

On an impulse, she summoned three or four mouse slaves and sent them in search of the prophet Rommel. She couldn't say why, but knowing whether or not he was still around would be of some comfort. As luck would have it, the deathly ferret hadn't gone far; he was dipping his feet in the lake just south of where the bird of leaves had taken off earlier.

He didn't give off any discernable mood when he entered her chamber. He merely looked her in the eyes and muttered, "Already?"

Ophiuchus stared a bit, trying her best to articulate her childish ill ease into something that would sound like something she would say, but her constant starting and stopping mid-syllable finally got on the taller mammal's nerves and he held up his paw to silence her. "Something's troubling you?" he mocked.

She threw up her arms and nodded succinctly.

"I for one know I gave you enough to go on."

"Yes, but…"

"Still you want more?"

"…yes…"

"Hmmm, strong leaders often do. And indeed, there is news. The Strega have attacked the Marrow-Vinjians!"

"What?"

"At Berlinger Station, with about twenty or so squirrels."

"The squirrels are with the Strega now?"

"I suppose. Hard to fathom how those savages think, but so far I can't remember anytime the Strega ever broke an agreement with them, if indeed they ever made one."

"Well, I suppose that is good news…"

"Yes, but potentially bad as well."

Ophiuchus considered this, somewhat disbelievingly, then posed, "Well, what of it? We bear no grudges against the stupid brutes, even if they do take after the humans in some ways. You know, they even make explosives?"

"True, but something tells me that Astran would make a very tempting target just now. He killed a few squirrels last year, didn't he?"

"Yes." Ophiuchus rolled her eyes. "Cost us a fortune in gold not to go to war with them. Wait a minute, why wouldn't you have seen this earlier?"

"Fortune telling doesn't work like that, as you well know.

One can only know beyond knowing what IS happening and deduce where it will lead. You saw so yourself, last night, when Astran and Tranah were fleeing from the scene of their attempted assassination…exactly what I said they would be doing. I'm surprised they got away before the army could identify them. As convinced as Marrow is that the Strega were the ones who destroyed his fence, you can still be damn certain he'd still have some troops to spare for you."

"…I…"

"Think. Even when you do your own scrying you never get much farther than something that's about to happen. Knowing beyond knowing is a very subtle art, and it drove your mother insane, which is why you only do it as a hobby."

"How did you…what did you have to bring that up for?"

"I'm merely trying to emphasize my point, but I fear my suspicions are being confirmed. Even as we speak, the vibrations of the world suggest that an attack on your son by savage paw is imminent."

Without awaiting response, he pulled a pouch of glittery golden dust, which he flicked at the ground by her feet, tossing up dirt and drawing a line of gold dust between them. He procured two more handfuls and crossed that line out, then dug his paws into the cloudy mist and swirled them around, waiting for shapes to appear…

✳   ✳   ✳

The artificial bird flew swiftly, though without grace. Astran, perched on its back, kept his eyes closed as he concentrated, driving it on. Below, the water was getting greener and more stagnant. They were in the general area but from their height it was impossible to tell where this secret entrance was supposed to be.

"Syrinx!" he called down into the bird, "could I bother you for directions?"

He meant she should come up top with him, a meaning she didn't miss. "Fuck your grandmother!"

"Oh." Said Astran, frowning. "So that's how it's gonna be?"

"Yeah!" Using the sound of her voice to pinpoint her, Astran, while still concentrating on the bird, dug his paw into the leafy shell and yanked the petrified lizard by the scruff into the chilling wind, holding her eye to eye.

"Glad you could join me." He grinned.

"You ornery faggot…" she hissed.

"Yak yak yak, now, you gonna tell me where this magical secret tunnel of yours is or do I find out how well you do the high-dive?"

"You wouldn't dare!"

"Just tell me where it is."

She squinted in fear at the ground below and found the spot. "There!"

"You're sure?"

"Unless you plan on throwing me down for a closer look…"

"Don't tempt me."

He willed his creation lower, skirting along the wind, curving upward on a draft, and following the current down and to the left, toward a small grouping of blooming chestnut trees.

"There!" Rommel barked, jutting his finger at the pattern in the smoke that resembled Astran's bird.

"What?"

"Your son's flying machine is careening toward a clump of trees." Corresponding shafts of dust took shape accordingly. "That one in the center," he said, and the others faded away as the one in the middle grew larger. "That one is a known hideout for radical squirrels. Look now!" A group of them had appeared on the most prominent branch. "I fear I was correct earlier. You're son doesn't even know they're there. See?" The smoke reverted to its original picture. "He's facing away from them. He'll never see them coming!"

"Good gods…"

"You've got to help him!"

"What?"

"If you're willing to co-operate, I can help you fend these beasts off until Astran is in a better position to do it himself. If you launch a spell at the exact place I tell you to, the squirrels will be confused, and Astran will gain the upper paw."

"He should have it already," the One-Eyed Witch muttered to herself. "Stupid, non-magic using…"

Without waiting for her consent, Rommel walked closer, wrapped his massive paws around her head, and concentrated on the exact location.

"Here…"

"Do you see anybody in those trees?" Astran called out.

"Nope." Syrinx did her best not to vomit. "I don't think anyone's been in one of them for decades. Why?"

"I don't want anybody to know we're here."

"Well, your giant leaf-bird can attest to that," she wheezed sarcastically, as Tranah, curious about all the shouting, came up top. Astran would rather she hadn't, as she might throw off the balance, but he redoubled his concentration until his head started to hurt, lifting them further away from the ground.

Suddenly, the bird jerked violently in midair. Astran's eyes snapped open to see fragments of broken leaf falling away from the bird's side. And, creeping up toward the wing…

"Fire!" Tranah screamed. "We're under attack!"

The momentary distraction was more than enough. Astran's concentration broke, and an instant later the bird fell apart beneath him.

"Jump!" he shouted, and did just that, not knowing or caring if the others had done so as well, and then he was falling…

Earth and sky flickered past him for a few heartbeats, and he gripped his staff tightly and braced himself for the impact.

When it came, it was far softer than he had expected. The water helped to bring him back to his senses, and he swam for the surface with all his considerable strength. His head broke the surface and he found himself bobbing in the current not far from the edge. Around him the others were struggling while leaves drifted downward like snowflakes. Astran growled to himself and swam for the edge. He made it, fishing his staff out of the water along the way, and hauled himself onto land.

He shook himself, spraying water everywhere, and shouted at the others.

"Get out of there, you idiots, the Strega will know we are here!"

He waited, seething, while they struggled out of the water. The mice were trembling in fright–typical of the pathetic creatures. Tranah looked angry, but at least she was unhurt.

There was no sign of Syrinx anywhere.

"Where in the name of King Shit is that accursed lizard?" Astran swore.

Ophiuchus, still entwined in the ferret's massive grip, felt a shiver run up the base of her spine, as if she'd made a horrible mistake.

Looking, appropriately enough, like a couple of drowned rats, Astran, Tranah, Barnabas, and the other two mice crawled ashore smelling like mold and coughing up enough water to keep several flowers alive for days.

"Where's Syrinx?" Tranah sputtered as soon as her voice returned.

"Forget her, you fool," a voice said from behind him.

Astran turned. "Bathin! What are you doing here?"

The ferret hissed at him, showing his needle-like teeth. "There are Marrow-Vinjian scouts in this area, you bonehead. Your racket will have alerted every single one of them. Now move, quickly!"

Astran saw the sense in his words, and followed him. The ferret darted away toward a heap of rubble overgrown with weeds. Astran, following him, caught the scent of other animals on the breeze, and his eyes narrowed. Was this a trap?

"Prepare yourselves for a fight," he muttered to the others as they caught up with him. Marrow-Vinjian scouts? he wondered. And the ferret couldn't have mentioned them earlier? Well, it's not as if he could see the future, he supposed.

There were, indeed, animals hiding in the brick-heap. As Astran moved closer, he saw a familiar figure emerge. The toga he was wearing was slightly less stained than it had been when they last saw him, but the shocked, hangdog expression and stench were identical.

"Chumsa," he snapped. "Why are you here?" Astran had almost expected with the hurried mood of the previous evening that Bathin would cart him off to Never-Never Land, never to be seen again.

The leader of the Wahid inclined his head. "Greetings, Astran. I am glad to see you have reached this place in safety."

Astran, shocked that the pudgy rodent knew his name, looked past him, toward the group of others emerging from the heap. "What is this? Why are you here?" he asked again, as the small group of a dozen or so he had seen at first now swelled into almost a hundred with signs that more were nearby.

'We are the resistance," said Chumsa. He waved his arm at the various types of rat surrounding him: members from several tribes, including the Lakova, Farj, and Farris-Ianist, and mice of all walks. "We have joined forces to fight against the evil of the Marrow-Vinjians."

When the full extent of Chumsa's quickly-formed militia had spread itself out for them, it was truly impressive. But, while it went unnoticed by the rats, the most profound effect was on the two older dormice, Barnabas and Trismegistus. Barnabas, who was beyond old but still with many years left in him, had, like many old slaves, long given up the hope of seeing his species being treated as equals. Trismegistus, younger and more clever, had been dreaming of the same thing, but had sworn to himself he wouldn't dare to truly conceive it until he saw it with his own eyes. Now, here it was before the both of them, mice and rats together as one, with no apparent separation in rank or stature, brothers in arms. Clopin, youngest of the three and more idealistic, saw none of that, but rather faithful servants willing to fight alongside their masters, proving their bravery and dedication to the common good. It gave Clopin a dollop of fulfillment knowing he could be as faithful as they, but his elders decided then and there that as soon as the chance arose they would have their freedom.

Astran looked impassively at them. If even the Least-Rogonians didn't stand a chance in outright combat against the Marrow-Vinjians, then what hope did this ragtag militia have? "I wish you good fortune, then. But I must be going." It seemed unwise to stay much longer, especially if there really were Vinjian scouts around. He could imagine what hell they'd catch if the imperialists found their two favorite groups, Least-Rogonians and separatists, in the same location.

"You must do no such thing," said Chumsa, showing a firmness that surprise his guests. "We have come so that you may join forces with us. Give us your strength, and together…"

Astran sighed. "Come, Tranah. We have no business with these fools. We must deal with the Strega."

That said, he turned his back and walked away, the ultimate sign of contempt. But he had never expected what happened next.

"There are ghosts down there, you know!" someone shouted.

Astran turned back around. "Huh?"

"Ghosts," whoever it was continued, "in the underground. That's where you're going, isn't it?" Astran wasn't foolish enough to give away his plan to someone who was likely to be captured in the very near future, but they continued anyway. "They'll lead you to your death if you let them."

"Yeah, so will he." Astran pointed his finger at Chumsa, then resumed the walk back to secret entrance.

Behind him, Chumsa shouted something. Astran turned irritably to look, and saw half a dozen warriors charging straight at him.

He muttered a curse to himself, and ran. The mice were already ahead of him, and Tranah followed. To his rage, Astran saw arrows shoot past him as he ran. They were trying to kill him!

He whipped about, forcing the closest ones back; then, when one from the back vaulted over another to launch an air assault, Astran gripped his staff with all his might and paused him inches above the ground, thrust his arms and legs back, in a T-shape, and, with three simple slashes at the ground in front of him, made deep cuts in the poor beast. One across the belly, one across his ribs, and a third straight down his solar plexus, forming an I. The rodent's stomach bulged and grew heavy, it was as if a lead balloon was dripping out of his middle. Astran raised him higher, causing the weight of the expansion to pull harder on the innards. Slowly, and meticulously, the great belly left the body cavity and sank slowly to the dirt, dragging intestines and colon, kidneys and spleen along with it. As the mass finally made port, the stomach contracted, causing the intestines to expand as the energy pulsated back into it's owner and exploded him into a million bloodless chunks. Without another word, Astran and party turned and walked away.

That seemed to discourage their pursuers.

Ahead, Astran could see the entrance. It looked like nothing particularly significant; just a small tunnel almost completely hidden by a large clump of weeds. "Nothing like first class, I guess."

Tranah, reminded once more of her missing companion, balked at her brother, but before they could have a go at it, Bathin had reappeared and planted his paws on their shoulders and directed their attention to the wreckage of the leaf-bird. It had an unhealthy, bluish glow radiating off of it. Astran and Barnabas leaned closer, but before they could get a better look the bird itself dissolved into the frothing water and the glow circled the isthmus and crept onto the ground. The rodents backed off just in time for the blue to surround the hole. They all moaned as what was surely an impassable barrier formed over their only real advantage, but instead, the edge of the blue broke out of its round shape and created, the silhouette of a large spider, which, sliced deep into the earth and placed the hole above their heads, at least two or three feet. From above, it was still recognizably spidery, but from their perspective it was just a jagged column.

Barnabas and the nearest dormouse, Trismegistus, pounced forward to examine the hulk of dirt. They sniffed and dug their paws into it; the soil gave way to their fingers.

"It looks solid, master," Trismegistus chirped.

Astran rubbed his chin thoughtfully, and puzzled over this and other things that were going on, "Tranah?"

"Yes?" she replied unenthusiastically.

"I think we're in some serious 'Is and Is-Not Territory' just now," he muttered, using one of his grandfather's pet sayings.

"What?"

"It 'Is bad' and 'Is-not good', remember?"

"Yes," she lied, since their grandfather had died before she was born, and she'd never heard him say that before.

"Still glad you came?"

"I never said I was."

"Fair enough…"

Astran stepped unhurriedly toward the dormice, weighing his options. On the one paw, they'd been shot down by the same rats who'd made this thing rise out of the ground, and it was likely that this was another trap. On the other paw, the whole bit could have just been saber-rattling on their part. Wouldn't it be a show of good faith to jump through their little hoops and allay their suspicions professionally? He turned back toward Bathin for advice, but the mysterious ferret had vanished once again. Astran shot a glance at the wreckage of his bird. Well, he thought, this is all very pleasant…

A ruffling of grass and the smell of familiar rats!

"Oh no, not these idiots again…" Tranah whined.

"Quickly!" the closest of the five rebels shouted. "The Marrow-Vinjians are coming!"

That settled that, then. Astran made a beeline for the mound, but upon touching it a shock ran through his body, launching him back more than a foot and leaving him feeling exceptionally weak. Before anyone could do anything the column glowed brightly again and jiggering splinters of light opened all across itself, outlining several shell-like portions, like a tortoise, which then broke off violently, leaving an actual spider made from the earth, much larger than they.

"Oh shit." Tranah wheezed.

The spider knocked the clumps of hardened dirt off itself and bent its legs lower to put its venomous jaws just above eye-level. They fell back into a defensive position. The mud-spider reared its hind-quarters higher, lifted one of the remaining clumps with its front legs and hurled it at Astran.

Dashing to his rescue, Tranah brandished her ax like a broadsword and deflected the projectile with a hard backhand that quartered it and sent the smaller pellets hurtling to their left. Undeterred, the monster launched clump after clump at them, which Tranah knocked away with ease. With each supposed success she dared to advance closer, but Astran, having regained his composure, knew that the beast was only baiting them. He flourished his staff pretentiously-no need to stand on principle just now–and made to launch a power spell toward the spider only to find that, except for a strong gust of wind, nothing much came of it. After a second attempt, which also failed, he figured it out: that thing had stolen some of his magic to bring itself to life!

Damn clever rats, these Strega, he thought. Without wasting a second he spun to the rebels. "Reinforcements! Now!"

They scampered dutifully back toward Chumsa and his ragtag militia. Astran barked at the mice, "Ideas?"

They chattered at each other in the native language of the mice, then Trismegistus, snapping his fingers and ramming his fist into his other paw at the same time, dug out a pebble from the dirt with his toe and flicked it nonchalantly at his master. Confused, Astran watched them as they huddled low to the ground, digging up more pebbles and arranging them in a small pile. Chanting in their ritualistic manner, they faced their master again and, using the wisdom of monks, lit the pebbles with mystic fire. Catching their drift, Astran lifted them as high as he could with his remaining power and launched them into the spider's mouth.

Tranah, caught by surprise, ducked reflexively, giving the beast an advantage.

"Master!" Barnabas shouted. As if their current predicament weren't enough, four Marrow-Vinjian scouts in lobster-back and tri-corner, swords drawn, were lumbering down toward them. They got close enough for Astran to smell the white powder on their breath, but that was as far they ever got.

At first it just looked like a purple blur. Something violet and flowery had plummeted from the nearest tree and was spinning like a top around the red-clad enemies, sending bursts of blood toward the sky as certain body parts hit the grass. Finally, as the last of the four heads was sent springing into the distance, the purple blur dropped into a recognizable shape: Syrinx, now mysteriously dressed in a loose-fitting robe, was crouched before him, carrying twin scimitars and a slightly apologetic look on her face.

"Sorry I'm late." She shrugged, the tinkling of further weapons hidden in the folds of her clothing ringing in Astran's ears. He wasn't sure which made him angrier, the fact that she'd reappeared in human clothing or that she'd reappeared at all.

"We'll discuss this later." He pointed toward the beast and his sister, who were making a very impressive show of fighting each other.

"Ah, yes, that. Should probably help her."

"If it wouldn't be too much trouble…"

Syrinx dived into battle, darting past her friend, and promptly relieved the spider of its throwing leg. As the monster stumbled, she and Tranah, reading each other's thoughts, flanked the horrible thing, ran up a leg on each side and stood on its back, plunging their weapons into its head! Though they'd hoped that would kill it, it merely bucked in pain, knocking them into the water but leaving Astran the perfect opportunity to launch what was left of his mystic energy into the spider's exposed underbelly. The force was enough to knock it into the lake, where it began dissolving almost immediately. Astran could feel his energy rising back up as he and his mice made for the isthmus to fish Syrinx and Tranah out of the water.

A million questions needed to be asked, but Astran decided they had wasted enough time already and he ordered everyone into the underground tunnels as quick as they could scurry. They didn't stop until nightfall.

✳   ✳   ✳

Ophiuchus, wringing her paws in agony, finally made up her mind and gathered all her mystical items into a single spot. She would need all the power she could summon. Racking her mind for all the right spells, she sat upright, channeling all her energies for several minutes, not a muscle in her body flinching. Slowly but surely a rift formed before her, a portal of sorts…

Resolving all her strength, she lifted herself back up and shuffled into the portal. She wanted to personally survey the damage this battle with the squirrels had done…

She reached the spot in the sky and fell to the ground with a lack of ceremony. It had almost killed her, this portal business. She pried herself off the ground and turned toward the trampled dirt where her children had just battled the mud-spider. She felt a rush of maternal concern, the likes of which she hadn't felt in years…only to be suddenly cut off. The first wave of arrows had missed her mostly, but three or four had clipped her behind the abdomen. As she sank to the ground in pain, she rolled toward her attackers: the reinforcements the rebels had gone back for had finally arrived.

Syrinx Silvereye, Chapter Fifteen:

|||||||||||||||||||||||||||||||||||||||||||||||||||||||||||||||||||||||||||||||||||||||||||||||||||||||||||||||||||||||||||||||

It was just after the bird was attacked by the One-Eyed Witch's spell that the lizard mercenary found herself spread-eagled across the peninsula where the isthmus connected to the land. She remembered landing in the water, but the harsh jut of liquid directly up her nostrils had knocked her cold. En route to her companions, she stumbled across a small chest in the tall grass, made out of hardened mud and silt. Her suspicions piqued, she knocked the lid of with her foot and found inside a flowing purple garment which, from a quick feel, was packed to the tooth with hidden knifes.

Not feeling particularly trusting of whom she suspected had placed this chest for her to find (and had undoubtedly fished her out of the water as well) she lifted the robe out of its container. A small but conspicuous roll of parchment fell from the waistband. Her suspicions confirmed, she unrolled it with a quick flick of the wrist. It read:

Silvereye,
There are two parties of Marrow-Vinjian
scouts in the area: one group of four,

which normally patrols this section of the
park, and another thirty-rat group
dispatched in response to last night's attack. It is inevitable, given
recent activity, that your friends will escape
the four who scour this area
looking for the rebels. You know our stance
in this matter, but you must get the
Least-Rogonians underground before the second
group swarms upon them. Events
are not spiraling in our favor, and until
we can permanently cement our
alliance, it is
absolutely imperative that Astran and co. remain alive.

Enclosed is everything you'll need for what
the Strega will likely throw at
you…

Sincerely,

M.S.

Ah, Syrinx thought, good old M.S. She wondered whose side he was on this week. She flipped the parchment over on a whim and found "Yours" scrawled in much sloppier handwriting near the lower left-hand corner. Well, she supposed, that was nice of him. Going over it once more, she noticed there was a postscript at the very bottom:

P.S. Beware of Lafitte…

Day Three
Marrow-Vinjians

Marrow-Vinjians, Chapter Sixteen: The Damned Fool

My dreams haunt me. I'm in the space beneath the Royal Bedroom. My Liege is ill at ease being lead by me. I am better suited, for I come down here often. My eyes are only just adjusting to the darkness when:

"Master?"

"Master!" The poor wretch bounds toward us. "Master, Whore has waited long for you. She has no more food, but Whore is pleased. Master is merciful to Old Whore, he is!" As she strokes my face with her knobby fingers, it is unthinkable that this female was once my queen. Her once plump face is now narrow, with the leftover skin hanging neglected off the bone…

"My Queen?" His Majesty looks on in shock.

She doubles over in horror. "Not Queen, Whore! Queens are clean, Whore is filthy with her Master's love."

"Go," I mutter. Sire trips and runs on all fours in the opposite direction.

I awaken.

I slip out and into the early morning, the dawn still hours away. The Station actually looks less pleasant in the dark, and the mud still hasn't dried yet. I don't see any lights from the mound; the officials our jittery contact had looking after the tunnel must have given up. I don't blame them. I wish there were more of a wind. It's far too quiet, and the heat from within the hollow tree is still clinging to my body like a second layer of clothing.

A mad impulse takes me. I duck low, evading what little moonlight there is, and head behind the mound, by the shore of the lake. I see a clump just where I stop, a female's dress and wig, one like Amin had on last night. Someone else has the same idea, it seems.

Feeling embarrassed and more than a little silly, I unbutton my uniform. I can't believe I'm still in my dress togs. Fully nude, I fold them carefully, and set my stovepipe in the center. My fur feels sticky, but the breeze quickly alleviates that. Given careful consideration, I lift my hat back off of my clothes, and remove my wig, set it down with infinitely more care than the rest of it, and pin it down with my hat once more. I feel exposed and vulnerable, my every neuron questioning what I'm doing.

I bend down, trying to assume a natural position. It feels strange, putting my front paws on the ground, and feeling my weight sink down on them. My nose is so close to the soil; it's intoxicating and overwhelming.

I start slowly, ashamed to move out in front of the world. Crawling on all fours is an instinct, but my mind refuses to grasp it at first. I'm half-tempted to dash back to my pile, reattach my wig and forget this mad experiment, to say nothing of memorizing the details of that dress so I could chide that female if I see her. I don't.

The dirt beneath my feet has lost all friction, and I'm going faster without even trying to. First along the edge of the shore and then gradually away, into the wild and unprotected, toward the squirrels and Marrow-Vinjia. I feel light.

I am not alone. It's only when I see her that I know there was a reason to be here; I can hear the beating of her heart. It beats surely, like a wild animal's; the flow of her muscles poetic and sensual. The two of us are suspended in time, alone in the universe, two objects in motion…

She feels the same, I can sense it. She taunts me with her energy; her vibrations emanate across the air, primal and fierce. There is nothing but her to me, and I her. Even now, as the world slowly blends back in, element by element, all of this is irrelevant. Who we are now is nothing. We have no identity, she and I; we are nameless like the larger animals, without culture or shame… Two strangers who matter more to each other than their own families.

We don't stray too far from the mound; we have sunk to the mindless freedom of instinct, which tells us to hug the water. It is safer there. Be afraid of the trees! How wonderful it is to react with fear, with honest terror to the world that is so large around me.

In short order, we have returned to where we each began, not ready to don our civilized masks ever again. Her eyes are blazing, heady with the same narcotic; she presents herself, and I melt into her. She is unknown to me. I know that, once we have broken and she affixes her dignified air, she will be a stranger. She, undoubtedly the mate of a proper Marrow-Vinjian gentleman, will hold herself high with a sophisticated air, sneer down her nose at the other rats who dare to parade in the bare. If she should ever see me again, assuming she recognizes me, she will cast her glance slightly sideways; not enough to arouse suspicion, but enough to let me know that if she ever looked in to my eyes she would have to judge me for what happened. I won't let her feel that way. I'll never look for her.

I step away while she redresses and sneaks back off toward the fence. One of our more fashionable settlements is on the way. If she hurries she'll make it before sunrise. No one will ever know.

Why? As I pull my boots back on after everything else, the animistic relief I'd felt seconds earlier has become remorse. I put my wig back it its proper place and stare out over the water. I know that this entire escapade has meant nothing, and perhaps would have been better had I not succumbed. I don't know…

I look to the center of the lake, where the deadly glow that destroyed our fence first blossomed. Will they attack once more?

There is a light out there. I have the warrior's sense, but only the sort one gets when staring down a known agent, not a fellow combatant. I doubt my folly has slipped unnoticed; what would the Strega make of it, I wonder? Humph, I hope they got some entertainment out of it, the cowards. Won't face us straight on, so they watch as we lose our composure from lack of sleep.

I hate them.

Within minutes of sunrise the Provincial Governor has reinserted himself emphatically.

"Lord Bloodford, it's simply the most wonderful thing. Our men, we've had them working all night, our very best minds, you know, all of them, and we happened upon a solution!"

None of us are truly listening. Astairelike, the oviraptor, is making quick work of the egg that should have lasted him through tonight, and Spoolnicker is glancing along the tree line for the squirrels. I find my thoughts elsewhere.

"Yes yes yes, it's the most wondrous thing, a marvel of simplicity in and of itself. A veritable Alexander's Knot. Not that I put myself or my men above yourself, your Lordship, but indeed, the solution was so perfectly obvious it's remarkable!"

Astairelike tilts toward him, like a plant following the sun. It's hard to tell what he's thinking; there are days when I think I'll never fathom what goes on in his head.

"We simply dug around it! Can you even conceive it, your Lordship? Of course, when it came to us, we were all so tired – it seemed like a joke. Of course, by then the situation seemed so dire it was worth trying, and sure as the sword on you hip, it worked! A second tunnel, just to the side of the mound, it's only been completed within the hour, we made such quick work of it, time being of the essence, naturally, but the most remarkable aspect of it is that it actually goes under that barrier. You could reach up and touch it! Huh, marvelous bit of business if I do say so myself!"

And without waiting for a response, he's off, most likely to brag about his Roman Triumph to anyone else who will listen.

"You know," Astairelike burbles, "for someone who talks so fast he should really have a much higher voice."

How I like that remark I can't say.

"So, gents." Spoolnicker joins the conversation at last. "Do any of us believe that?"

"Hmm," I wonder. "If they'd given up they would have simply let the barrier drop."

"Only a fool would believe that the Strega would never imagine anyone digging from the side," Astairelike postulates.

"If they simply lowered their defense, we'd think they were setting a trap," Spoolnicker says.

"And wouldn't enter," I add.

"Whereas," Astairelike jumps up, alive with activity, "if they let us think we've got the best of them…"

"THAT would be the perfect trap." I smash my fist into my paw, my finger smarting where the pigeon pecked me yesterday. "However, we can't ignore the possibility that this is their sideways way of challenging us to a straightforward fight."

"There certainly isn't any other way to get in," Spoolnicker adds. "Even if we went to one of the other entrances, they've had a whole extra day to prepare for us. Odds are any other entrances on this side of the lake will be sealed of by the time we get there."

Astairelike picks a portion of yolk out of his teeth. "Well, we've walked into traps before."

"Doesn't pay to be too optimistic," I murmur. "They've already shown they won't let anything stop them. Even if we travel through the Fountainhead and into the most populated routes, we can't trust that they won't rain down Armageddon simply because there are innocent tribes present. I suspect by this point we're all the same to the Strega."

Astairelike giggles. "So, we really DO have to go through the Land of the Blind."

It certainly seems that way. Everything we've heard of it tells us that the Citadel has no power there. That is the keep of the heathen god Sivad. This just keeps getting better and better.

"Well," I relent, "tell them to pack you more food. It'll take us at least two days to get through the Fountainhead."

We approach the makeshift entrance dug unceremoniously into the side of the mound. We're just getting on our way, Astairlike climbing first into the hole, when the Provincial Governor, a true politician, signals for us to halt, and stumbles forward for still more talk, this time in a voice loud enough for even the Least-Rogonians to hear, I think.

"My friends!" he begins presumptuously, addressing the

crowd that has gathered, rather than us. "Given the status of things, perhaps I too should go. As far as the Fountainhead, at least. This obstruction will still be unknown to the tribes we make trade with. They must be informed!"

Wow, he can actually bullshit with a straight face, I'm impressed. Astairelike, however, is not so forgiving:

"You know, if you're worried about getting re-elected, it IS a lifetime post…"

The crowd laughs, which the annoying fool takes with a smile. The governor grandstands a little longer, plays the hero for his audience, then has his own rucksack fetched in as ostentatious a way as possible.

"Well?" Spoolnicker whispers.

"It's none of my concern if some nobody politician wants show off for the unwashed masses," I sigh, wanting very badly to begin already.

"What if he slows us down?"

"I hardly think he'll want to come the whole way."

"I would, if I were governor here."

"Well." I draw my sword from its sheath. "I'll just assure His Majesty I only had his best interests in mind."

Marrow-Vinjians, Chapter Seventeen: A Day At The Races

The tunnel is incredibly murky. The glow on the other side of the barrier, for whatever reason, doesn't extend to the interior. I know all tunnels are dim, but this place is especially hard on the eyes.

The official opening of the tunnel goes straight into the ground, but the actual passage tilts at a 135 degree angle for ten yards before reaching the Fountainhead, which is a hundred yards straight down and wide enough to fit a full-sized statue. This particular tunnel was intended for rats who walk on all fours. We have to stoop to fit in. Granted, we could make like the natives and save some trouble, and back pain, but with our weapons and supplies it would make us lose our balance, and with the momentum we'd build up we'd miss the spiral planking that corkscrews around the Fountainhead's perimeter and plunge straight down the empty space in the center. That doesn't strike me as terribly pleasant.

Neither does our political friend. Convinced he's on some

epic quest the likes of which even we've never encountered, he's enhanced his supply of food with three handsome grappling hook sets, which I doubt he'll need, as he's only going as far as the entrance. The twit is probably gushing over what an impressive portrait he'll make just now, should anyone ever care enough.

We're not making much progress: we have to walk with our backs bent over our tails to keep from tripping as the path slopes more steeply. After an hour, during which the Governor has never stopped talking, we seem to have gone only about thirty feet. I think the others are an inch away from killing him; I wouldn't mind, except that under the circumstances it would look terribly unprofessional.

"You know," Spoolnicker interrupts him, "this Fountainhead's a thousand feet straight down, I hear. You sure you're up to it, old rat?"

"Oh, it isn't the distance," he replies cheerfully, oblivious to the insult, "especially if you've done it more than once. No, it's having to go around that boardwalk that circles down. It's so monotonous…" I cut him off before he can go on and bring our movement to a halt.

We wouldn't be stopping, except that Astairelike's caught his foot, his bad one, in some loose dirt that sank beneath him. It shouldn't take but a second, but while I'm prying him out, Spoolnicker gasps! I look up, the barrier is still behind us. It is as if we've been walking in place the entire time, only we haven't… the hole is no longer off to the side. The barrier is following us.

"I wonder," the governor drools bewilderingly. "Do you suppose it's solid on this side as well?"

At first I think he's being foolish, but then I get his meaning. The barrier might only have been solid from the exterior, but passable on our side. Highly unlikely, but it wouldn't hurt to find out.

Spoolnicker shifts his weight, pulls up his bow, and touches the end of it against the glowing green wall. It passes through! He pulls it back before he loses his balance, but the governor is overjoyed. He doesn't even speak before he's shoved his hand through, marveling at how strange it looks through the light. The three of us turn once more to conspire, but are distracted by a sizzling noise. Instinctively, we look at Spoolnicker's bow. The edge that tapped the wall is bubbling, melting away! The bowstring snaps violently! The wood vanishes into a whiff of steam. Before we can even look up, the governor screams!

He's yanked back his paw, which at first looks merely burned, but the red scarring across his skin vanishes almost as immediately as it grew. As if a thousand mites were eating at his fingers, his tissues spasm and die off.

I'm not paying attention to him. The three of us are staring hard at the barrier. It flickers, almost winking at us. They would do something like that, wouldn't they?

It's moving toward us! A split-decision, and the poor governor's fate is sealed. Spoolnicker grabs the governor's ruck violently. I cut the straps and bash him in the skull with my hilt. Astairelike jump-kicks him into the green light. The governor starts melting almost instantaneously. We take off running, Spoolnicker portioning out those grappling hooks, and then tossing the pack over his shoulder. The barrier's gaining speed! We have no choice, we ball down on all fours and sprint. It matches our speed step for step, remaining just behind us, mocking us with the painful death it plans to mete out.

We reach the Fountainhead and the promised wooden spiral, but we do not stop. On pure adrenaline we surge forward, my stovepipe hat fluttering away, and leap across the emptiness to the other side. Spoolnicker falls short, but catches his hook on the edge and lowers himself to the walkway below us.

The barrier doesn't stop. It barrels through the portal like a cannonball and soars across the air, coming straight for us. Astairelike and I, kicking Spoolnicker's hook free, bolt off of the edge, aiming recklessly at the other side. Our diagonal fall steers us away from the panels beneath the one we entered but we barely catch the next one down with our hooks.

The green monster slams against the wall we leaped from, pauses for a second, then slowly drops downward.

"Oh, great," Astairelike moans.

"Follow me!" I shout, slinging my legs under my arms and flinging myself backward, heading squarely for the board opposite me. I can chuck my grappling hook at the board a few levels down. Astairelike free-falls, only to be caught by Spoolnicker. Taking a cue, Astairelike grips his ax and whips his chain down to me; two of them drop straight down four or five levels before yanking me down with them. In my other paw I still have a death grip on my own line, but as Spoolnicker gets a good footing on his level he gives Astairelike's chain a hard tug, ripping my hook through the board, and freeing me to whirl it around and catch the next lowest level on the other side.

With Astairelike firmly gripped around his neck, Spoolnicker dives, his arms flat against his sides, to the levels beneath me. We've got to do something quickly. The light is following closely, and we're still less than a quarter of the way down!

Still we leap, back and forth, without pause. Flipping and kicking, catching every stray splinter with hook and lariat, pulsating lower and lower in the greatest acrobatic formation that no one would survive to tell about. With every coil and recoil we sink maybe seven or eight feet.

There's a cart about five levels down. Not all of us will fit, but one could ride it all the way down. Spoolnicker eyes it. We land about two levels up from where the cart is, my fall being broken by a second cart full of wine barrels. My ankle twists sharply, and I foolishly pause to clutch it. Spoolnicker, the damn fool, stops to wait for me, despite Astairelike's prodding objections. He's pulled an arrow out of Spoolnicker's quiver as if he's making to horsewhip him, but the barrier has caught up. We pounce at the same time, my foot knocking a barrel off the cart, Astairelike's arrow scraping across the light and catching fire. We meet in midair, grabbing each other's paws, our force spinning us around to grant us more momentum.

Astairelike dislodges himself and goes into free-fall. Spoolnicker hits the inside of the cart like a comet and knocks it into motion. The barrel has landed a few feet in front of him, and Astairelike chucks his flaming arrow at it, exploding it and sending Spoolnicker's cart careening onto the level below. With split-second timing he clutches his now-useless bow and propels his cart like the world's fastest gondola, making wonderful time in spite of how taxed his arms must be.

My stop to coddle my injury has allowed the fatigue in my own arms to catch up with me. I can barely grip the edge of the wood to launch myself off again; fortunately, Astairelike collides with me soon after takeoff. Placing the soles of his feet on mine, we back-flip off of each other, and I shoot right toward Spoolnicker while the little mouse is by himself at least two levels below us, hanging on with the skin of his ax blade. I land right in front of the cart, sidestepping it and jumping in from behind. We lean forward and he rows with all his might, catching up with the mouse finally, but Astairelike jumps up too exuberantly, causing us to lose balance and pitch the cart off the wood and back into the hollow center.

I don't know how long we plummet in our cart. I look down, and all I see are curious fools gathered near the bottom to watch the madness. I watch them transfixed until the cart begins to rotate downward, forcing us to watch the barrier chasing us instead.

The cart rotates back toward the bottom; the time has come to abandon ship. We scramble out with a good amount of air left beneath us, I give the cart one last good kick after jumping, so it won't land on top of us.

There's nothing we can do now but brace ourselves for impact. I feel someone old and feeble collapsing under me as I and my men hit the ground at last. We dash to our feet, to all fours even, as the light barrels down on us. We stumble over some peasant and make for the tiny cavern that leads to the other tunnels just as the barrier crushes and incinerates all those fools who stopped to goggle at our adventure.

Only two feet away is the path to the right – which leads to the land of the blind, the other leading to where any sane rat would want to go just now. Alas, our shiny green friend springs out of the soil in front of the left fork. We bank as it expands like a bumper to force us into the Land of the Blind, ceasing and solidifying into green granite as we leave the domain of the Strega and plunge into the keep of Sivad. We grind to a halt and overturn just short of a cliff! It feels as if my lower half is melting away and attempting to drag my torso with it. My adrenaline is long gone, my breathing short and labored.

I'm not sure, but I think Spoolnicker says something like, "Well, saved us two days…"

Just before passing out, I look over at the granite wall and spy my stovepipe hat sitting idly, unmolested if slightly dusty. The wall that burned and killed everything in its path but the wooden boards must have pushed my hat along with it, in case I should need it. They're mocking me, I just know it.

Marrow-Vinjians, Chapter Eighteen: The One-Eyed Man Is King

||||||||||||||||||||||||||||||||||||||||||||||||||||||||||||||||||||||||||||||||||||||||||||||||||||||||||||||||||||||||||||||||||||

The Land of the Blind is a rectangular underwater cave that could easily house an entire parliament of bears were it not completely sealed off save for a few small tunnels. The ground is cold and the air is stale with the scent of rats who died long ago and the stench of a nearby predator.

Not far from here, beneath us actually, is what used to be Warren's Burrow. Seventy years ago, the Capra-Vinjians waged a war with the combined forces of the Lakova, Shrii, and Farris-Ianists over that sacred land; for it had once, according to legend, been the home of a race of underground hares who, before being wiped out by the Strega five centuries ago, had been the pre-eminent mystics of the park. My great-grandfather led the charge and forced the savage rats off the land. And now, supposedly, it's the realm of an evil god. If I had to guess, I'd say the Strega don't expect us to make it out of here alive, which is why we're not dead right now.

We're perched along the edge of the cliff, my head dangling over, as I survey the ground below. If we follow a small path that's been carved into the wall of the cave we'll reach a crudely fashioned but enormous pyramid that the current inhabitants have mocked up over the entrance to Warren 's Burrow, probably as a vestige to the devil they worship. Without a word, we start down.

I feel a little gray around the gills as we follow along a path leading to the pyramid and ending near its top. The structure is cold but vibrates beneath our feet as if it were breathing; the ceremonial engravings trip us as we climb over the peak and balance carefully on the wall. Just seven feet below is a trapezoidal opening, which one could theoretically jump straight down into and enter the pyramid much quicker.

"You know," Astairelike says, forcing himself to speak at last, "when I joined the army, they never said anything about scaling pyramids."

"They said to expect the unexpected," Spoolnicker snaps.

"I hardly think they meant anything like this."

"Well, don't worry, I'm sure that eventually someone will come along, we'll kill them, and everything will get back to normal."

"Normal is over-rated, if you ask me…" That voice!

He snakes out of the opening below us. Before he can even breathe we've jumped him, my sword against his throat, Spoolnicker's bow binding his arms, and Astairelike's ax against his forehead. He doesn't resist.

"Not that happy to see me, I take it?"

"How the devil did you get down here?"

"That green light disappeared two hours ago. I'd have said hello, but you were asleep when I came in. If I hadn't put that wall back together after I broke it down, some Lakova scout might have gutted you by now."

I glance back up. The barrier had seemed intact when we'd come to, but we hadn't been quite so interested in going back, with all the lost time we had to make up for.

"What're you doing here?" says Spoolnicker.

"Well." Metatron stands up, lifting us up with him. "It's like I told you. My only interest is making sure that no one involved in this little game of yours has any advantage over the other."

"Who else is there?"

"Your friends, the Least-Rogonians, for one."

I don't say anything. He clearly thinks we've overlooked his claim to have taken down the barrier and put it back up, to say nothing about how he keeps turning up. Best to play the gullible card a little longer:

"So, why are you telling us this?"

He shoots me a look. "I just thought you should know. This is all getting rather interesting, from where I'm sitting…"

"How wonderful for you," Spoolnicker spits. "Except that every time you come around there's trouble."

"Me? Trouble?"

"Don't be an ass! First there's the attack on Marrow-Vinjia, then those damned squirrels!" He throws a punch, but the ferret's height and flexibility prevent it from connecting.

"Um, if you'll recall, those squirrels were already there, and that most unfortunate decimation of your homeland happened long after we met."

"I don't care!" Astairelike screams. "Why don't you get out of here before you bring Sivad on us?"

"There's no such thing as Sivad."

"What?"

"I was just inside that pyramid. There's nothing there."

"Nothing?"

"Nothing but some rat bones and remnants of the ancient hares. To be perfectly honest, I don't think the Blind exist either. Look at this place, it's a ghost town."

"Well." I sheathe my sword. "That's one less thing we have to worry about." I signal the others to let him go.

"If I were you," he says, his voice slightly more cordial, "I'd go in there and look around. You might find something of use; weapons, shields, that sort of thing."

"We have weapons." Spoolnicker glares.

"Yes, a broken bow, an empty quiver, a damaged ax, and a sword that won't stand up to any magical attack higher than 'Pick a card, any card.' Well equipped, you are."

"We don't need magic," Astairelike growls.

"Think about the Strega for a second. After everything they've done, do you really think a sword is going to do you much good?"

If he wasn't so tall I could cut his head off for that. "You," I bark, viciously, "stay out here."

He scratches his neck noncommittally as I signal for the others to enter the opening. Fortunately, the narrow hallway we have to maneuver through is tall enough that we don't have to crawl on all fours, giving us at least the impression of dignity. It leads us to another cave, smaller than the main one, but large enough for a small empire of rats (or a single tribe of hares) to live very comfortably. The walls have a dim glow; not pervasive, but hinting of an orange light. It is considerably warmer in here than it was outside the pyramid. There're one or two graves near the entrance, but most of the area looks undisturbed. It doesn't seem to dawn on my friends, but I'm filled with a kind of sentimentality; I'm standing in Warren's Burrow.

It's strange, but in my mind's eye this chamber is flooded with a mist like flickering candlelight, the walls bright and vibrating like muddy orange water, reminding one of a lovely,,,morgue. It brings a twitching sensation between my eyes and goes further back, sending a strange sensation along the top of my shoulders and into my spine. I step without meaning to, surveying this hall of glory, with nonexistent whispers in my ears, guiding me to every spot where a proud rat lost his life in that famous battle. Here… there… No matter where I step a still portrait blooms before my imagination, magnificently painted: a Vinjian in full battle dress atop a Shrii, feathered and painted, his crude ax useless against his killer's forged steel blade; a Vinjian gripping a Lakova by his scalp, forcing him to his knees as another soldier of the empire swings his ax, preparing to disembowel the poor savage; two Farris-Ianist braves looming over a fallen soldier, eyes bloodshot, unaware of the three Vinjian archers taking aim; a Lakova and Farris-Ianist in duel, each with sharpened bone weapons at the ready, destined to kill each other; an entire squadron of our foot-soldiers surrounding a massive Shrii, three headless bodies at his feet, a fourth gripped in his hand, a fifth atop a long spike. So many images, all of them with lifelike eyes that look straight at me.

A pure radiation of epic death, an intoxicating invitation to join the long run-out brigade; it grips me around the neck. I have a childlike fancy to run off with these ghosts into a leather-bound history and never return. It's the stench of this place, the way the floor moves slowly under me. I cannot help but think, as my dreaming recedes and the shadows creep back over me like hypnotic acid, that I am very small.

Metatron, who's followed us in, speaks:

> *"In Egypt's sandy silence, all alone,*
> *Stands a gigantic leg, which far off throws*

The only shadow that the desert knows:
'I am great OZYMANDIAS,' saith the stone,
'The King of Kings; this city shows
The wonders of my hand.' The City's gone,
Naught but the Leg remaining to disclose
The site of this forgotten Babylon.
We wonder, and some hunter may express
Wonder like ours, when thro' the wilderness
Where London stood, holding the wolf in chase,
He meets some fragments huge, and stops to guess
What powerful but unrecorded race
Once dwelt in that annihilated place."

"What the screaming hell is that?" Astairelike sputters, confused by this sudden interlude.

"On A Stupendous Leg Of Granite, Discovered Standing By Itself, In The Deserts Of Egypt, With The Inscription Inserted Below," purrs the ferret, citing that poem's title.

"What? Speak English!"

"That was English."

"Well, speak better English, then."

He chuckles, then turns back to me. "Still, it is a rather poetic setting…for all the good it did them."

I can't say I disagree with him, but time is of the essence. "I thought you said there were weapons down here?"

He looks disappointed, "Of course. They're over there."

"Where?"

"Just around that bend down there…"

He indicates another small cave toward the end of the cavern. The four of us move pensively, entering a small room that our party can just barely squeeze into. Metatron has to double over just to avoid scraping his head. The three of us turn to protest when the floor illuminates below us, exposing an intricate circular pattern that rumbles a split-second, then descends quickly. In no time at all, the ferret is standing comfortably at his own full height and the lot of us is facing what looks like the unfortunate collision of a graveyard, an Aztec temple, and a weapons cache. Around the outside, save the small elevator where we're positioned, is a plethora of freshly dug graves, largely unmarked in the traditional sense, but a sizable number adorned with swords, axes, picks, spears, shields, and other means of waging war, all expertly crafted and untouched by rust or grime.

In the center is a triangular structure. I hesitate to call it a pyramid, but whatever it is it is made from the bones of animals much larger then myself. Between the many cracks and gaps there is a dark blue flame, pulsating as if it desires to be free. If it is supposed to be imprisoned by the bones or merely generated by them I can't say, but as soon as I give it any real thought my attention is diverted slightly lower to the statue that surrounds this oddity. A long sandstone replica of a snake, scales thrusting outward like small spikes, with a rattle like a scorpion's tail, a hood like a cobra, a pointed head like an anaconda, and an exaggerated mouth like the egg-snake, fully opened and with so many fangs exposed it looks more like the jaw bone of a piranha. This is like no reptile that Mother Nature ever made. This is their heathen god, Sivad.

Not wishing to broach the subject just yet, I turn to Metatron, "Whose graves are these? I don't recognize the make of those…"

"That flame," he ignores me, "rather amazing, wouldn't you say?"

I don't answer, but he doesn't notice. "Supposedly those bones are from the hares themselves. Allegedly, that fire just sprung out of nothingness the minute they erected that structure, and ever since strange things have been happening to anyone fool enough to come near."

Well, that's comforting…

Spoolnicker sputters, "Look, we're not here to learn ancient history. Let's just grab something and get out before the natives catch wind of us."

"Nah, how dem natives gon' do thatch, reckon?" a lackadaisical voice calls out.

From out of that snake's mouth, comes a vole! Less than three inches tall, whiter than ivory, wearing a tattered Capra-Vinjian uniform far too large for him, hanging like a judge's robes, dark circles burned under his eyes, and spider webs hanging like thick, matted hair down the side of his head.

"Dem folks up 'ere, I hanna heard mucha dem since the last time a rat came thumpin' down to see Ol' Reuel." He motions up to the apex of the cave, where hundreds of what look like tiny stalactites perch directly above us.

"Bats?" I whisper.

"How do you suppose they survive down here?" Astairelike twists his mustache nervously.

"Well," I pose, "I suppose if hares can survive down…what's so funny?"

The vole quits his mocking wheeze and smiles at me. "Up 'ere's no bats, nosah, ain't the Blind, neither. Some-wars betwixt, I reckon, but dang if Ol' Reuel can make much t'it."

"What's going on, Metatron?" I look but he's not there anymore.

"They're not planning on waking up on us, are they?" Astairelike asks him.

"Can't say for sure, nosah. That big ol' snake over there, him says all sorts, but never makes n'mention of them. Can't even say too clear 'bout why I ain't up there wit'em."

"What's that supposed to mean?" Spoolnicker snorts.

"Pick up one of dem swords, 'ere. You see, sho'nuff."

Letting his ego get the better of him, Spoolnicker snobbishly turns towards the nearest grave, one with a well-crafted pick-ax jutting from the head of it. He plucks it as it he were selecting a flower and spins it cockily, not noticing that immediately overhead, one of those strange stalactite creatures is beginning to vibrate, struggling at first, but then erupting from its pose like a velociraptor hatching from its egg. Before I can get a good look at it, it…oh my God in heaven, it's MELTING!

It dissolves into steady stream of clay-like magma urinating out of the precipice and into our midst, hitting between us with more force than one would expect, morphing into a ball that spins horrendously, elongates into a cylinder, then a block, and finally into a more rodent-like shape. The beast that bears those wings is like no mammal I've ever seen, nor any monster I ever encountered in a fever dream. A head somewhere between a proper bat and an Irish bulldog; a strong but diseased-looking body, like an anteater, with claws to match; sharpened bones sticking out of holes on its chest, insect-like feelers flowing from them and twitching in the air.

The devil gives an anguished scream, then, before we can do anything about it, he stabs his claws straight through Spoolnicker's chest, almost as if it were a spirit. No blood squirts out of him, nor does he spasm like so many impaled vermin I've seen in my time. It opens its mouth as if to eat him; it inhales sharply, and a stream of purple smoke flies out of Spoolnicker's eye sockets!

The skin on both of them is bubbling effusively. Spoolnicker's strong features contort into something like the demon that's attacked him, the beast transforming into something closer to a rat. Before it can cut and run, Astairelike and I have it ensnared around the neck and beheaded, respectively. Before he notices that the body's reverting to its original shape, the little mouse has upended his ax from its chain and commenced dicing the remains into smaller portions. The fury and zest with which he performs this is enough that lifting the ax after every cut nearly flings him completely off the corpse and into my lap.

Meanwhile, Spoolnicker's shifted back into his old enormous self, no worse for wear but badly shaken, unable to hold his pick-ax or even stand upright with fidgeting at the thousands of imaginary aphids that must be crawling on his skin just now. Astairelike, finally bucking himself off his demon, pivots on his supporting paw and springs after Ol' Reuel. He hurls his chain lariat, hoping to repeat our victory over the demon, but Reuel, as if catching a punch, hooks the chain and, in a shocking turn, elongates the fingers of his other paw into pointed metal butcher's knives! He knocks Astairelike sideways with the blunt side of his paw and faces him down, still smiling, but less sincere in his hospitality. "Dem folk up t'the ceiling, 'sa way of doin' that. Never did figure why…" He retracts his fingers, but not without clipping Astairelike's nose right between the nostrils. It was a simple flick, but at first glance the cut looks rather deep.

"It's because I want them to," a melodious voice pipes over Reuel's shoulders. I wish I could be surprised that it looks to be coming from the snake wrapped around the blue flame, but I honestly can't.

"Never did say why. Least-ways, I can't remember nothin', all that gum-flapping 'bout everything else…"

The voice chuckles. "That will be all, Reuel."

The vole shrugs and walks off, slowly. Spoolnicker with the tiniest grip on himself re-established, looks that stone lizard in the eye, or, rather, what would be the eye in real life. "Another vole?"

"Fresh out of voles, sorry," it deadpans. "I had more a few years ago. Can't say I know what happened to them."

Astairelike, gripping his nose as hard as he can, wheezes to me, "Bedford, is that who I think it is?"

"I'm afraid so, Astairelike," the snake intones, "but you need not worry. For now I'm not inclined to harm you, anyway. I am Sivad, God of the Harvest, and ruler of the Blind."

As interesting as this bizarre scene is, I don't think it to our benefit to linger much longer. I would just grab another weapon or so and cut and run, but how to do it without ending up like Spoolnicker? More importantly, how does one run from a god?

About the first point, he reads my mind. "I'm afraid you can't take a weapon from my graveyard with suffering those consequences. If my subjects don't steal your 'sight' and in turn die, they can never become one with me, and assume less painful forms. It's fortunate that you came in a group; most of our visitors blunder in by themselves, and the original follower simply escapes. Or tries to, anyway. So far no one has left the Land of the Blind without my say so. Their starvation-riddled graves dot the entire Main Cave." He chuckles to himself again.

"Why?" Astairelike spurts before he can stop himself.

"You see those pitiful beasts up there? Can you think of a better way to prove your loyalty than to become one of those?"

"A lot of volunteers, are there?" Spoolnicker spits.

"A mortal rat doesn't volunteer so much as he's volun-TOLD, but it's the same thing in the end. A god likes to be appreciated, even if he has to force it."

"That's the most horrible thing I've ever heard," Astairelike marvels.

"Well, there's not much else to do. If I could ever think of something better I might not put them through all that. Then again, I'm pretty hard to impress, and besides, it's not as if I have many visitors."

"You could make yourself a new statue, snakes have nothing to do with your chosen field," I say.

"I'm impressed! You seem to have a great deal of wit about you, which is not terribly common in those who blunder into my keep."

"We didn't blunder, we came here on purpose."

"I know, and under such extraordinary circumstances! The last time the Strega used the Citadel that way it brought Ol' Reuel down here. Clearly you are their enemies, and therefore friends of mine. No sir, by 'blunder' I meant that you entered my temple. I've never met anyone who did so on purpose."

"What about the ferret?" Astairelike bursts, confused.

"…Ah. Him. Oh, I could tell you about him, but what good would it do? You wish to make war with the Strega and have little time to do it. Why shouldn't I help you?"

He does have a point. Because of the Strega, he's the last of the pagan gods, at least, that's what history claims, though he gives us no real reason to trust him. I need a sign first.

"Those things up there…"

"Yes, those. I'm not even certain how I came up with them in the first place. They used to burn offerings of hashish back in the old days, but we've run out."

"That's not what I was going to say."

"Well, that's not important. Oh, you will bury that poor fellow, won't you? I try to keep it neat around here, if at all possible."

Spoolnicker's still not convinced. "What does that have to do with…?"

"So." Astairelike buts in impatiently, "All we have to do is pull out some more weapons, kill the bats when they turn into rats, and you're just going to let us go with brand new magical weapons?"

"I wouldn't go so far as to call them magical, but that's the basic idea, yes. I might change my mind, and then again I might not. But if it's magic you're interested in, you might try putting those weapons into that fire there for a second. All sorts of good energy in there." I don't doubt that under all that rock he's smirking at us.

We turn to each other.

"Are we really going to believe any of that shit?" Spoolnicker whispers.

"Well," I rub my eyes, "I say it's a bad idea to trust him."

"So do I." Astairelike cracks his neck. "But I can't imagine what else we'd do. I mean, it didn't do you any harm going through this ritual of theirs."

"No harm! I felt as if every limb on my body were being eaten by typhoid-infested cats!"

"But you are still alive," I point out, and without waiting for another word I make for Reuel. "Sir, while we don't believe a word of what you've told us, it seems unwise to decline your offer."

"A smart decision, on both ends," Sivad intones knowingly. "Incidentally," he throws a spotlight on to a rather garish sword with a circular hilt and Arab curvature to the exposed portion of the blade, which in this light looks almost red, "you might be interested in THIS sword. It belonged to you grandfather. At least, I'm assuming it did, seeing as that's his grave and all."

"You seem to know a lot about me, don't you?" I mutter to myself, not intending for him to hear.

"Oh, I know much about you, Bloodford." His voice grins. "As many as you've killed, they say the Angel of Death himself will come to collect you at the appointed time." Death himself, eh? Well, that's a new one…

I grip my fingers around the hilt, unwittingly freezing a few seconds. Call me sentimental, but as great a man as my great-grandfather was, to hold his sword, silly looking though it might be now…

"For King and Country," I whisper, and pull Excalibur out of the Stone.

Christ, the pain!

In less than half-a-second a monstrosity has fallen upon me, hugging me close around the shoulders and blinding me with smoke. Even if it's coming out of my own sockets, it feels as if I've breathed in pepper spray. I can feel my body boiling alive; every hackle of my skin stinging, the air bubbles forming beneath it make it feel as if it were no longer connected to anything. The bones themselves, as if to make up for neglect, begin rotting at the ends and then growing exponentially.

None too soon, I sense Spoolnicker's pick-ax being dug into my attacker's skull. As soon as I can see the brute, and the thing that he killed, I know all is well, but still involuntary firings of electricity spasm through me. I lollop ridiculously as Ol' Reuel laughs and laughs.

"Hoo, frere, you worse 'an 'em frogs come down once ago. Dem's jumping all around, you betcha."

"Frogs?" Spoolnicker asks, not grasping the connection as well as I might.

"Yassir, came on down with they hocus pocus, pick up a boocoolotta weapons, had all 'em leapfroggin' 'round like a hurricane of gunnysacks." He scratches his chin, then laughs. "Heheheh, leapfroggin'. Get it?"

"Lovely," I spit, having regained control over myself.

"Your turn." Spoolnicker glares at Astairelike.

"Yes, well, I think we'll be skipping my turn," he says defiantly. Not having the patience, I lean back and kick, my foot catching a shovel by the hand-grip and launching it into his stomach, knocking him down and fooling the ensuing bogeyman into thinking he took it. We catch the thing as it tries to escape, but we deliberately take our time killing it.

"Or not," Astairelike coughs once he gets his voice back. "Not works too."

Sivad is laughing heartily at our expense, but we're ignoring him; Spoolnicker takes a closer look at Astairelike's new weapon, then his. "A shovel? Who fights with a shovel?"

"A shovel's a very useful weapon," I reply. "After you kill someone, you can dig a hole for them."

"Speaking of which…" Sivad sings.

"Yes, yes, we're getting to that," Spoolnicker grunts. Turning to the white mouse, he says, "Well, you've got the shovel, hop to it."

"Actually." I step in. "YOU do it."

"Me?"

"You're a lot bigger than he is. You'll get it done faster."

As helpful as I'm willing to delude myself that this has all been, we've fallen even further behind schedule. After stepping and fetching enough before Sivad to avoid any more deistic insanity, we lash our new weapons across our rucks, replace our old ones (Spoolnicker having fixed his bow and snatched a paw full of arrows that weren't on any particular grave), and make for the entrance to the main cave. Reuel's accompanied us so far, much against my own wishes.

"Eh-na," he belches when we cross into the main cave, "Why y'all got you weapons on ya backs like 'at?"

"We figure we shouldn't use them too much," Astairelike admits, though the decision was more between Spoolnicker and himself.

"I mean," Spoolnicker adds, "look what they've done to you."

Reuel looks a bit confused at that, so at least we haven't offended him. I shall be sure to redress the both of them as soon as we're out of earshot.

"Say," he replies at last. "You din put 'em in the fi-ar yet!"

It's true, but as for myself I wasn't in any hurry to get too close to it, if indeed it was the fire that killed all the Capra-Vinjians. I quickly change the subject. "Reuel, how far is it to the other end of the cave?"

"'Bout eight hours," he giggles to himself, "by the way the frog hops."

"Thank you." I smile insincerely. "What are you staring at?"

"Nothin'. Right fine coat cha got."

"Yes, well, it's new." I don't like that leer he's giving me.

"Sho is. Can't reckon how old 'is'n is. When I got it once ago it was pretty tore up."

"Well, I can," I say, hoping to end this conversation as quickly as possible. "That's from the Capra dynasty. Capra the…V, I should say."

"Hmm, that were once ago. Maybe someday I'll have a new coat like yours." He gives me the eye, and I reflexively grab my hilt. He turns and scampers off without a word.

"Think he'll make trouble?" asks Spoolnicker, finally composed again.

"I honestly can't say," I reply.

"Anyone else no longer care?" Astairelike snorts.

Neither of us respond.

Marrow-Vinjians, Chapter Nineteen: Thieves In The Temple

"And the humans train their females to do that?" Spoolnicker eyes me suspiciously. "Can't imagine why."

We've been walking for four hours. By now we've run out of things to talk about, so I've been filling them in on my last visit with His Majesty.

"Well, you wouldn't think it, but it does please the eye in an odd sort of way. Most likely, there is some small subtlety they're more attuned to, else we would have caught on before."

"Well, naturally."

"I don't know." The little mouse has finally stopped his gulping. "In my lifetime, we've always been taught to ACT like humans, not BE like humans."

"What does that have to do with anything?" the great black rat grunts.

"I wear a human's clothes. I believe in the human's code of modesty. I don't believe the lack of clothing makes a female any more attractive, the way they do. That is the difference between animals and humans."

"Humph. You got philosophical all of a sudden."

Astairelike starts talking, about how he ended up in the army and the things he's seen, while Spoolnicker interrupts him every few seconds to make some snarky comment. I'm not really paying attention. I can't help but feel that our encounter with Sivad went down too easily. I think he might have something to do with that ferret, but what? And, more importantly, are they trying to set us up for something?

I glance over my shoulder; I'm whaled by the sudden appearance of Reuel! Almost an entirely different specimen than he was just a few hours ago: dark circles under his vacant, enlarged eyes, and sneering, for all the world, like that squirrel who killed himself in front of me yesterday. He has a glow like the barrier around him. I go for the sword on my rucksack, but I can read in his face that he will not harm me just yet. Spoolnicker moves to question him, but Reuel's sharpened his fingers and before I can draw my blade or Astairelike can stance his weapon, we hear a shrieking whistle much louder and more piercing than we've ever encountered.

All about us the ground breaks open and shapeless points, like an alligator's teeth, jut slowly upward. Surrounding us on all sides are the bodies of those long-dead, mostly rotted away, but fearsome and luminescent like their spectral counterparts. Low, guttural wheezing comes from unused portions of dead rats' lungs. The lot of them stalking directly toward us, claws extended, teeth bared.

Astairelike pounces, but I catch his tail and fling him in the other direction. He meets one of the beasts in midair, swinging the concave end of his shovel handle against its neck, almost hard enough to bash its head clear off of its neck. Before the mouse reaches the ground another corpse leaps at Spoolnicker. The two immediately behind me jump in unison, but I duck and they collide with Spoolnicker's assailant, who's been thrown in my direction.

I tuck and roll, grabbing my old sword in my other paw and charging the flank to my right. I've managed to behead two of them before the heavier new sword throws me off-balance and allows another corpse to grip my wrist and fling me to the ground. Dodging his snapping teeth, I ram the butt of my hilt into his temple, which stops him long enough to allow me to force the blade against what would have been his throat. A sideways cut destroys the cartilage but leaves his head on his body. I take opportunity of the slack in his grip to fit my other sword under his neck and behead him entirely, though his grip almost doesn't loosen before the next rotter staples his teeth into the dirt by my shoulder.

He pulls back and clutches my coat-collar; I attempt to repeat my scissor trick on his midsection, but the lack of a lower body doesn't loosen his paws. He's driving me to my knees, until Spoolnicker, complete with a scrambling dervish on his back, runs the devil down with his pick-ax aimed like a lance. He moves to give the rider on his back the same treatment, but Astairelike jumps on top of it, the weight dropping the zombie to the ground, and plucks the skull off with his bare paws.

Scrambling back to our feet, we take our normal fighting positions as the horde tightens their circle around us; we attack first. The pain in all of our muscles is becoming more distracting than it normally is this early in the fight, and the monsters still standing are far enough away that we're afforded the chance to gasp in pain. My knee, especially, is barely holding me upright. For once, Spoolnicker makes the first move, butting the first attacker and hooking the back of it's head with the inner curve of his pick, dragging it along and over his outstretched leg. This proves to be an error in judgment on his part; the amount of time he's spent on his posturing has given two other wraiths a clear shot at his arms. With a burning pain all over my body, I fling both swords straight for them; they hit the devils between the eyes. Astairelike, ever vigilant, hands off his shovel to me and jumps for Spoolnicker's shoulders, his chain swinging before his foot even hits the ground. He lands and his ax somersaults into a distant opponent, whose resulting spasm catches and yanks his chain, propelling him forward as he grabs the sword nearest him and hurls it back at me. I knock a zombie down with the inside of the shovel, flip it around, and catch the sword on the back of it like a lawn dart. Before that thing can get back up, I've plucked my great-grandfather's sword from the back of the shovel and deprived him of his head.

My knee still troubling me greatly, I settle for using the shovel as a shield of sorts, to hold them off while I slit their throats. I'm fighting more or less by myself; the little white mouse is still skipping around from group to group, as is his custom, but Spoolnicker, enraptured by his newfound usefulness in close-quarters combat, is far too busy impressing the audience in his head to be of any help. My bait-and-switch technique is working so far, but for the life of me, I can't figure how they keep coming. By my estimation, with as many of them as we've chopped into little pieces, the field should be clear by now. I grunt and moan, as my arm gets heavier and heavier, with still no end in sight. I struggle to divide my attention enough to get a bead on Reuel.

There!

I push myself as hard as I can, but I fear if I do very much more of all this ducking and pouncing with my sword my knee will break. I suspect that within seconds I will either be over-whelmed and suffer a dog's death; Astairelike, returning to the center of the formation, takes my side, propping me up. Spoolnicker, backing towards us, is covered in sweat and breathing heavily. I think that his obstinacy has been beaten out of him finally, and the familiar signal spurs through us as his back makes contact with ours. If we're going to die, we will die like soldiers!

A wind, of all things, picks up. The sudden force pries several of our attackers off the ground and dashes them against the cave wall. Another picks up from a different direction, and then another. The winds cross and strike at each other, circling around in a shrinking loop, the three of us in the center. From the other side of the cloud of dust, I can see the form of a massive snake jolting toward where Reuel was just standing. It snatches him and carries him into the wind in its mouth; crossing the threshold it shifts into a large hare with hawk-like claws instead of feet! With one foot he nearly crushes our party, digging his talons into the ground to protect us from the tornado he's created, with another he holds Reuel high.

A form, like the one that squirrel coughed up, is oozing out of the vole's nostrils like a traumatic head-wound. It's contorting his face the way fire warps a piece of paper. I suppose the poor little devil's had his vocal chords crushed already, or else I'd be able to hear him screaming. It's hard to get a good look at Sivad; I try shifting my weight around but my movements make him tighten his grip.

The substance that bled out of the vole's head is trailing like a kite now, oblong with globules at the end, with a long, waning trail that leaks back to his orifices, still tenuously connected to him. The rodent is still alive; somehow this horrid cyclone hasn't sandpapered the last spark out of him just yet. At long last he retches and vomits, the last traces of his possession eking away, caught in the updraft and raising higher and higher. Sivad drops him dead on the ground and stands full upright, pushing us further into the earth, raising his ears, as the tornado bends at center to funnel the withering mass away from us. The winds follow and the air is still at last. Sivad pauses to take long, gasping breaths before he even looks downward at us. He doesn't bother to look at Reuel's limp body; instead he looks directly at me, his expression confused. I can't say I've ever seen a face quite like it, but sufficed, I can tell this is not the same god we were dealing with earlier.

He loosens his claws at last, but before we can stand up he's pinned Spoolnicker back down, the sharp end of his talon a swallow away from impaling him in the throat.

"Please don't." A familiar and discordantly polite voice echoes through the silence: Metatron!

"This doesn't concern you," Sivad mutters, which is still plenty loud.

"Yes, it does. I need them."

"Go eat shit and kill yourself!"

"Charming, but if you'd stop letting your baser impulses rule you for a moment, you'd let them go immediately."

"They brought the Strega into my keep! I demand justice!"

"And justice you'll get, but you won't get it properly unless you let them go on and fight the Strega themselves."

"I don't care! I've kept their foul false magic out of my domain for years without any help from any mortal rodent, and I damn sure don't plan on asking for it now!"

"Look!" The ferret raises his voice finally. "There is something much larger than you happening, and I will not be robbed of my crowning glory just because you can't get over the possession of a worthless vole!"

Sivad seems to struggle with that point. "But," the god starts out, "I… they… Reuel…I must…"

"Then you must. Just. Don't. Kill them."

He flashes a self-satisfied smirk and makes to leave us. I don't get the impression he's really helped us, judging by the way Sivad's begun breathing heavily again, like a bull readying to charge. The ferret reads my gaze, even if he's not looking at me:

"I just saved your life," he mutters. I doubt that he means it.

Sivad lifts his claw off of us, but we're unable to move. He cricks his neck menacingly, and with that my body jolts upward involuntarily, followed by Astairelike and Spoolnicker, then the corpse of Reuel. Our bodies rise off of the ground until we're right at the level of his nose, then slam back into the wall, our arms are pinned to our sides. I can barely breathe.

He looks away from us, waves one of his claws magically, and out of nothingness comes a bottle of human whiskey, nearly as tall as he is! He picks it up with one claw like it was nothing, breaks the top open with a single talon, and gulps the whole thing down in a single go; he belches, then hurls the bottle at us. We feel the full brunt of the glass as it smashes our faces and bounces onto the floor, shattering into a trillion pieces.

"Bet you thought that was REALLY funny, didn't you?" he snarls at us. "I try to help, he says you won't do shit, then you go and do me like that. And this is exactly what he said wouldn't happen, and then it does. He doesn't care that he didn't hold up his end of it. Fucker… Just because he's got some plan, thinks he's a big shot, does he?"

Spoolnicker manages to get some control over his body, enough to suddenly gasp loudly for air.

"SHUT UP!" Sivad barks at him. "I have enough on my mind just now. How they got in, how those wheezy little shits got their power…look at him," he indicates the dead Reuel, "and just what the hell I'm going to do with you?" He grins at this. "Oh yes, I've a world of shit planned for you three. No more mister nice god playing along so the…hic…the friends of the ferret can do what the ferret wants. No sir! By the time I'm done with you your innards will look like a can of fuck exploded!"

He rams a talon into Spoolnicker's midsection! Spoolnicker yowls from pain, but my experienced ear tells me he's not about to die, a disturbing prospect if it means what I think it does. And indeed, upon retracting his claw there's no hole in his stomach, and as he continues to groan from his injury, it's lifting like a fog, perhaps as if it were healing instantly. Without giving us any time to digest this he backhands Astairelike, cutting his neck so deeply, I shouldn't be at all shocked if his spinal column was severed! And, again, his wound heals without delay. I can barely see it except for the reflection in Sivad's demented eye. It's not pretty.

"Are you enjoying this, Bloodford?" he smirks sedulously, taking a sabbatical from chopping up my archer.

He leans forward, eyes filled with murderous contempt. How dare he look at me that way! I no longer care about anything else; I steel my nerves and spit at him. I didn't plan on hitting him in the eye, though.

He doesn't react so much as he simply stops in place, all but frozen, until he finally slumps his shoulders, rears his neck until it's fully extended and moves as close to me as he dares.

"That's the way you want it?" he chuckles sinisterly, his expression wider than a clown's. "OK then…"

He puffs his chest out, exhales slowly flings his arms out to the side, clutches his talons closed and, in a way I can't truly explain, the space around his claws looks as if it were warping, contorting to his grip, as if he's grabbed reality itself! The stone wall cracks around us, as if it were contorting into a set of hands. I can make out individual fingers now, they crush against my chest, and my companions'. The wall is breaking apart, the hands that bind us are the only parts not crumbling onto the cave floor below.

With a wicked smile, he brings his claws together and the remainder of the cave wall shatters, tearing at our skin like buckshot; the hands, afloat, dip a little lower, but with a wink and a flourish, as if he were dealing cards, the hare spreads his arms and our hand-prisons burst through the air, circling his head like a lariat, then his talon, and, once he's finally grown bored, he shoots us back towards Warren's Burrow, crashing through the pyramid and down through the ground, our bodies being torn at like meat in a sausage grinder, before we finally plummet, face first, into the dirt beside the graveyard.

I'm not quite as together as I was a second ago. I feel myself blacking out, but I can swear I hear him shouting at his minions, something about freedom and…oh, it doesn't matter now. Even if the now-dripping sea of oncoming liquid assassins were to reach us this instant, I would rather die here than put up with this madness much longer. Even if I were to hear a roar like the one Metatron unleashed when he charged the squirrels, and sunk his gnawing teeth into the airway of one, releasing so much blood into his lungs it would drown Sivad; even if I saw him charge like greased thunder into the space between us and the enduing horde, rounding us at blinding speed and forcing them back with the same unseen weapons he used to shoot one of the last surviving squirrels down from the tree, melting them into puddle which one cannot see them recovering from…

Oh, wait, that just happened.

The thought of being rescued by him a third time doesn't sit well in my stomach. "Show-off," I swear under my breath, as he mows down all the foul creatures around us and cracks open the stone fingers around Astairelike and Spoolnicker.

He makes just as grand a proceeding coming back, but instead of collecting me he stops and shouts, "Give me your sword!"

"I'm a little tied up, just now."

He cracks just enough of my binding open to free my arm. "Give me your sword!"

I've had enough. "Why should I trust you?"

"Because for now it serves my purposes for you to be alive," he says, and before I can respond he tries to snatch my hilt from me. I respond by removing my blade from it, but he simply loops behind me, picks up the whole assembly and dashes through the horde once more toward Sivad. He manhandles me thoroughly, wrenching my arm around, slicing through the mud-men as if I weren't even attached. Sivad backhands a large portion of rock at us; Metatron dodges and doubles back toward the blue flame near Sivad's statue. Forcing my sword arm out straighter and longer than nature intended it, he aims me dead at the flame!

My blade makes it all the way to the hilt before the ferret flicks around absentmindedly, as if I were a rag doll, and heads back toward the mad god. He reaches his feet and circles around him like a shark, drawing his attention toward my glowing sword while he puts his free paw back into his vest, clutching whatever it is he keeps killing with, and deposits one in Sivad's kneecap. Once the omnipotent giant buckles down to our level, he knocks me off of the sword entirely and thrusts it into the hare's chest, barely missing his heart, and I doubt that was by accident.

"What," the ferret says, "did I JUST tell you?"

"Go to hell, Mr. Big Shot!" the god wheezes weakly. The

hordes are evaporating without his presence to sustain them. Astairelike and Spoolnicker have left their safe perch and rejoined me by Sivad's feet.

"You know the problem with the Norse gods?" Metatron continues. "They kept forgetting that they weren't immortal. They only lived forever because of the Golden Apples. But what happened when someone cut down their tree, huh?" He twists the sword like a corkscrew, maximizing the pain but still not hitting his heart. "You, my friend, have just eaten your last apple…"

"Fuck you," Sivad whimpers, glaring so hard his eyes are turning a shade of azure. I become aware of a humming noise directly behind us. Having finally gotten back into our familiar groove, Spoolnicker feels my impulse and turns first, gasping as a warp opens! We three instinctively draw our weapons and take position, fearing some new menace might be sicked on us, but once our backs are turned, Sivad spreads his talons and kicks us into the portal.

Day Three
Least-Rogonians

Least-Rogonians, Chapter Twenty: King Marrow I

||||||||||||||||||||||||||||||||||||||||||||||||||||||||||||||||||||||||||||||||||||||||||||||||||||||||||||||||||||||||||

t was in the early hours of the morning that the One-Eyed Witch, captured and afforded the best medical aid Marrow's army could give her, regained consciousness, just in time to see the still impressive facade of Marrow-Vinjia, its outer wall already almost completely rebuilt. At first, in her groggy state, the pieces did not fall fast enough into sequence; she wondered why it felt as though her stomach had been clawed at by a falcon, but after she noticed her body was very heavily bandaged, her paws were manacled tight with steel and some type of animal skin, placed just behind her back where she couldn't gnaw through them, and, finally, that she was in a makeshift cage, being slowly brought before a building that was made to resemble what the humans called 10 Downing Street, that the reality of her situation sank in.

Hardly had she arrived before she'd been brought through the empty streets and into the palace, and into the private chambers of King Marrow himself. He stared her in the eye, his deformed figure completely erect, giddy with excitement at his new toy. He waved the guards off. He personally wheeled her cage over beside his enormous bed, then vaulted on top of it and lay on his belly, looking her straight in the eye.

"A most fortunate coincidence, my dear, if I do say so," he said.

"Humph," she spat. "Give me one reason why I don't zap myself out of this cage and blow you across the lake!"

He rolled toward the wall and fished a spare cigarette from under his pillows, then rolled back to her. "Don't suppose you would mind, would you?"

Smirking defiantly, she tensed herself and willed a small flame before her. Marrow leaned into it accordingly.

"Ah, it seems I was right about you. Not only are you smart enough to not attack a regent, but to be cordial to your captors. Don't worry. As soon as Bloodford returns from the Citadel I shall be more than happy to send word of your capture across the lake, and your subjects will have ample opportunity to rescue you."

"You mean…but I'm surprised, Marrow. I'd have thought you would have sent your favorite pet to scoop me up personally."

"Had I had time to prepare, I certainly would have. The propaganda value would have been astounding. As it is, it was some faceless nobody, so I shall have to give credit to the entire army, which always plays well but is very hard to make a statue out of." He paused from congratulating himself to take a long draw from his cigarette. Ophiuchus, glad for the silence, turned her glance to the floor beneath the two of them.

"She's still down there, isn't she?" she asked. In her mind, her sister was long dead, her skeleton picked clean by decay.

Marrow tsk-tsked and muttered something about not

throwing something away just because it wasn't pretty anymore, but when he picked his voice back up it was about something else entirely. "Do you really think that pathetic excuse for a son of yours can actually face the Strega and survive?"

"He's your son, too!" She found herself growing angry at him for reasons which didn't seem to make sense. It was not so much that she was confronting him after all these years, but the fact that… well, the fact that Marrow held such a low opinion of his offspring was actually an insult against himself, in a way. Marrow, to his credit, ignored her.

"So, the rebels who shot you…"

"I don't know anything about that!"

"No, I don't suppose you do. You never seem to know anything until it's too late. Take Octavia, for instance. All the power you and your mother had between you and you never knew the next in line was defecting to marry *your most hated enemy*… Still, Father always did have questionable taste in females, my mother excluded, of course."

His arrogance was breaking her patience, the casual way he was dismissing the poor wretch that he'd probably killed. Not that she'd felt sorry for her sister, but in principle it seemed cruel.

He seemed to read her mind. "I don't see how you're in any position to judge me, Ophiuchus. I didn't do anything to your sister that she didn't do to Capra IX before me. The only difference is the old rat had a bad heart and died before she could really get to him. Besides: abandoning your husband to steal the rat your sister married, who just happened to be the ruler of the Vinjians? Betraying and becoming a traitor to betray a traitor? Your fellow Least-Rogonians might find this sordid little bit of forgotten history to be very interesting, if only I could leak it without putting my own neck in the noose."

He paused and inhaled smugly. Both of them knew that neither would ever reveal the truth, but the fact that he'd been the one to broach the subject put him very much in the lead.

"Astran," she started weakly. "Bloodford will never get there before he does."

"That remains to be seen, my dear." He gripped his paw around her chin and forced her to move, eying her cannily. "You know, you're not bad looking, despite the years." Ophiuchus didn't know how to take the compliment, but she decided negatively. "Except for the eye. Tell me, did Octavia do that, or your mother?"

"My husband." She took a small modicum of comfort in the shocked look on his face. "Right after he found out about Astran, he got me pregnant with Tranah, then grabbed his ax and cut me so that no male would want me. Then the damned fool killed himself."

"Curiouser and curiouser." Marrow patted her chin. "Well, that's no longer my concern."

"Oh, and what is?"

"Whether I should publicly execute you, or lock you away and tell everyone you're dead."

Least-Rogonians, Chapter Twenty-One: Lafitte

All through the night before, Astran and company had circled the spiraling passages that lead from Syrinx's secret entrance; these caverns seemed to have no end of access to the ground directly beneath the mainland, but it took nearly six hours for it turn back toward the water, and even still they first had to travel downward. The main party had made camp at last, while a scouting party consisting of Trismegistus and Clopin, reported back that, while in sight, the beginning of the true underground was still at best another three hours off.

They were sleeping in shifts, keeping watch; Astran and Tranah had drawn the short end and had the worst shift, the second to last one before dawn. The dormice were curled in a circle behind them, Trismegistus slightly off-kilter, with Syrinx three-quarters of a meter behind them, posted with her eyes toward the way they'd come.

"Astran?" Tranah squeaked, her voice softer and more childlike than normal.

"Huh?"

"I know I probably should have asked earlier, but, what *exactly* is it we're doing?"

He quickly summed it up for her, but she barely noticed. He was tapping his staff with his fingers distractedly. It was hard to ignore.

"Not exactly...erm, well, you know what I mean..." She turned away.

It only took a second before the silence was too awkward, even by Astran's standards. "You, uh." He cleared his throat. "You handled yourself pretty good up there. With the spider, I mean."

"I thought so."

"I mean, who'd have thought, my little sister...actually useful for once."

She shot him a sly, sideways glance, "Well, I'm good for something other than that rope trick, anyway. Never could get the hang of much else."

"Pretty clever of them, though," he ignored her, "stealing my magic like that. A lesser mystic would've been powerless against that thing."

"Uh-huh. Right, whatever you have to tell yourself..."

"Oh, be quiet."

"You know, now that I think about it, I think you've done more magic in the last two days than I've seen you do in my entire life."

"I have not."

"Well, sure. I mean, think about it: you launched those guards at the cat, you summoned that ghost thingy to frighten

Mom, you blew off that tree branch, you made a bird out of it, you flew us all across the lake, and then you fought that spider with me. That's a lot of very powerful spells. I don't think I've ever seen you do a large spell before except for that whole bit when the frogs came…"

"I gave Mom that scar."

"Huh?"

"Well, you weren't born yet, but Dad cut Mom's eye out right before he died. When you were little, she tried to grow that eye back. I wouldn't let her."

"Personally," a strange new voice croaked, "I think the scar becomes her…"

He was a Norway rat, a putrid shade of yellow, clothed in a smoke-colored tunic and floppy peasant's cap, and in very short order he was flanked on his right by Tranah and Trismegistus, with Barnabas and Clopin completing the circle around him as he stared, bewildered, into Astran's eyes. Without time even for anyone to breathe Syrinx had launched herself, broadsword drawn from within her cloak. The stranger caught the sword between his palms and flung himself backward; Syrinx, still airborne, was tossed callously over Astran's shoulder.

Acting as one, the dormice lit a match each and formed a triangle around the newcomer, while Tranah bared her ax, and her friend loosed a set of daggers from her sleeves. The stranger had turned to face Astran again; the mystic's eyes never left him. Clopin, less used to flame than his counterparts, grew anxious and menaced the stranger; still clutching the broadsword, he whirled counter-clockwise and lopped the flaming heads of the matches off and, catching the scruff of Clopin's neck with his non-dominant paw, took him as a hostage.

Everyone but Astran backed off.

"Rude," the mystic muttered, squinting his eyes and concentrating hard on the sword. He tightened his grip on his staff, and the blade melted.

"Hmm," the shocked captor muttered, "no matter." He reached behind his back and drew from its hiding place under his tunic an ebony-handled circus whip! Knocking Clopin down, he whipped his lash about and lassoed Astran's staff right out of his paws, flinging it far enough behind all of them to be of no use during a close-quarter's fight.

"I don't actually need the staff," Astran threatened.

"You know," the stranger mused after a long silence, "it's been a while since I used this tunnel, but I certainly don't remember there being a welcoming committee."

"Who are you?"

"That's not really any of your business. Besides, if this is how you treat strangers I'd hate to see what acquaintances have to put up with."

"Yeah? Well…" Tranah groped for words. "It serves you right for sneaking up on us like that!"

"Listen, little girl, I've been prowling around these tunnels since before you were born, and I'd certainly like to think I'm old enough to know what serves me right. Now," he said as he climbed over the genuflecting Clopin, "if you'll kindly get out of my way…"

"Wait." Syrinx spoke finally. "You wouldn't by any chance be Lafitte, would you?"

"Depends on who's asking."

"That's a yes."

"Well, who might you be, then?"

"Syrinx Silvereye."

"Never heard of you."

"And these are Astran and Tranah of the Least-Rogonian tribe."

Lafitte glared at Astran. "You I've heard of. And what of these?" He motioned to the dormice.

"They are the priests from our temple," Tranah added helpfully.

"Little violent for holy mice, aren't you?"

"We're also money-changers," Trismegistus replied.

"Ah. So, who are you all running from?"

"What makes you think…"

"Please, they only built this passage for thieves and smugglers, not exactly somewhere you go for a day trip."

"We're trying to get to the main tunnels." Astran took charge.

"Oh?" Lafitte eyed him curiously. "And you just happen to come through the secret entrance?"

"It was convenient."

"Yes, well, you've picked a helluva route for yourself, kid. This little cove empties out into a patch of nothing, and it's a goddamn labyrinth getting back onto the main roads. You'd have been better off going through Greenshire."

"Greenshire's on the other side of the lake."

"It is? Huh, well, that's what I get for only ever using the back door, I guess. So, any of you foundlings have the slightest clue where you're going? You know, even in the main network, there's certain routes where if you go far enough down you're not coming back."

"Do you know how to get to the center of the lake from here?"

Lafitte's eyes lit up. "No, but I can get you halfway. After that it's basically a straight line… so long as you don't piss anybody off, anyway…"

Least-Rogonians, Chapter Twenty-Two: Octavia

‖‖‖

The Marrow-Vinjians had gone to great lengths, whether they realized it or not, to turn Ophiuchus into her sister. At Marrow's insistence, they'd bathed and dressed her, while the King looked on, in one of Octavia's old dresses. The One-Eyed Witch took little notice. The initial burst of adrenaline had worn off and the exact damage she'd suffered was becoming apparent, and what strength she'd held on to she spent on planning. Hers was a most undesirable situation; at full strength she could very easily disintegrate Marrow and his immediate guard and muscle her way out of enemy territory, but she was not at full strength, and it was as this dawned on her that she took into account just how many soldiers she'd have to go up against, and how easily they could overwhelm her. The Vinjians had defeated larger groups of Least-Rogonians than her, after all.

No. As always, her plan would require subtlety. There was also the problem of Marrow himself. Since she'd last encountered him he'd more than likely killed her sister, who had been much more powerful than her. Clearly, he had some advantage he could just as easily use against her. The sun was coming up and the king had called for his breakfast; since she had no true plan for escape, she was willing to accept his hospitality until he forced her hand.

Her captor, who seemed determined not to notice her, went about his normal routine, which involved eating a very large breakfast with an entire barrel of wine from The Fountainhead. The servants had brought in a table that was far too long and placed it in such a way that Marrow could eat from it without leaving his bed. Ophiuchus was freed from her bindings and placed to Marrow's left, with only an entire squad of archers to keep her from making her move. Several plates of chocolate were brought out and the king tucked in without giving anyone else in the room a second notice. Ophiuchus, having never seen chocolate, was wary that he might try to poison her, but finally decided that his ego would never allow anything so easy to overlook. She ate in silence.

Marrow polished off four or five plates before he even looked at her, then, surprisingly, he waved off his guards and turned to face her. He waited until the last one left his chambers, then spoke. "I've decided what I should do with you."

"Oh?" she quipped dryly.

"I think the fate of Cleopatra will be good enough for you."

Ophiuchus had no idea who Cleopatra was supposed to be, and mentioned as much.

"She was the Empress of all Egypt , and the lover of not one but three great kings. When the third lost his taste for her, she was overthrown and dragged through his capital in tattered rags like a circus whore."

"That's a little excessive…"

"Yes, well, the help expects it." He chuckled at his joke. "You should be happy that I would give you so grand a send-off, witch. I'd think you'd expect a peasant's death by my paw."

"I'm more surprised you're not trying to keep me for yourself."

"Oh, no, I got all I wanted out of you."

"It must be hard not wanting anything anymore…" she leered.

"You really have no idea what your sister's been through, have you?"

"Whatever you did to her is fine by me," she glared done at the table, but his odd grammar confused her. Octavia was dead, wasn't she? Why was he talking about her like she was still alive?

"I have trouble believing that." He got up and moved his bed, revealing his trapdoor.

"Giving me a tour of the dungeons, eh? Funny, I had thought even you would have the decency to just kill your prisoners like I do."

"No, this is a very special prison." He extended his paw, gentleman-like, to help her down. "I come here when I need to relax."

"Not having a female will do that to you."

"Who says I don't… you really don't know, do you?"

"Know what?"

"Oh-hohohoho, you know, I always figured you for the clever one in your family. Even your old mother knew, not that she did anything about it, but those last few months of her wretched life she made it very clear."

"What're you talking about?" She descended the ladder. "My mother died two years ago, and I certainly would have known about…"

"Master, is that you?"

Ophiuchus froze on the last rung. That voice!

The mass of rags shuffled toward her, the eyes blank, showing no sign of recognition; the wretch almost instinctively nuzzled at her, as if the sound of voices had made her hot and lustful. Ophiuchus gaped blankly at her. The poor beast finally recognized that she was not her "Master", but still she stroked at Ophiuchus' ears demurely, as if she were pleased that her master had sent her a female rather than himself. The One-Eyed Witch cringed with every touch, all defenses splintering as a glass ball thrown at a concrete barrier shatters into trillions of jagged shards.

"Ah." Marrow's tittering voice crawled from halfway up the ladder. "Still the old hypocrite, Ophiuchus."

"Master!" Octavia pushed her sister aside and pounced at the king, whipping down his trousers and licking at his stomach. She wasted no time getting toward his manhood, which she lapped at hungrily; aside from a grin, he seemed not to notice.

"What've you done to her?" Ophiuchus screamed, horrified.

"What she did to my father after my mother died, except that I have the decency to use an actual cage."

"Master," Octavia wheezed between gulps, "does Master want Whore to nuzzle the female for him? It would please him so…"

"Perhaps later, slave. Right now…"

"You!" Ophiuchus swore, gathering every drop of energy she had and firing a ball of acid at him; he never flinched, not even as Octavia bowled him over and threw a shield between the ball and the two of them! The attack melted her charm all over the floor. Ophiuchus sank, weakened, as her sister applauded herself.

"Master! Whore has saved you, reward her!"

Marrow grinned and pulled a good sized splinter off the wall, which he struck her across the face with five times in succession.

As the leader of the Least-Rogonians looked on in shock, he grabbed Octavia by the snout and whipped her around, throwing her to the floor and taking her so roughly that her jaw pounded into the floor! The wild demon that filled him cracked his mask so thoroughly that Ophiuchus briefly thought he might have transformed into someone else. After he'd satisfied his lust, he straightened his wig and re-affixed his trousers.

"A real charmer, your sister." He spoke in his normal voice. "Perhaps, instead of killing you, I'll let her teach you some tricks."

Ophiuchus was paralyzed with every bad emotion known to rats, quivering without meaning to, but somehow still able to summon a stinging tone. "You."

"Me?" He grinned horrifically as Octavia stood back up, her paw running along his inseam.

"You've taken…" the One-Eyed Witch stammered.

"Only what is rightfully mine," Marrow barked, his facade breaking.

"Ha." Ophiuchus retreated into her mind and presented a defiant visage. "So this what the Vinjians expect from their leader…"

"The Vinjians will expect what I tell them to expect!"

She screamed, righteous anger being her only defense against the fear.

The veins were throbbing on both sides of his forehead. "You think I'm supposed to care about a bunch of backward rodents who hound me night and day to explain the most basic of human concepts to them?" He screamed and slapped Octavia hard enough to knock her out. "I never wanted any of this!"

"You sure don't act like it!" Ophiuchus choked back tears for her sister's well-being. She couldn't explain it, but it was as if all her hatred for his sister had disappeared.

He wheeled on her, grabbing her scruff and forcing her to meet him eye to eye. "You know what my family were before all this? Clerks! Call us nobles, barons, landed gentry, we were CLERKS! Then dear old grandma married Capra VIII and years later I'm set for life as the second son of a mighty king. I was going to leave this rat-trap, I was going to be a hero in the wars. But no! My mother dies and Father remarries. Father dies and this whore becomes Queen! Then my brother gets himself killed in the Battle of Thirty-Seventh and Broad Street and I'M next in line to marry her! Then she plunges our nation into financial ruin and I have to sink every coin of my family's money into keeping this pitiful little speck of land solvent. So, of course, you'll excuse me if I'm not overly concerned about some pitiful little wretch that natural selection would have thrown to the wolves were it not for me! If I'd let her go on the way she did, there would have been violent revolution and every unearned misery I had to endure would have been all for nothing, to say nothing of centuries of history your little traitor contented herself with urinating on!"

Ophiuchus couldn't hold back anymore, she wept. "My sister…"

"You didn't care about her then, did you?"

"I had you!" She fell to her knees as he spun around and retreated into his chambers, locking both of them away. She darted for Octavia's limp body and flung her arms around her. "This is all my fault!"

She kept muttering that it was her fault, not knowing why…

"Oh, Tavy," she cried, "Tavy, what has he done to you?"

"Whore," Octavia whimpered. "Whore must please her Master…"

"Tavy, don't say such things!"

"Whore will show you how to please Master, Master likes his females to please each other."

"How can you say that? Don't you know who I am?"

"You are Whore's new friend. New friend will help Whore please Master!"

In desperation, Ophiuchus tried to gather her magic to put the poor brute out of her misery, but the bizarre tragedy of it was too much. She raised her paw to slap her, but the look of lusty anticipation in Octavia's eyes stopped her dead in her tracks. Instead she crouched down and bawled, while her sister, blind with Marrow's poison, lifted her dress and lapped at the base of her tail.

Least-Rogonians, Chapter Twenty-Three:
The Final Dormouse, Clopin

fter much thought, Astran and Tranah decided they didn't care for Lafitte much; in the three hours they'd been trudging along since breakfast he hadn't said a word to them, but kept humming to himself as if it were a beautiful day for a picnic. They, in turn, hadn't tried talking to him either; or each other, for that matter. It seemed that the more their path corkscrewed and angled lower into the earth, the less they had to talk about, even though Tranah was bursting with questions and Astran was at least worn down enough to answer her. But it was Lafitte's smug expression that really irritated them: it was the look of a pirate chieftain, superior and smarmy.

Syrinx had stuck to the back of the party, just behind the dormice, who were crouched low and deferentially as always. She stared intently at this hideous yellow rat who had taken it upon himself to guide them. Never mind that she knew he would be trouble, but even without knowing his name she would have sensed something off about him. She couldn't put her finger on it, and wouldn't force his paw until the last possible moment, but still…

The boredom had finally become unacceptable for Tranah, who tapped Astran on the shoulder. "Where do you suppose we are, exactly?"

"Just under the westernmost Ocanom village, Seychelles, which would put us about five hours away from the center of the lake, were we walking straight there," Lafitte whistled merrily.

"Ocanom?"

"Well, most of them are on the other side of the lake, but their leaders had enough foresight to start up some trading posts here, like the Capra-Vinjians did a few years back…which was smart, because they look less like savages that way and the imperialists leave them alone, mostly."

Astran squinted at him. "You speak harshly of the… Vinjians…" he bit back calling them "Marrow", not entirely certain why, "and yet you follow after their fashion."

"Well, I'm really more what you'd call an 'abolitionist'."

The dormice immediately straightened, which Syrinx alone was there to make note of. Astran and Tranah, however, had never heard that word before. "Abolitionist?"

"Yes, I go from place to place, making all sorts of ties with rodents, and when I get fed up, I 'abolish' them!" He stopped walking to crack his neck; as soon as the siblings had passed him, he turned around and winked at Barnabas.

"Loner type, huh?" Tranah yawned. "Well, I can see why you'd want to spend so much time down here."

"Oh, I don't know. There's a lot of potential down here for anyone willing to try for it."

"Such as?"

"Well, take me, for instance. I was strolling around on the other side of the lake, minding my own business, when this hare approaches me."

"Hare!"

"Yes, and the oddest thing it was. Seems he was some sort of god, which would explain how he would survive that far underground, but anyway, he said it had been forever and a day since he had any company, and he'd be willing to grant me anything I wanted. Sounds too good to be true, doesn't it? So I ask him, 'What's in it for you?' 'Nothing, but if you wouldn't mind giving me your soul, I might be willing to go so far as, say, filling your boots with gold every morning for the rest of your life.' Now, I have to ask, god or not, who just goes around offering to fill someone's boots with gold? Well, I felt a little sorry for him, since he obviously went so long with no one to talk to that he thought it would take exactly that to get someone's attention. Anyway, it never hurts to have a steady supply of lucre around, so I say, 'Well, I wouldn't mind the gold so much, but I'm a bit loathe to give up my soul.' So, we worked out this deal, where he'd get the soul of the first rat I saw the next morning, thinking I'd go straight home to the wife and lay out my boots. But I got him! I walked around all night until I met this vole, Reuel, I think his name was, and kept him talking until the sun came up. So, Sivad got what he wanted, and I got more than he planned on giving me."

"How so?"

"I cut the soles off of my boots and hid them in a cave down at the very bottom of these tunnels, and ever since the cave has been bursting with gold coins. Which, I suspect, makes me the greatest trader in history, if I do say so."

"Wow," said Tranah.

"Why," Lafitte purred, as he glanced slyly at the dormice again, "I'd go so far as to say two or three rodents could live off what I've got stashed away. But," he rolled his eyes, "that's just me. Always thinking of what other people could do with my gold."

"That's an odd thing to think," Astran said.

"I don't *think* so," he chuckled at himself, "the more you think about what someone else would do with your wealth, the less you do it yourself…"

That brought the conversation to a stinging halt, and no one spoke again for another hour or so. The dormice, however, were acting very strangely, from where Syrinx was standing: they kept shifting their posture from bent and humble to upright and proud, as if trying it out before committing to it. The constant cricking of their backs did not escape Astran's notice either. He fell back and whispered to Syrinx, "Something weird going on here."

"I don't trust him."

"I wasn't talking about him, but now that you mention it…"

"We should have been there by now. If we keep heading downward like this, we'll never make any progress. I'd bet the Marrow-Vinjians are as far the Shrii's territory by now."

"Where's that, exactly?"

"Not sure, but I know it's not this far. Besides, why should we keep going deeper? I'd say we're at least half-a-mile down by now."

"Hmmm, I say we wait 'til we're just under the Strega's keep, or reasonably close, then just blast our way straight up. They won't be expecting that."

"I wouldn't."

"Why not?"

"Remember what he said: 'There's certain routes you go far enough down you're not coming back.' And yet he keeps pulling us down."

"Is that what he normally does?"

"How should I know?"

"You obviously know him, or at least know of him. Don't you remember? You called him by name when he first showed up."

"I might have heard a little, but not anything useful."

"And you've heard?"

"He's someone we should keep our eyes on."

"You're right, that's not very useful…"

The Dormice huddled closely together as they walked, speaking in hurried sign language lest they should be overheard.

"That rat," signed Barnabas, "could he really be what he says?"

"It's possible," replied Trismegistus, "but how could he help us? He's showing our masters through the tunnels!"

"But you heard what he said, enough gold for two or three rodents to start a new life. Why would he say that unless he wanted us to hear it?"

"Have you two no loyalty?" shot Clopin. "Some stranger comes along and suddenly you'd abandon your masters over some loose nonsense?"

"Clopin, I've served rats longer than you have," winced Barnabas, "and I can tell you, what we have is hardly living and certainly no way to die. Don't you want to be free?"

"I don't believe what I'm hearing! All these years we've kept the temple and you never complained, then this mysterious traveler comes out of nowhere, bragging about something that's probably not even true, and now you're talking about freedom!"

"Don't you want anything out of life?"

"I want to know when my next meal is coming. Is that so wrong?"

"What say you, Trismegistus?"

"I'm with you, but Clopin has a point. We can't just trust some stranger without knowing for certain…"

Their frantic hand motions had caught Tranah's attention, and they quickly dropped the subject, but as Barnabas pulled ahead of the others, he whispered, "The gods sent him to us."

In the afternoon, they broke for a late lunch. Astran, feeling hungrier and much more fidgety than he could remember, barged through much more of his rations than he should have, while Tranah merely picked at her food, and Syrinx didn't bother to touch it. The three of them were sitting apart from the others. Astran and Tranah, being forward thinking individuals, couldn't comprehend why a rat of such age and experience should chose the company of inferiors over theirs. Tranah was struck more by the novelty of it, but Astran seemed to pan a much deeper meaning from it; at least, he noticed that whenever Lafitte seemed to say something raucous or wild the elder dormice beamed with admiration, while Clopin looked increasingly uncomfortable. Once, almost accidentally, his eyes and Astran's locked, and the slave's expression became one of pleading. Astran turned back to Syrinx, who had her gaze stuck squarely on the back of Lafitte's head.

"Syrinx?" Astran muttered, drumming his fingers ever louder against his staff.

"Hmm?"

"I'm beginning to suspect our friend might be trouble."

"Probably."

"I suggest we rid ourselves of him, quick-like."

"Hmm, I wonder…"

"Eh?"

Syrinx fished into her robes and pulled out a folded up bit of rawhide. As she unfolded it, Astran deduced its purpose and tore it from her. "All this time…you had a map?"

"If I may…"

"Please, I'm practically drooling." And he was, briefly, toying with the idea of eating the map, but decided against it.

She unfolded it all the way, and cleared her throat authoritatively. "If you will notice, this map only covers the official, respectable rodent's routes. As the way we've come is less than respectable, it's not on here, so it wouldn't have done much good until we got back on the main route."

"Well, all right then…"

"So," Tranah interrupted with her mouth full of food, "how will it help us now? We're still not on the main route."

"Yes, well." The lizard traced her fingers along the ink paths, but the map covered both horizontal and vertical layouts and it was all too easy for her to lose her place; never mind that she wasn't too certain what she was actually looking for. "What was that name he said?"

"What?" Astran coughed.

"The Ocanom village he said we were under a few hours back."

"Oh," Tranah chirped, "it was 'Sea Shells', or something like that…"

"Good, because he said it was only five hours away from the center, and if it's been about that long or so, we'd probably not be too far off if we started heading upward." Syrinx ran her fingers across the hide rapidly, trying to locate Seychelles . "Ah! Here it is. Now, let me just… Wait, that's not right. The path from Seychelles does lead straight into the Strega's keep, but if you follow that back to the surface, it puts you here. Now, this entrance over here is the one closest to where we came in, and if you follow that, you would have to change directions here, here, and here, and that would only put you about here, even if you were heading downward, but since we've gone this way, that means…"

"It means the old bastard is taking us in the opposite direction," Astran growled. He snatched up the map angrily, meaning to crumple it up and hurl it at the dormice, but upon doing so he saw Lafitte, surrounded by Barnabas and Trismegistus, leaning uncomfortably close to the three of them.

"Master," said Trismegistus, "the old rat says we should be going now."

"Does he? And which way shall we be going, sir? Further downward?"

"It would strike one as the best bet," Lafitte grinned.

"Well, Mr. Lafitte." Astran stood, gripping his staff like a rifle. "We've decided we'd rather not be doing that. Thanks anyway, though."

"Oh," said Lafitte, eyes glowing, "I think you'll be going on."

"Surround him!" With Astran's order, Tranah, Syrinx, and Clopin had drawn their weapons and blocked off any escape route. Barnabas and Trismegistus drew their matches but had yet to light them.

"Slaves," Astran tilted his head in annoyance, his flaming pupils boring straight into Barnabas, who was by then too accustomed to obedience to truly disobey and cursed himself with a single tear as he slowly lit his match. Trismegistus silently pleaded with him not to, but when the fire was lit he sank to his knees, confused and overwhelmed, his new found hopes dashed and no clear picture of what to do. Taking advantage of the pause, Lafitte again retrieved his circus whip and snapped it around Tranah's neck!

Three things happened at once: Syrinx abruptly removed his dominant paw with her twin scimitars, and the hand was replaced by a spectral glow, which went unnoticed as Astran shot directly into Lafitte's chest a beam so powerful it set the yellow brute's shoulder blades shooting off in opposite directions. The skin, muscle and tendons were completely burned away, Lafitte went to scream, but instead of sound he issued out a monstrous orb, too large for him to have swallowed it!

This thing, appearing lighter now, rolled toward their feet. It filtered into the air and sifted back into the soil, wheezing out, "You'll not take the Citadel!"

The charred hulk that was Lafitte dropped to the floor, but the rat himself, in phantasm form, remained. "I suppose I should thank you for that. That monkey suit was getting a little heavy."

"What?" Syrinx coughed.

"I wouldn't worry about me, miss. Just an old troublemaker, and I can see my bag of tricks won't do any good now…"

"Tricks?" Trismegistus mouthed to himself.

"Well, I'm off, then." Lafitte excused himself and floated off in the direction he'd been leading them in, until he finally evaporated and was gone.

"What was that?" Tranah stuttered.

"My mother," Syrinx said, sheathing her blades within the confines of her cloak, "would call him a jack-o-the-wisp. They get you good and lost." She grinned to herself, remembering what her friend had written: P.S. Beware of Lafitte…

"Nothing to do but head back, I guess." Astran pulsated, twitching worse than any junkie you're likely to meet. It was while he was wiping the sweat off of his forehead that he almost tripped over Trismegistus, who had lain face down, prostrating himself mercilessly.

"Master," he whimpered over and over. Barnabas and Clopin each shot their superior a hangdog look of solidarity.

"Astran?" Tranah leered.

With a backhanded flick of his staff, Trismegistus was hurled into the opposite wall with such a thud that all involved thought he was dead. Without thinking, Tranah dashed to his side to render aid. The old mouse was alive bad badly hurt, and it would be a long minute before he regained his breath; pitifully gulping in short, violent bursts of insufficient strength, he fought for air. Tranah glared at her brother, but he'd turned his attention away from that slave. He moved toward the other two, who held themselves submissively, Barnabas much more so than his younger friend.

"I'll deal with YOU later," he spat. He waited until Trismegistus was back on his feet, then, still drenched with sweat, he gave an abrupt motion, and led them all back the way they came.

Least-Rogonians, Chapter Twenty-Four: The Phantom Prince, Marrow II

||||||||||||||||||||||||||||||||||||||||||||||||||||||||||||||||||||||||||||||||||||||||||||||||||||||||||||||||||||||||||||

*O*phiuchus' husband had been dead for twenty-two days. By tomorrow, her daughter Tranah would be born, and she was convinced that, in spite of everything that had happened, she'd suffered enough, and deserved to look at her children with two eyes. It had been such a mad dash over the last several days: pouring over her mother's texts, the scrolls the frogs had brought with them, and other, secret sources. She could no longer remember exactly what she'd culled together to create her liquid remedy, but no matter. She sealed it off in a vial and retreated to her private chambers, where the final step, combining it with the entrails of a newt, would create the clay-like panacea.

She stroked her stomach tenderly. By tomorrow, she thought, I'll be looking at you with both eyes, and your father's wrath will pain us no longer. That stopped her. She hadn't reckoned, she now realized, on how Astran would react. Unlike her husband, her son had known all along he was a bastard. Exactly whether or not he knew who his *father was she could not say, but she'd gotten the impression he felt she deserved her deformity.*

No matter.

The corpse of the newt had been brought there for her. She dug her knife into its stomach, splashing the foul-scented organs all over her floor. She would only have to endure it for a second. She readied the vial to dump over the muck when a cough from behind interrupted her. Astran, at the age where he was quickly becoming an adult, was slumped against the doorway with a murderous arrogance in his expression.

"What is it?" she barked, ashamed of how startled he'd made her.

"I'm trying to figure something…"

"What?"

"The Capra Dynasty ended with Capra VII. But his daughter married somebody else named Capra, so how was he Capra VIII? Wouldn't he be the first in a whole other line of Capras?"

"No," she answered warily, not certain she liked where this was going, "that's wrong. Capra VIII was the crown prince, but the female he married was from a house that was also headed by someone named Capra. Their family was in line to take over the throne anyway, should the main Capras be wiped out."

"Vinjian politics are hard to follow. For example, how can Octavia be Queen when their laws clearly state that you need to have an heir to retain the throne?"

Ophiuchus shot bolt upright. "How long have you known?"

"Known what?"

She turned away. "That doesn't concern you!"

"When my aunt's a traitor, and my mother sleeps with her husband, that doesn't concern me? Good Gods, how long were you going to keep it from me?"

"It doesn't matter anymore."

"Mom, I'm the bastard son of the enemy, and the rat who raised me killed himself over it; it matters plenty!"

His mother slumped over her lizard carcass, weeping. "Don't you ever mention that horrible vermin again! He almost killed me, and then you'd be sitting here without a mother or father. How would that suit you?"

"Sure. Don't ever talk about it. If nobody remembers it, it never happened. Just like with your eye. You think you can just grow it back, and everyone will forget the head of the Least-Rogonians raped his wife, and maybe they'll never ask why…"

"Stop it."

"And maybe they won't bother to find out that it's all because their precious Astran is really…"

"STOP IT!"

"Prince Marrow II!"

She froze. In all her days she hoped she would never hear him says those words. "How did you…"

"Oh, everybody knows. My face is famous throughout Octave-Vinjia. They think I'm her son. They think she sent me abroad."

Ophiuchus dropped her vial, missing the blood and absorbing into the dirt. "I don't want to hear this!"

Astran stepped forward, ready to bark a prepared speech at her about how horrible she was to hide her shame like this, and how easy it would be to pick up and leave and be given a princely welcome in their enemy's territory, but Ophiuchus had leaped for her husband's staff, propped against the wall. She wheeled around on him, but he caught it with one paw and, forcing it to remain still with a strength that greatly outstripped his size, his will began to overpower hers, and the staff glowed with a familiar light that Ophiuchus would never have expected from her own flesh and blood: a killing spell!

His strength finally pulled the blazing staff to eye-level, and, with *a war whoop, Astran rammed it square against her head. Between her protective charms and his lack of experience, he couldn't have murdered her that way, but he succeeded in killing the portion of her face where her eye was. Now nothing in the world would bring her sight back; no panacea can bring back the dead.*

Astran fell, and his mother stared at him, frantic and confused. It was unbelievable.

The guards quickly appeared and dragged him to their prison; it was just then that the pain took her, and she had to be dragged back to her bedding to give birth. She tended to baby Tranah for three days before she could stand to think of her son. Leaving Tranah to her wet-nurse, she ventured up to the mound by the shore with raven feathers marking the doorway. Inside there were rows of iron-lined water pits, covered with heavy oak lids; the guards led her to the one farthest from the door. With a decided lack of ceremony, they forced open the lid of Astran's pit and hoisted up the crucifix that shackled him. As he gasped for breath, he glared at her, and something about his expression reminded the One-Eyed Witch so much of his father, Marrow.

She tiptoed, trembling, up to him and placed her paw on his face, wiping away the stagnant water. Overcome, she threw herself on him and sobbed hoarsely. He didn't move, or speak, or even seem to notice her at all.

She brought him home and they never spoke of it again

So, Ophiuchus dreamed, having forced herself to sleep after she could no longer stand to look at this pitiful wretch – the sister she never knew she'd loved so dearly.

The whole way back, Astran fumed and vented his anger by blasting long strings of flame in quick bursts every few seconds to light their way. For their own safety, the others had allowed him to take the lead, although it was quite clear he had no idea where they had gotten to, and none were too keen to bring this up but Syrinx, and she preferred her lizard served raw. Tranah, all but crouching behind her companion, was making careful note of Astran's posture; it was probably just her imagination running away with her, but he just wasn't walking like himself. He looked more like their mother. She could finally see why he drank so much, he'd just replaced one addiction with the other.

"Syrinx?" She swallowed.

"Eh?"

"Still have that wine on you?"

"No. Wait." She fished around in the folds of her cloaking. "Yes, yes I do." She retrieved a paw-sized metallic flask. "Not much, though. Why?"

"I think my brother could use a drink…" She snatched it up and dashed ahead to tap her brother on the shoulder. He stopped belching flames all over the tunnel but otherwise remained perfectly still.

"Yes?"

"Something bothering you?"

"We're lost."

"Yeah, we were just talking about that, actually." She jiggled the wine just behind her brother's ear. "We should probably stop and get our bearings."

"It'll be dark soon."

"It is dark, we're underground." She smirked mischievously.

He crouched down dejectedly and took the flask from her. She half-expected him to quaff it back in one stroke, but instead he sipped pensively, almost afraid to drink it. Tranah filed that observation in the back of her mind, and while she was there she put one or two other thoughts together; she was deciding that maybe she didn't like her brother using magic so much.

"Well," Astran mused, "this is a fine mess."

"It's a regular Alexander's knot," Syrinx agreed, having spent so much time trying not to get cooked by the ill-tempered rat that even she was lost.

"A what?" Tranah stared.

"Well, the humans had a king named Alexander, a while back. He was out conquering the world when he reached a forgotten empire that had been without a ruler for hundreds of years. Their king back then had created a mighty knot, about seven feet long…"

"Seven feet?!?"

"Yes. When he died, he left an edict that the rightful heir to his throne would be the first person to untie the knot. No one ever could until Alexander came along."

"Poor little things." Tranah held her chin. "Imagine, all that time without a king over something stupid like that. How did they ever get anything done?"

The females shared each other's misery, but Astran, his ears pricked up and taking a much larger sip than before, cleared his throat. "How'd he untie it?"

"What?"

"Alexander. How did he untie the knot?"

"Oh, um, he cut it open. With his sword." Astran's eyes lit up, but it went unnoticed. Syrinx continued, "Still, seven hundred years and the answer was right in front of them…"

Astran stood bolt upright. "Tranah, do you figure it's dark outside yet?"

"It would have to be, we've been down here all day."

Astran's fingers acted out computations in his head, his

tongue clicked up and down, he tightened his grip on both his staff and his drink, which he finished in a single gulp. "Everyone get together in a circle. NOW!"

The dormice, eager to get back into their master's good graces, snapped to position, but Syrinx and Tranah stood numb.

"Astran," his sister whispered, "what is it we're doing exactly?"

With a boyish twinkle in his eyes, Astran tapped his staff against the ground and the two were pulled like iron to a magnet into the circle. "Cutting the knot," he laughed.

"Are we going to regret this?" Syrinx snarled.

"Probably. Everybody bundle close together, I don't want to take up more space than is necessary."

Barnabas and Trismegistus grabbed at Syrinx's robes; she grabbed Tranah's paw, while Clopin climbed up on Tranah's back. She, in turn, clutched Astran. He smiled maniacally as a viscous red foam formed around them, leaving just enough air, but sealing them off completely. Clopin, deduced Astran's plan before the others.

"Master, the Strega, this area is their domain!"

"The Citadel," Astran ignored him, "it keeps the water out, right?"

"Yes, but…"

"Good!" He clenched his fingers and the barrier closed around them completely; he focused hard on dividing his mind, the way he did with the bird, making it exist and fly at the same time. The ground shook around them on all sides, below and above. A series of yellow beams glittered out of the dirt immediately beneath them, and with tremendous force the party was blasted upward through a thick layer of earth, and then another and another. The lights contorted underneath their feet and became like a golden tree in rapid bloom.

They broke through the final crust of the underground and instead flowed unimpeded through the murky depths of the lake. The water got brighter, and with all the grace of a leaping whale the tree exploded out of the water and bloomed with a trillion leaves and branches, with their pod balanced on top.

Astran relaxed the section of his brain that had sealed them off; the five gasped desperately for oxygen and quickly dispersed on to the less crowded branches.

"DON'T YOU EVER DO THAT AGAIN!" Syrinx screamed, which gave Astran no end of delight.

"Worked, didn't it?"

"Oh really? And exactly what did all that accomplish?"

"Well, now that we're up here, we can judge our relative position to the center of the lake, and adjust our route accordingly."

"We got lost, and your first thought is to thrust a giant battering ram up through the tunnels and play lookout?"

"I like to call it lateral thinking."

"Uh-huh. And while you were thinking laterally, did you stop to consider what we'd do now that we've just thrown a giant-sized gauntlet into the faces of the rats who're trying to kill us? I hardly think they'll just roll out the welcome mat for the male who just issued a huge 'Fuck You' to their symbol of power. No wonder your mother doesn't trust you…"

"If you're *quite* finished, would you mind getting off your ass and assisting me with the whole 'figuring out where we are' part? Because if you could, that would be great!"

Tranah, who'd moved to the edge of the branch she had chosen, called out, "We're on the other side of the lake from where we started, I think."

Astran's face turned serious. "That would put us in Marrow-Vinjian territory."

"Yet another reason this tree was a fabulous idea," Syrinx screamed.

Astran willed his branch to bend over by Tranah's, scanning left and right, his brow creasing. "Something's going on. Ordinarily, they have two outposts watching over the lake; there, and there. Now, with the alarm Mom raised the night before last, there should be even more. They're not there, now."

Tranah was impressed, but something about that didn't seem right. "How do you know that?" she whispered. He didn't answer her. His focus was drawn to a disturbance from distant Vinjia, just now becoming visible in the early evening moonlight. In his mind's eye he crossed the water and retraced his steps from the night before to the wall of the city, and from that night further back into the past, to when Tranah was a little one, through the entrance and down the streets to the stately replica of 10 Downing Street. It was right as his instinct pinned down the royal palace that a ghostly shape, pure white and stark against the evening black, came winging toward them, wailing like a banshee. Astran glared at it until it stopped an inch away from them, the familiar face calling out to both of them.

"Mom!"

The tree shattered and the two rats were sailing across the wind; their companions fell into the lake, making such a large splash that the wave reached all the way up to Astran's feet! Astran winged his sister at breakneck pace across the great expanse toward Marrow-Vinjia. Within seconds they'd crashed into the water and landed on all fours in nearly the exact same spot they'd stopped that night. Without a word, Astran robed himself with flames; Tranah stared with a twinge of fear as her brother, almost unrecognizable, emerged in full Vinjian drag, decked in finery befitting a duke or cabinet minister. His sister coughed, and before she could even lift her paw and excuse herself, a wave rushed across her body and left her in garb similar to the infamous Lafitte.

"I'll explain on the way," he said. It didn't matter now if Tranah learned the family secret, their mother was in danger. Taking her by the forearm he dragged her toward the almost completely rebuilt wooden barrier. Other rats, dressed in their Sunday best, shot them confused glances as Astran pulled up to a hidden gate and rapped sharply.

"Free!" a voice called from behind the wall.

"Rat!" Astran replied.

"Native!"

"Born!"

A series of clanks and murmurs spat out and the secret door opened.

"You'll forgive us, my Lordship, but we hadn't any record of anyone important going outside the fence tonight," a stuffy rat in an undertaker's suit approached them. When he got a good look at Astran, he fumbled into a bow and quickly led them inside, keeping his head bowed deferentially, very similar to the dormice.

"Did His Majesty receive word of my arrival, yet?" Astran sighed, acting as bored as possible.

"No, My Liege, your return is quite unexpected."

"Good." His voice became haughty. "Our king would have made such a spectacle, and I haven't the mood for it tonight. Call for a transport and bring us to him straightaway."

"Forgive me, sir, but all our vehicles are presently in the city."

"Really? Whatever for?"

"One of our lesser opponents is making war with us. Nothing

a night or two of hard work shouldn't eliminate, but I'm afraid it's still an inconvenience. I say, what have you got with you, there?"

"A Shrii concubine. A gift for His Majesty."

"Ah, yes, well, will you been needing an escort, My Liege?"

"No. I would rather go unnoticed for now. I'm certain I can find the palace by myself."

"Very good." The undertaker puttered off.

Unsure of where to begin, Tranah blurted out, "Who was that?"

"His name's Danglars. He works for the king in some way or another."

"How do you…wait. Stop. What are we doing?"

"We're in disguise," he hissed, imploring her to keep her voice down. "They think I'm someone important, so as long as we play it cool we should slip in and out of here unnoticed."

"Ha. And you think I'M irresponsible."

"Calm down, I know what I'm doing."

"And that's another thing. How do you know what you're doing?"

"These rats have very contradictory customs, but once you've figured out which is used for who, they're not that hard to learn."

"And where did you learn these, exactly?"

"Remember when you were little, and I used to run away all the time?"

"…Oh, you didn't!"

"Shut up."

"Right. And when was I going to find all this out?"

"Trust me, little sister, you ain't seen nothing yet…"

"What?"

"Just be quiet and act like a concubine. Concubines don't lose their tempers like this."

"I don't even know what a concubine is. I couldn't understand half the words that vermin was using. What the hell's a ' Liege ', anyway?"

"You'll see…"

At last, he led her past Bloodford's estate, resisting the urge to point it out to her, and up the stairs leading into the palace, where the guards wasted no time in rushing him inside. Without a word spoken to either of them, all manner of important looking rodents had descended upon them, correcting their outfits as they walked and leading them toward the king's private chambers. An elderly rat to the front was silently prompted to run ahead of them, and as he circled around the bend of the hallway, Tranah suddenly became desperately aware of how close she was to King Marrow! The rat she'd wanted so badly to just rush in and decapitate now seemed like a murderous hydra ready to pounce at them, and though she had not yet set her eyes on him, she began to regret that she'd ever wished him wrong, lest he should smell it on her. She gripped Astran's paw for comfort. He said nothing, but squeezed back.

They passed the portrait of their mother and were left alone, finally, at the doorway to Marrow's chambers.

"You're sure this will help Mom?" Tranah squeaked.

"Just cover your ears and let me do the talking." He knocked. The door seemed to open itself.

"You know," an unfamiliar voice muttered, "for all the fanfare, I'd have thought Bloodford had made his way back already; but I see it is only you."

"Hello, Father." Astran bowed respectfully, while clenching his fists closed.

Tranah, at first, didn't react. It was as if her mind wanted to break out of her body and scream, "It isn't possible!" But after she'd caught herself, she realized this was all some plan on Astran's part. He was clearly impersonating this Prince of Vinjia; that was it. His magic must have disguised his appearance to everyone else but her; that was it, it had to be. A weak smile caught the corner of her mouth; to think Astran would do something this ballsy to save their Mom...

"Your return is ill-timed, I'm afraid. Far too much on my plate..." Marrow droned on, not looking like he cared what he said.

"Well, I won't hold you up, except that you've got something that belongs to me, and I'd like it back. Sentimental reasons, you understand..."

"Of course. I didn't think you'd come all this way for a social visit, not the way your mother raised you."

Huh, Tranah thought, guess old Queen What's-her-face must not have been the saint everyone made her out to be.

"Then again, there is the question of why I should return this thing of yours, boy. After all, what did you ever do for me?"

"You know exactly what I did for you, sir. Same thing my mother did, and everyone else who knows what I know. I dare to think even your precious Lord Bloodford *knows*."

"Humph, you really think I would tell him?"

"Frankly, yes."

"Shows what you know."

"Still, I am rather busy, so if I could just collect..."

"You still haven't told me why, boy!"

"You know exactly why." He tilted his staff toward the slouching king. Tranah was confused. Did the Marrow-Vinjians know magic?

"You would really do something as crazy as that, over something you don't even value?"

"No, but I might just on general principle."

"Hmmm, very well, but we both know how it will turn out in the end, for both of you."

"You sound awfully sure of that."

"It is the destiny of everyone involved. It has always been that way, boy; no matter how much you try to drink it away, sooner or later you'll have to take your spot. Take this as a sign of good faith…" He opened his secret door and disappeared underneath the floor, returning moments later with their mother! She bore all the scents of being raped and urinated on. With a sharp turn of his head, Astran found himself staring down the impassive face of his father, who merely belched. "You'll be back."

Throwing his princely robes off to the side, Astran whipped a ball around them and shrank the three of them into a mote of gray light. He rushed them out through the halls and up through the night sky over the inner city, upending carts and merchants, and back to where they'd landed outside the gates. Once back in normal form, Tranah, not knowing what to think, held her mother close and turned her head to her brother, who only held up his paw to silence her. "Trust me, you're better off not knowing."

Astran helped his sister lay their mother on the ground, where he summoned his energies and healed her as completely as he could. When Ophiuchus reawakened, she didn't respond to Tranah's tender affections or Astran's protective stare. She stood up slowly, still feeling weak, and looked back at Vinjia, her face awash with anger.

"Tranah," Astran whispered, "I think Mom could use a minute alone."

He led his sister a few feet off. She couldn't take it any longer. "Astran, what is going on? And don't tell me I don't need to know! I've been not knowing this entire time and I don't know how much more of it I can take!"

"After this," said Astran, "we need to go and find Syrinx and the others. We're going home. We failed."

"But…"

"With the Strega on the warpath like this, Marrow won't get any closer than we did. It might be years before anyone can make a play for the Citadel again. It's over."

"But…"

"GAAAAAAAAAAAAAAAAAAAAAAAAHHHHHHHHHHH!"

They wheeled about, and the first thing that met their gaze was a pyre as high as a human building, with their mother limping forward, arms raised straight upward. In her rage, she was razing Marrow-Vinjia to the ground!

Day Four

Marrow-Vinjians, Chapter Twenty-Five: In The Kangaroo Court Of The Maharajah

||||||||||||||||||||||||||||||||||||||||||||||||||||||||||||||||||||||||||||||||||||||||||||||||||||||||||||||

It came as a tremendous surprise when we found ourselves on a lily pad hundreds of feet above where we just were, but it was more the sudden change in temperature that affected us. It was shortly after midnight, and when one is used to having a wooden barrier around their home, or at least a sensible distance between it and the water, the chill of early morning on the lake is almost unbearable.

The opening is still behind us, but I don't expect to go back through it anytime just soon, particularly if Metatron decided not to kill Sivad after all. Astairelike looks all around, having better night-eyes than either of us at the moment; we're nowhere near the center of the lake, but we're still much too distant to be reached by any rodent.

I keep my eyes glued onto the portal, knowing full-well

that the ferret will be poking his unwelcome head through it any second now, and I will not be taken by surprise anymore. Sure enough, no sooner do I finish that last sentence than his familiar dead eyes poke through. I take pleasure in catching him off guard, but he recovers quickly, and somehow manages not to sink the lily-pad that is already miraculously supporting the weight of three others.

"You know," I drop all semblance of chivalry. "I'm beginning to suspect that you're not the humanitarian you claim to be."

"Is that sarcasm, Bloodford, or are you really that big of an ingrate?"

"Look," Spoolnicker bellows, "we're starting to get a little tired of your whole 'mysterious benefactor' business…"

"I've already told you," Metatron interrupts him, "for now we have concurrent interests…"

"And what happens when we don't any longer?" Astairelike jumps on him.

"I wouldn't be vitriolic if I were you three, especially since I've gone out of my way to save your lives. More than once, I might add."

"Yes," I glare, "and at least twice it was from trouble that you caused in the first place!"

"You never would have gotten out of that cave if you tried to sneak past Sivad unannounced," he counters, "and his trying to kill you minutes after I warned him not to is the result of his own stupidity."

"Yes, but why would he listen to you in the first place?" Spoolnicker yells. "Who are you?"

"Somebody who knows, and somebody who knows is very dangerous…" is all he'll say.

"Look," he cuts Astairelike off before he can say anything,

"it's been forty-eight hours since the Strega used the power of the Citadel to destroy your homeland and kill dozens if not hundreds unnecessarily, both in Marrow-Vinjia and Berlinger Station. In those past forty-eight hours, you've been attacked almost constantly by a tribe of otherwise useless vermin who just happen to hold the most powerful weapon in all of Creation, and if you don't stop them this weapon will end up in the hands of your tribe's sworn enemies… that is, if they don't exterminate the lot of you first. Why the hell are you so concerned about me?"

He does have a point.

"Now," he resumes, having calmed considerably, "right now you're in the frogs' territory. I don't know much about them except word on the street is that this particular tribe is in talks with King Marrow; some sort of alliance. They might be able to offer you some sort of haven for now…"

"Haven? Where? We're in the middle of the lake!" Astairelike spurts.

"It's better than nothing, especially with Sivad…"

"Didn't you kill him?" I ask.

"No, he managed to escape when I was distracted by the portal, but I did manage to grab him…" he looks down at his paw, where we notice for the first time that he's dragging the corpse of Reuel.

"Now why would you bring him along?" Astairelike sounds more worn-down than angry.

"Well, I can't say for certain, but if you'll remember what he said earlier, the frogs have been in Sivad's inner sanctum. Most likely to gather weapons. With any luck, the tribe of frogs that happens to happen upon you will be one of if not the only sect that has been in that cave. There's a chance they'll remember him."

"Wait a minute." Spoolnicker holds up his paw. "That uniform's more than a hundred and fifty years old. Anybody who knew him would be dead by now…"

"Just because the uniform's that old doesn't mean he is," the ferret counters. "Besides, if he didn't know this particular group, the ones who have had contact undoubtedly told others about him; I certainly wouldn't keep such an odd experience to myself. It's beyond slim, but I think there's a chance that one of them might recognize his body. That could be worth something."

"Unless they think we killed him," the white mouse whines. "I say we chuck that lifeless thing into the bog, go back whence we came, and get on with it."

"Sivad might come back," the ferret warns, handing me the flaming sword back.

"And there's just as good a chance he won't," I curse. "Any other detours will cost us too much time, and we were just starting to make progress the other way." I can see the failure of my argument before I even make it, but I don't care just now.

"Fine." The ferret shrugs noncommittally. "You do as you please, but I think *they'll* be wanting a word with you first." He points out into the early morning mist, where a boat is floating toward us. The familiar overwhelming odor of frogs reaches my nostrils, and while I would never say I was happy to see them, it is nice to be faced with something familiar. There's a splash; upon a closer look there're three of them on the boat; one of them's jumped off, undoubtedly to scout ahead. I'm relieved when I see his head pop out of the water, since I have no doubt that although it's currently supporting the weight of me, Astairelike, Spoolnicker, and the corpse of Reuel, this lily pad would sink into the freezing depths if the slimy amphibian were to join us.

He looks us up and down, surveying us and sizing us up.

"Vinjians," he says aloud to no one in particular, then turns to signal his companions. He gives us another once over, and notices the dead vole. Curious, he swims around, then lets out a gulp. "Reuel!"

I swear to Christ, if that ferret saves our skins one more time I'm going to kill him.

In short order the boat's run alongside us and the leader of the three has introduced himself as Main Scout. He doesn't look at all fazed by our portal, but he does seem to recognize Reuel and is especially curious as to how four Vinjians have suddenly fallen into his lap. I don't tell him much, it's really none of his business, but he quietly listens, nods a bit, then directs the conversation back to Reuel. "How did he die?"

"Rabbit killed him," Astairelike says, probably trying to set up his stupid "asking too many questions" line again.

Main Scout doesn't fall for it. "You." He looks back at me. "You're Bloodford, aren't you?"

"That's what they tell me."

He chuckles. "The Maharajah will want to be seeing you, then."

The whole way back to his master's home, Main Scout never says a word to us, nor do his companions. Astairelike and Spoolnicker, I notice, are having some difficulty dealing with the smell of them. I myself am only doing marginally better, but the way they stare at me one would get the idea that I was an old hand at dealing with these creatures, and how dare I not tell them before?

I use the twenty minutes of our voyage to ponder our ferret friend more thoroughly. When we first met him, he asked us if we were going to see Chumsa, then vanished. Given what he's gone on to do, that was undoubtedly for identification purposes, making sure we were the right rodents. Later, following the destruction of Marrow-Vinjia, he shows up at Berlinger Station, picks us out of the crowd. Why he was there, I don't know. He sees the squirrels before we do, warns about them, then scampers. We go into the tunnel; he reappears and warns about the attack. He helps us fight them off and disappears again. We go into the tunnel, get attacked by the Strega once more, and hours later he conveniently shows up again, and lures us into Sivad's pyramid. Weapons, he says. True, in the end the sword I gained there mortally wounded an immortal god (and, by extension, would cause great damage to someone who draws power from a mystical artifact but is otherwise a normal rat) but by bringing us down there, he somehow caused Reuel to be possessed by the same Strega energy that came out of the squirrel we killed. Reuel tries to kill us, Sivad saves the day, and then turns on us, when wonder of wonders, the ferret is there again, fending him off with nothing but a cryptic warning. It works well for about a minute, until the god changes his mind and throws us to his pet devils, and again the ferret just happens to be there, saving us and bringing us to the surface, "unintentionally". And he just happened to know that the frogs would recognize Reuel's body.

I'm beginning to suspect a pattern here.

A quick re-establishing of my feet on the ground, and I'm better prepared to assess this strange detour of ours. From the air around these things, I can tell that they are both unhappy and desperate about finding us. I doubt very much that we were being looked for, but after retrieving us they don't seem at all anxious to get back to what they were doing. They're taking us toward one of the little nothing islands that periodically dot our half of the lake. They're basically clumps of dirt and grass where hardly anyone could put up any kind of permanent settlement. I don't even think you can see it from the other side of the lake.

The water's turning marshier by the row, and the stench of wet frogs grows thicker and thicker. I don't know how I'm going to manage being diplomatic if the smell gets any worse; I feel on the verge of an aneurysm as it is. I listen for the characteristic ribbitting, but hear none. We run ashore, and without further word, the other two frogs shove off and circle around the island, heading back the way we came. Main Scout remains with us, but he looks more interested in Reuel's body than the living rodents in his charge. Perhaps they mean to bury the poor fool here.

He sticks his webbed hand into a pouch I haven't noticed before, which is just out of sight in the grass. He retrieves a handful of what looks like golden glitter, which he scatters carefully around the vole's body like an outline. The powder burns into the ground almost immediately; whiffs of smoke surround him. Main Scout swirls his hands around in it, making patterns in the steam, but Lord knows what he'll get out of them.

All around the island one frog after another pokes his eyes just above the water, looking from the smoke to me and then to each other. I don't sense a threat, indeed, I feel for the first time in days that I'm in familiar territory; should things turn worse three Marrow-Vinjians can certainly handle these creatures. I hear a loud paddling behind us! It's the Maharajah I met in His Majesty's chambers, just before… He looks more troubled than my fleeting impression of him would have led me to believe possible.

"Bloodford? Oh, merciful Tade! Everything's gone horribly pear-shaped. Tell me, when is the rest of the army arriving?"

"I'm sorry?"

"I know you're only scouts, but surely there are others around? I know your reputation, but even you can't be all the help King Marrow has sent!"

"What are you talking about?"

"Don't you know?"

I've had enough. "Sir, we've spent the last two days underground on a mission for His Majesty, so any machinations of yours are beyond us."

"Underground? UNDERGROUND? You mean…you don't…how can you possibly not know what's been happening? Your king has retreated into the city, my goals for empire are being challenged, and the Least-Rogonians are moving to capture the Citadel! HOW CAN YOU NOT KNOW?"

He moves to strike me, but Spoolnicker steps in, grabs his wrist and forces him to the ground with a thud. Spoolnicker half-nelsons his arm behind his back; I put my sword to his throat just in time to ward off the other frogs who've sprung from the water to aid their leader.

"Now," I say as calmly as I can, "let's not do anything foolish. You clearly need our help; now, if you can just explain to us why…"

"Why! The goddamn Strega is why!" he sobs quietly to himself. "When they attacked your kingdom the second time…"

"Second time?" Astairelike spurts.

"It was earlier this evening. They burned down the portions of the wall you'd rebuilt and leveled Marrow's palace. He retreated with his guard into their stronghold in the city. Oh, that I should see the day that our strongest ally retreats from the park."

Outraged and confused as I am, I press him to stay on subject. "Ally?"

"We had an alliance with your people. It was signed just before the initial attack. Marrow promised to provide us with military aid in our quest to unite all the tribes."

"How can a rat army aid a frog army?" Spoolnicker hisses.

"It was merely a symbolic one. Even among the amphibians, Vinjia is known and revered. With the threat of his army in my back pocket, the unification was all but signed. But some hours ago the stronghold was attacked, worse than the last time. They moved the entire tribe away, and now the other frogs think that Marrow has been vanquished, and those who would stand to gain by keeping the tribes separate are challenging my claims of military strength. Without the Marrow-Vinjian army I shall be ousted from my position in the hierarchy of the lake, and most likely overthrown within my own tribe!"

Spoolnicker releases him and he retreats into a fetal position, or as much of one as an egg-born can manage.

"I'm sorry." I stand as straight I can. "But we have our own mission to accomplish, and if what you say about the Least-Rogonians is true, then it makes it doubly important that we do so."

"Don't you care about your tribe's honor?" one of the other frogs curses.

"He doesn't know," the frog next to him hisses.

"Know what?"

"There've been reports," the Maharajah sniffs, "witnesses, squirrels, frogs, birds. When Marrow's palace was destroyed, there was a female spotted amid the wreckage. She ran off, but a lot of rats saw her. They say it was Queen Octavia!"

A dagger rams me in the chest. "Nonsense!"

"There are many witnesses."

"I know nothing about that!"

"Octavia would never have sided with us. Don't you see? We need Marrow just as much as you do."

"Are you trying to blackmail us?"

"No!"

"Bedford." Astairelike grabs at my sleeve. He's got that look he has whenever he knows I'm not telling him something, but he's motioning for me to leave.

I try to get away, but the frogs circle tighter around us. "What is it you want, sir?"

The Maharajah straightens up and re-assumes his air. "I've made contact with Marrow, through our mutual connections that have branches in the city. He's reluctant to offer us aid, but he tells us that if we'll find that female and get rid of her, he'll send all the aid he has at his disposal…"

Disturbed as I am at all this, I can't help but smile at how ignorant he's being. With our hold in the park momentarily weakened now that our ancestral seat of power is temporarily absent, My Liege will need almost his entire army just to prevent the Farj or Farris-Ianists from making a power play or some as-yet unknown relatives of the Strega leaping in to avenge the Wahid. Really, the only portion of his forces he could spare would be the three of us, and we're unavailable. "You do know what that entails, don't you?"

His expression is grim. "No, Bloodford, I think it is you who doesn't know. You see, we know what your mission is, and where you stand as far as progress is concerned, and the progress of your enemies. Main Scout!"

"Yes, Sahib."

"What agent do we have among them?"

"Silvereye, Sahib."

"Ah, our very best spy. You see, there is nothing that happens in this park that we frogs are not aware of. Not even the squirrels, or even you, can claim as much. We've known for centuries what your people have yet to discover; we know, for example, that to get as far as you should have gotten by now, you'll need to travel through an entrance to the underground that no one knows about but me, and I happen to know that that female who happens to look so very much like your long dead Queen just happens to be heading in that direction. So: we assist you on your mission, you beat the Least-Rogonians to the Citadel, King Marrow remembers us, and this mysterious look-alike suddenly vanishes from the face of the earth. Everybody wins."

Save for the shaman tending the corpse and the Regent in front of us, the slimy beasts have assumed fighting positions. "Rather unsporting," I quip dryly.

"You're accusing me of cheating?" He's grinning so widely. Fortunately, this has an oddly calming affect on the others. "A Marrow-Vinjian calling me a cheater, that's funny," he manages at last.

"I'm glad to see you've gotten your temper back," I whisper snidely. "You weren't doing so well at first."

"I see now why Marrow keeps you around," he purrs disdainfully.

"Of course," I add, nonchalantly, "a servant can't have two masters…"

"Hmm?"

I draw the sword and display it vertically. "Your people went down into the Land of the Blind for these weapons. I notice you don't have any with you."

He doesn't answer.

"Your guard seems awfully small for a frog of your stature."

He still doesn't answer.

"Maybe…" I don't finish that sentence, but more than one of his followers back down.

"Where is this entrance exactly?"

His eyes dart suspiciously, but before I can press him farther Main Scout calls out, "Sahib! Sahib!"

Glad for the excuse, the Maharajah brushes past me to the dead vole.

"Yes?"

"He was possessed by the Citadel, Sahib."

"Shit," Spoolnicker grunts, "I could have told you that."

"This is…" The Maharajah doesn't know how to finish that sentence. "Is there any chance…" He turns back to Main Scout.

"Already he speaks," the shaman purrs, as the vapors swirl over his head and take the form of Reuel while he was still alive, tattered uniform and all. I barely blink at this.

"What's all this, then?" Astairelike approaches, suspiciously cordial all of a sudden.

"He will describe to us his possession," Main Scout intones flatly.

"Why should we be concerned with that?"

He draws a long breath and exhales slowly, debating whether he wants to dignify me with an answer.

Ugh, no matter where we go on this mad campaign there's nothing but delays. Spoolnicker's right; a nice, straightforward raid on the squirrel settlements is just the thing right about now. I mean, honestly… Why are my hands shaking?

The shaman swallows most of the smoke with one gulp from his enormous mouth, slowly allowing columns of it to escape as he speaks more slowly than anyone I've ever met.

"A doubt had he in all his master's doings, and dreams had he of actions unperformed, the master became a monster in his eye…"

Huh. That's interesting.

"And in his plagued states the rodent would ask himself where his loyalty should stand…"

I suddenly feel very uncomfortable.

"And the voice that came in reply seemed that of his own, but it was the voice of the fire which had come from beyond him, so much a part of him it seemed he never felt the strings fitting around his arms, or the burning hands that guided him after…"

I fidget with my collar, unable to deduce why I'm suddenly feeling a pinch of sympathy for the poor Reuel. Could what he have been going through been anything like the anguish I've had over the last few days? I mean, ever since that night, Octavia… These frogs know all about it; or do they? They could be wrong, bluffing…but so much has happened that makes no sense to me… No, it couldn't possibly be, but I wonder…

"Are there any other agents of the Strega?" the Maharajah asks him, wiping away his sweat perfunctorily, as if it disturbed his hearing.

The shaman stirs up more smoke, and takes another swallow, but before he can reveal whatever secrets he's learned impulse gets the better of me and I cut him off before he can speak. "We'll do it!"

"What?"

"You say you can help us make up the time. We have no choice."

The Maharajah looks struck dumb that I've capitulated without trying to bargain, but none the less delighted. He snaps his fingers and his minions retreat into the water immediately, he himself only lingering long enough to give a self-satisfied grin. Main Scout, being forced to actually swallow all of the smoke now that there was no one to listen, shoots me the evil eye. Is it because of the inconvenience? Or did he see…why couldn't I stand to hear what his vision had brought? Why?

The shaman unceremoniously rolls Reuel over and into the lake, watching him float away as he prepares the boat once more.

Spoolnicker walks over, but plops down on his back on the crude wood the craft is made of. I take a wasted second to make myself as presentable as I can; Astairelike grabs me by the elbow.

"Something you're not telling us, Bedford?"

I ignore him. I don't want to think about it, the idea that I might be going mad, or…

The Elder Hares, Chapter Twenty-Six: Metatron

The ferret had calmed down considerably; Sivad had been acting irrationally, but by opening the portal and sending Bloodford and company to the surface of the lake he had inadvertently put everything back on schedule. Hell, he may even have sped up the process! After summoning Main Scout and foisting his rodent pawns into the hands of the Maharajah's right-hand amphibian, he returned to the Land of the Blind, staring down the wounded hare with a look of utter contempt.

"You know," he said as he waved his paw and created a lit cigarette from nothingness, "I suppose I should thank you for that. Saved me a heap of trouble. It's hard figuring out just what you need someone to say to get someone else to do what you want, but actions speak so much louder than words."

"Fuck you," the dying deity spat.

"Hardly. You know, Sivad, the problem with you is that you've forgotten where you came from. I remember our once-proud god of the harvest before he started drinking himself under the table and had to be thrown out among the mortals. Were I still the same being I was that day I'd have considered it an extremely poor joke to think that not only would you be the last one standing, but feared in ways we never imagined…"

Sivad coughed up several chunks of blood, but said nothing.

"Oh, don't play that old silent treatment game with me. You and Hurucan used to go at it like that from dawn to dusk, and I'm as damn sick of it now as I was then."

"I…don't understand."

"Sivad, I always knew you were stupid, but don't tell me you never figured it out! I remember the day we sent you away you had enough brains left in your head to shout at me, 'You'll be next, you stupid shit!' And, in a way, you were right…"

"I…Gukumatz?"

"Yes."

"But, no, you can't be Gukumatz. He was a…gods can't become angels when they die! And angels of death were never alive to begin with!" Sivad feigned terror, while silently calling out to his unholy minions.

"Oh, you can believe it's me, Sivad. I was born a god, same as you, and cheated death when that inferior vermin the do-gooder turned on us. For all his bluster, Hurucan was actually one of the least powerful of all of us. You called him out on it once, remember? You called him a 'pitiful excuse for a…'"

"'Worthless piece of crap that can't do shit,' yes, I remember, but, it just can't…"

Metatron, having shape-shifted back into the hare known as Gukumatz, flicked his cigarette into Sivad's wound. "I practically created the Citadel all by myself, but he got all the credit because it was his idea! It was only a matter of time before I discovered the secret of true immortality!"

"But…"

"Oh, don't get me wrong, it had its downside. When I watched as all my friends marched into the oblivion of the afterlife I felt a pang of guilt; and when the beastly ferrets, mindless puppets, all of them, bound my wrists and robbed me of my freewill, I felt betrayed; and as the decades passed and I was forced to usher more and more souls into darkness, a voiceless manservant of the unseen equalizer, Death, I nearly went mad. But then I discovered something else! When you snatch the soul of a hero, it fills you with a sort of high, a state of ecstasy so brilliant it blocks out everything else but the feel of raw power coursing through your body. So I began to specialize in heroes. At first it was just to feed my addiction, it just took control of me! But I found that while it had the more immediate, tactile benefits, the power that filled me stuck, so that it not only felt like I was stronger, I was actually gaining power. Soon I was able to influence the outcomes of conflicts just to create and kill more heroes, and I tell you, just about every great battle between rats, mice, squirrels and anyone else in the last century has all been because of me. It takes such minimal prompting, and if free will starts to get in the way I just give another light nudge and it all works out the way I want it. Take now, for instance; I took control of Reuel's mind and attacked Bloodford, and now he'll believe anything I tell him because I rescued him. Of course, I was only expecting to save him from those hordes Reuel summoned, but your ad-libbing added a real zest. I swear; I'm so close to achieving my goal and you go and speed things up even more. I could almost appreciate it."

"What do you want with him?" he coughed, discreetly steering his hordes in a semi-circle around the treacherous wretch.

"You surprise me, Sivad. I would have expected you to burst out with accusations or insults for me. Very well, since you insist on talking shop: I am the only living angel of death. 'Valkyrie' would be a better term, actually, by this point. I've been getting back my freedom, piece by piece. I'm almost entirely corporeal as it is, which is why the others can see me. But it'll take a whacking amount of power to finish the job…such as what could be gained from taking two heroes at once; like, say, Bloodford and Astran of the Least-Rogonians. It's amazing just how simple their minds are, how quickly they'll turn on themselves if their secrets become known by others. Like Bloodford's habit of talking to himself, or how Astran doesn't really hate his mother as much as he thinks he does. So you tell one that he's crazy and send the other a message that he thinks is from his captured mammy, and they end up right where you need them.

"Even the Strega were willing to kick in with their little mud-spider, and everything else they've done. How does that saying go? 'It's the fear of death that makes monsters of us all'?

"With everything I've done, they're bound to kill each other, and a few years down the road, the city rat Chumsa will lead his little resistance and rid the lake of those pesky little Strega and I will reign as the only god around. Pretty good, eh?"

"Yeah, except I already knew all that." Sivad grinned. "You told me. When you used my possessed sword it showed me your mind and all your secrets. And this whole time I've been sitting here and playing dumb, you never bothered to look behind you…"

Gukumatz reeled as the mud-bat creatures all charged him at once, melting and changing, to cake him into an inescapable prison of earth. Within seconds, Gukumatz, once more in the guise of Metatron, reached into the recesses of his clothing and launched the invisible projectiles between the eyes of each and every beastie. Without so much as a whisper they fell dead to the ground while the ferret very calmly restored himself to his former immaculate state, trying his best to furrow his brow at Sivad but unable to contain his laughter.

"That's it?" He lost his composure entirely. "After all that, that was the best you could come up with? You know, I'm not the least bit surprised we got rid of you. How someone could be so stupid? Pathetic!"

He fashioned another cigarette out of the thin air and squatted down by Sivad's seeping chest, callously blowing his smoke into the angry hare's face. "I almost feel bad about killing you, you know. And it's not because I feel sorry for you, even though you do deserve every ounce of pity. No, you might find it hard to believe, but the prospect of being the last of the elder gods is frightening. I will give you that. But" he laughed mockingly, "you didn't turn out so bad, and besides, with all those lovely rats to worship me, I just might make a better go of it as a single god than the whole pantheon ever did."

Sivad snorted in disgust at his hubris, but the ferret took no notice of it. Sivad took a close look at his former cohort and noticed a certain calm around him, a glassing over of the eyes. It was the look of one who thinks he's won the game before it's over. That might be his undoing yet, Sivad thought.

"Well." Metatron finished his cigarette and vanished it. "I have a few loose pieces I should kill off before I'm done. Be a good chap and die while I'm gone, won't you?"

Least-Rogonians and Marrow-Vinjians: Chapter Twenty-Seven

We float past a speck of land, small and uninhabited, and Spoolnicker finally speaks. "You don't suppose…"

"Octavia is dead," I slur, not looking at him.

"Well, obviously, but the whole situation…"

"Octavia is dead."

"It just seems a bit strange, is all."

I draw my sword out from its sheath, not for any real reason, and stare at it for a second. His Majesty himself gave this sword to me, and I've always treasured it. I pull the other sword from my rucksack. As we shift closer to another nothing mound of dirt, I grip His Majesty's sword like a dagger and plant it into the passing shore, and slide my new blade into the old sheath.

"Well," Spoolnicker starts again, "if it really was her…"

"It's not," Astairelike barks. "There was a funeral…"

"Well, she might have faked her death. I mean, humans do it all the time, and we're always trying to be like them."

"Don't be an ass."

"I'm just saying that if it does turn out to be her, I'll have a few choice words before we dispatch her, seeing as how everything's all her fault."

"You shouldn't speak of such things," I wheeze, squinting my eyes hard, hoping to drown them out.

"Think about it, Bloodford. Sure, we've always been all right, us Vinjians, but right around when she took over it all went to Hell. We had a chance, a damn good one, too, of wiping out the Least-Rogonians, but we didn't. And now, in addition to having to face the old geezers under the lake, we have to worry about them getting there first."

"I don't see how that would change anything," Astairelike muses. "Even without the heathens, the Strega would still have the Citadel."

"Well, of course, but if they weren't around to make trouble and stir all the mice up, we could just hold our own and wait for them to die off instead of mucking around in the middle of the lake while our home's been attacked twice in the last few days."

God, why won't they stop talking?

"What do you mean, 'stirring' all the mice up?" Astairelike puffs out his chest.

"Well, if the blighters weren't there with their slavery, all you lot wouldn't be pestering the government with your complaints instead of contributing like we do."

"And just what do you mean by that, Spoolnicker?"

"Well, for starters, all you mice ever do is complain. Say we treat you like 'Second Class Citizens'. Say rats always get preferential treatment. Say anything you like, but name one mouse who ever contributed to Vinjian society in the way that any of us have. When you get right down to it, a mouse is really just half of a rat, and with nature the way it is, your species is damned lucky to have survived this long without our natural predators having made quicker work of you than we."

Astairelike grips his shovel with a murderous rage in his eyes, but does nothing. I think he's too tired to fight him just now, but I don't feel at all sorry for him.

"So, anyway," Spoolnicker continues, "I'll be sure to bring that up with our impostor right before we kill her. Might do a body some good to vent the old spleen out."

"There's another raft coming!" Astairelike bellows foolishly.

A smaller, circular vessel is ambling toward us. There is a strange looking lizard, decked in a flowing purple robe, rowing it. I can tell from the way that it holds itself that it's carrying weapons.

"Main Scout!" it calls with a female's voice. Our guide looks startled to see her.

"Silvereye! What are doing here? You're supposed to be…"

"I know what I'm supposed to be doing. The situation's changed."

"Where are the others?"

"They got separated in the confusion."

"You should not be here, you must return before they regroup."

"Don't you get it? It's all over. Nothing they do can affect the outcome of all this."

"You are certain?"

"The rebels are a bigger concern, now."

"That is most fortunate. Now, go, before they suspect anything…"

She rows away. I honestly couldn't care less about what they were just talking about but I just have to ask. "Rebels?"

"Surviving members of the Wahid and some outcasts from other tribes. Your army killed most of them yesterday."

"Huh," Astairelike wonders.

"Told you we should have killed Chumsa," Spoolnicker coughs.

"You said no such thing," I moan.

It had taken little time for Marrow and his court to evacuate the dollhouse village and retreat into the city. It took a while longer before Astran and Tranah could drag their mother's limp body away from the eyes of their enemies. From their hiding place under a tree near Berlinger Station they watched as hundreds of noble rats scurried in anarchy, the whole of their society burning away and casting off into the early morning breeze. Tranah gazed with numb fascination as the stately dresses and stiff collars were clutched from burning fur and flung, trampled, onto the ground, as the modest, human-acting rodents resumed the natural nakedness of their breed. The ones whose clothing had not caught fire were dashing fervently in hopes of whatever could be hoped for; some were looting, others trying to impose order, some taking advantage of the chaos and violating unsuspecting females and children.

This dollhouse village, made up of some of the finest buildings on Earth, in effigy now only resembled Atlanta as it burned. The cardboard ghetto that had been flung together was the first thing to burn.

"Astran." Tranah grasped for words, but even if she had them she would not have been able to say what she really wanted to know. He put his arm across her shoulders and she hugged him tight, but felt displaced by the fabric that wrapped his body being pressed against hers.

"It's not our fault," he coughed, stroking her behind her ears. "It's them. They did this."

"Those poor fools. What did they do to bring this upon themselves, Astran?"

"Not the Vinjians, sis."

She looked up at him, the truth gnawing at her brain but not strong enough to break through. "So, what happens now?"

Astran sighed. His shoulders shrugged and his body lost every ounce of pride it could carry. "We'll go home, lick our wounds, Marrow will come back and rebuild this Kingdom stronger than ever, many of our tribe will die of their retribution, and neither of us will be any noticeably closer to taking the Citadel. In short, all this will have been for nothing."

"It just can't be…"

"The sad truth of it is, we probably would have been better off just leaving her there." He motioned toward their mother, who was now regaining consciousness. "You see that, Mom? See that fire over there? That's you, setting us back a couple hundred years over nothing!"

"Where…is…he?"

"My father? Probably a dozen miles away by now. And if he isn't plotting his revenge already, then thirty other minor players are out there looking to take his place. I hope you're happy with yourself."

"My plan would have worked." The One-Eyed Witch struggled to her feet. "All you had to do was get underground as quickly as possible and you would have gotten to the Strega before Marrow even thought about making his move, but no. You had to go gallivanting around on their side of the park and force me to intervene. If I hadn't had to come get you I wouldn't have had to force his paw. Now his rats are probably at the Strega's keep even as we speak."

"Don't you get it? You've just undone years of Cold War. Now every little nothing clan is going to come gunning for their spot, and who's going to get plopped in the middle of it? We are! Congratulations, Mom, you've just killed us all."

"You think you're so smart, Astran. 'Oh, my mother's a cheating whore, I'll just do the opposite of what she says so I'll always be right!' You think I don't know the way the world works as well as you do? We had the upper paw, we had the element of surprise, we could have won! We could have won." She sank back down. "And now…this has happened."

"Fine." Astran disregarded her and looked back at the rioting Vinjians. "It looks like things might be settling down. At the very least, anyone looking for a fight has already left. If we make for the water, we can probably snag some debris from that fence and propel it back across to our village. With any luck, we'll get back in time to prepare everyone for the upheaval."

"Astran, where's Octavia? Which way did she go?"

Her son stared at her, befuddled. "Mom, Aunt Tavy's dead."

"No. She must have run off, which way did she go?"

An arrow pierced the ground between the two of them; Astran jerked his head upward. A grinning squirrel with a black longbow was directly above them.

A flourish of the staff and a bullet-like shot of flame knocked the savage right off of his branch; his body hit the ground with a deafening thud a foot or so away from them.

"Forgot about the squirrels," Astran sighed. "Come on, we've got to get out of the park. With everything else that's about to happen we don't need to be getting shot at as well."

Ophiuchus dutifully rose, without any expression at all, and trudged toward the park's entrance. Astran picked at the dead squirrel for anything that might be useful but his search yielded nothing. He made to follow his mother, but Tranah was still there, riveted to her post. He hadn't noticed it, but she'd been stock still for several minutes.

"Tranah?"

"'Father'?" she repeated, too stunned to speak.

Syrinx stroked with increasing rapidity, but it brought her no closer to the shore; a steady eye on the barbecue pit that had once been Marrow-Vinjia was distracting enough to throw her off course. Even if she knew where Tranah and her family had gotten to, she had no plan as such. She hadn't even thought of a lie to account for her raft. After all, they'd been willing to overlook the mysterious appearance of her cloak only because the circumstances required constant movement. Now that quiet retreat seemed necessary it would have been imprudent to assume such a trusting neglect would come so naturally again.

It had been simple, really. The ever-mindful frogs had fished her out of the water again and loaned her their raft, but it was none of her friends' business if the frogs were involved or not.

Deciding that Berlinger Station was the most likely place for cover that Astran would seek, she finally turned away from the fire and set course for the outpost, thrashing her arms into the lake to make up for lost time.

As she pulled ashore, she was struck by the lack of scent; not a single rodent was nearby. She scanned the horizon, but, barring someone hiding among the highest treetops, there was no one to be found. That thought occurred to her as she craned her neck as high as she could. It was hard to see them in the darkness, but along the uppermost branches in all the nearest trees were dozens of squirrels, many with bows and arrows. Syrinx stood fixated, a thousand courses of action blurring together before she noticed the first wave of arrows flying down toward her. With a flapping motion she threw the bulk of her cloak in their path and the arrowheads had dug it into the ground instead of her, pinning her to the spot. She could hear the next wave being cued. She quickly dug out the most convenient blade and cut the constraints from her body, dashing naked for the tree line, only to lose that blade when a reflexive maneuver to deflect a projectile caused the tip intended for her to flash straight through the hilt, splintering it and rendering the whole weapon ineffective.

Dashing into the forest, she became conscious of a howling mass behind her. A small party of them was following her. She stopped and stood with her back against an old tree, thick enough to hide behind and quickly circle around to avoid capture. After listening for what seemed like forever she finally made her move, flinging herself around the right side and dashing past a small hill, staring at the uneven ground before her and willing herself to run faster. She paused by another tree just long enough to look back behind her before blindly pressing onward, unaware of the enemy to her front. She just passed a large rock jutting in front of the hill, concealing the entrance to a sort of underground bunker made by the rock formation, when she finally made eye contact. The enemy took aim with his bow and fired, just missing her shoulder. With all the grace of a dying antelope she flailed near to the ground and ducked behind the rock, hurtling into the bunker so quickly she reached the opposite wall before even realizing it was there.

She spun. The enemy was there at the entrance, his weapon

slung lazily in his hand. With no other choice, she charged full boar at the hunter and grabbed him by the skull, bashing the back of his head against the rock, spilling brain like yolk from an over-ripe egg. She crashed into the squirrel's body; she'd put her whole weight into the blow, and was unable to stop. Stumbling over the twitching corpse, she launched herself full tilt back the way she came, knowing full well that, since her opponent had come from that direction, there were likely to be more. She dodged fallen tree-limbs, sometimes crawling on all fours to make her way.

She bent low and followed her trail back toward an embankment by the lake, figuring it would be the last thing they'd expect her to do. The impressive horde was so tantalizingly close, but this was most irrelevant. She crept toward the edge, hoping to just stick her head over and scan for a safe hiding spot without giving away her position, but it wasn't to be. The earth gave way beneath her and she plunged into the lake, the loud crash almost deafening after a long time of hearing nothing but the heaving in her lungs.

Raising as triumphantly as seemed practical, she all but dived back down into the water as the nearest squirrel, mere feet away along the muddy lake shore, leveled his arrow at her and fired. Getting back to her feet, she tried once more to charge her opponent but the mud below the water's surface kept her from gaining any real speed. The enemy had taken aim again, and it was only the freak collision with a floating bit of debris knocking her off-balance that saved her. She serpentined onto dry land. With better footing underneath her, she got a good pace and bore down on her opponent, leveling him with a haymaker and trampling him into the mud.

Grabbing her unconscious combatant by the throat, she dragged him out of the water and back through the trees until her arms gave out from the strain. While the brute was still out of it, she filched his quiver and bludgeoned him with it repeatedly. She was in the process of fishing an arrow out to impale him through the heart, just to make sure, when the bulk of the search party caught up with her. It seemed that they would rather kill her with their bare paws after all that running she'd put them through. Clutching the bow she held like a baton she launched into the crowd with the intensity and bombast of a riot cop, the kneecaps and throats of the greater rodents seeping with blood. As quickly as it had begun, it was over, and Syrinx was the only one left standing.

She looked back to the treetops but not a soul was there to be seen. They'd spread out to other parts of the park. Syrinx ran back to her robe, but found to her disappointment that they'd stolen all her weapons, leaving only the map of the underground.

Even before we reach the isthmus that connects the frog's private land to the main shore, we can see Metatron waiting for us. He's standing, arms crossed, in front of what Main Scout tells us is the secret entrance to the underground. I vault over the edge of the raft, losing my wig in the process, and swim the whole two yards to shore. I have myself at full height and saber at eye-level before he can get a word in, but with a flat-pawed wave and the disinterested tone in his voice, his magic still works over me.

"She's over there." He points to the peninsula as I shrink back down, swearing under my breath at him. He hears me but says nothing.

I make my way into the dense grass but not far. The sound of her whimpering is enough to stop a cat, it is so pitiful. She's not much farther. As I come across her, at first I think I'd mistaken an egg on the verge of hatching for Her Majesty; she's removed all her clothing and curled into a ball, tilting slowly back and forth. I am, of course, filled with the same revulsion as when I first saw her three days ago, but I am curious. As fragile as her mind must have been in My Liege's care, this sudden shock of not only having her home destroyed but to have somehow found her way, naked, to a portion of the lake no Marrow-Vinjian noble has ever been to must surely be all too much. I wonder if she's broken completely or if this strange turn of events has jostled her back toward sanity?

"Blood…" she whispers.

"Yes, Your Highness?" I kneel instinctively, throwing my coat around her, even though it is soaking and surely colder than the air.

"Blood…ford…is that…you?" her eyes are unfocused and her breathing erratic.

"Yes, Your Grace," I shush her comfortingly, deciding it's worth the risk to touch her, steady her, the way I've done for other soldiers after particularly fierce battles in the past. She repeats my name a few times and starts muttering to herself. I clear my throat a few times but she doesn't respond. I wonder what to make of all this, until I once more appear beside myself.

"What are you going to do?" I ask.

"You're not real," I respond.

"Of course I'm real, I'm you."

"Get out of my head!"

"You can't hide from the situation forever, Bloodford. Don't you think it's a little odd that you talk to yourself for years, almost as long as you can remember, and it's only after a few highly suspicious appearances from a ferret that knows far too much, a magic show by a frog you've just met, who, we've also learned, consorts with spies and serves a master who's willing to blackmail you, that you question it? It's all highly convenient, if you think about it."

"This is all the Strega's doing."

"If I were you, I'd be more concerned about that weasel. He shows up completely unannounced whenever you don't know what to do, and he kills someone, a squirrel, even, from very far away, just by pointing at him!"

"But, that would mean…"

"If your life has taught you anything, it's that the only person you can trust is yourself. Look at you, you can't even do that now."

"Bloodford." Metatron's voice rings out, scaring Queen Octavia so badly she wrenches from my arms and hurtles off into the grass. "I'd stop talking to myself if I were you," he adds quietly.

"Your friends have arrived."

I feel as though time has gotten faster. I see Metatron standing, pillaresque, as my companions rush toward me, but there's a cry to my rear. Her Majesty is screaming, venomously, and looking as wild as any heathen Least-Rogonian. The very moment she grabs at my shirt collar, Astairelike launches himself at her. He takes her by the throat and brings both of us to our knees; the pain in my leg from the fall, which I've been ignoring thus far, blares throughout my entire body. The little mouse flings her aside and pounces on her, digging the heels of his muddy boots into her side, up and down, with so much force I'm surprised he doesn't crush her instantly.

Spoolnicker dashes to his side and backhands him with his bow, sending him a considerable distance. Before he can open his mouth to explain, the mouse attacks him. In the confusion I scoop Her Majesty up and pull her back the way she came. With tensions so high, I can't be too surprised when, after catching me out of the corners of their eyes, they pause to turn on me. I take my scabbard off my belt and bat them with it, pushing Her Majesty along as they continue to advance. Finally, I give her one great kick and fling my weapon wildly, pushing them back, but the moment I take my eyes off of Her Grace Spoolnicker gets by and seizes her. With one arm around her throat, he fumbles with his quiver until he grabs hold of his final arrow, which he clutches like a dagger against her throat. I'm certain he means to simply kill her here, but both my and Astairelike's cries stop him.

"Why?" he asks. "Why the hell are you two so crazy all of a sudden?"

He never gets his answer. As "sudden" leaves his lips a fine tipped arrow hits him in the center of the ear and comes out neatly on the other side. Astairelike and I turn toward the squirrels in the nearest tree, but Astairelike is caught in the chest before either of us can do anything. I just barely deflect an arrow with my sword, but Metatron, dashing as fiercely as he did into our last battle, scoops me up in his arms as I, dazed, grab Her Grace by the scruff. As he pulls us into the water, I see something large and circular rising up toward us. It hits us, and everything disappears…

Shortly after the deaths of Spoolnicker and Astairelike, the Maharajah returned to the Isthmus. Main Scout, who had watched the massacre unfold with minimal interest, was struck with a sudden headache; in his stupor, he could swear he heard the ferret's voice, but when his headache cleared he looked down and saw the Maharajah sprawled dead before him, and his face was covered with blood. Before he could so much as proclaim his innocence, the other frogs had knocked him out and imprisoned him. Days later, after a mock trial, they tied heavy weights to each of his limbs and carted him out to a trash can filed with paper. The set the contents ablaze and hurled him in. He was dead before the first layer of paper had burned...

Having decided that, ironically, Marrow-Vinjia would be a safer place to hide, Syrinx slipped past the many faces of the night and well into the charred wreckage of the once great compound, her purple-clad form going unnoticed against the multi-hued embers and smoking black skeletons. Moving into the center of town, she noticed a structure that looked far less burnt than the rest of them—a replica of what the humans called 10 Downing Street.

"Funny," she thought. "I always wanted to meet the big cheese."

With no guards around and the sole remaining citizen concerning himself with putting the finishing touches on the female he'd raped, it was a simple matter to walk proud and erect through the front door. It was clear from the get-go that the building was completely abandoned, but since she was there, she supposed it wouldn't hurt to have a look around and plan her next move.

Just at the top to the staircase there was a coat of arms which had not originally belonged to Marrow's family, or any other rat, tacked onto the wall. Feeling a little childish, she went to knock it off the wall, but found that it was actually a switch, which opened a secret passage. Following it, she came out from behind a portrait in the hallway beside the Royal Bedchambers. Replacing the portrait, she was shocked to find the unpleasant face of Ophiuchus staring back at her. Marrow certainly must have been crazy if he kept something like that around; Syrinx didn't even understand how Tranah and Astran could stand looking at her in person.

She pushed his door open and marveled at the luxury the old pervert lived in. She bee-lined for his enormous bed, where he had many important looking papers spread out. Most had letterheads on them and appeared to be boring, state-related items that were of no real use to her unless she wanted to build a fire. Others, larger and more impressive looking, included detailed maps of the underground, Berlinger Station and someplace called "Cold Harbor Lane", which, near as she could tell, was in the city somewhere. The only two that really caught her attention were a pair of letters, right by his pillows. The first was crackling and yellowed with age:

My love,
Fate may have been unkind to both of us,
But I know now that our life together can never be.
You really do love my sister, deep down, I think,
And I want the boy to live somewhere where
He won't be thought of as a half-breed.
I know that no-one can ever know the truth,
But your people talk, and they will know that
Their Beloved Queen bore no children of her own.
I will always love you,
Ophiuchus

"Huh," she said to herself, "the two warlords had a baby together. Imagine that. Wait a minute…" She snatched up the other letter:

Father,
I must not visit with you anymore.
I don't give a damn about Mother or what the others
Will think, but it just cannot work.
Tranah (Mother's other child) is getting older
And needs a big brother to look after her.
I always dreamed that one day I'd be a
Permanent member of the Vinjian Court
But for now, my life as "Astran" of
The Least-Rogonians is the only life I
Can afford.
Humbly,
Marrow II, Prince

"Holy shit!"

✳   ✳   ✳

Having finally emerged from their hiding place near where the fall had dropped them, the Dormice made their way toward Marrow-Vinjia. Clopin's protests that they should find their masters fell on deaf ears; Barnabas, firmly in control, insisted they make for the hated enemy and freedom. Clopin begged them, cajoled them; it simply couldn't be that Vinjia's mice were free, it went against the order of things, they would never have what the rats had. Trismegistus slapped him repeatedly until he stopped talking, and went along with the both of them.

"Merciful Pul," Barnabas exclaimed at the ashen wreckage.

"What do you suppose happened?" Trismegistus coughed.

"Our dreams of freedom just went up in smoke," Clopin barked sarcastically.

"Enough of that, now," the eldest croaked, "I've been waiting my whole life for this chance and we're not going to miss it because of a little fire."

"You don't suppose Master Astran did that, do you?" the youngest replied. "You'd look awfully foolish trying to get away with him standing right there."

"Master Astran would be dead by now, Clopin."

They barged forward, taking a cursory glance and decided that the least damaged building would be as good a place as any to seek shelter and food. If anyone important was there, it was possible they could gain acceptance into this strange new society–to defect, to use the term Trismegistus was sometimes fond of using. More so than the old mouse, Trismegistus had put thought into his freedom. The old rodent had wanted it simply as a thing, to not have a master over him, controlling his life, dictating the smallest details of his day, controlling his food and his schedule. Trismegistus wanted it more as a chance to be equal, to carve out a sizable chunk of the world for himself, to be someone important. As the nearness of his dream washed over him, he allowed his fancy to fly, supposing all sorts of wild ideas, even entertaining the notion of returning to the Least-Rogonians' land and freeing other mice like himself.

Then, as they headed for the entrance to the least damaged building in the village, Syrinx Silvereye ran smack into them coming out of it, bringing the crushing reality back down upon their heads. Well, the heads of the two oldest. Clopin was beside himself with happiness.

"Mistress Syrinx!"

"Huh? Oh, it's you three." She worked her way back onto her feet. "Where's your master?"

"We do not know." Barnabas walled in his tears.

"Well, we need to find him." Syrinx glanced at the rolled up letter in her hands and grinned evilly. "I've just realized he owes me a great deal of money."

"Mistress Tranah will be elated to see you," Clopin effused.

"Who? Oh, right, the female… Yes, we should probably do that. Find them, I mean."

"Perhaps they have returned to our home," Trismegistus choked.

"You're probably right. Hmm." she pulled out her map and glared at it. "If we cut straight across here, from Berlinger Station, we can travel diagonally to the city-side of the lake and come back above ground in Least-Rogonian territory. Should only take a few hours. With any luck we'll beat them there."

"Mistress…still has that map?" Barnabas stared, cockeyed.

"Yes," Syrinx replied dismissively. "About the only thing, really. Those gods-damned squirrels stole all my weapons…" She was talking more to herself than to him, which is why she failed to notice the queer look of purpose in Barnabas' eyes, or the motion he made to Trismegistus. As soon as Syrinx turned her back to lead them to Berlinger Station, Barnabas plucked up a board from another wrecked building and caught her square at the top of the neck. Trismegistus snatched her while she was off-balance and pinned her down, while Barnabas hammered away at her skull until only the leaking pus of her brain was left attached to her spine. Clopin shrunk back in horror.

"Now," Trismegistus screamed, prying the map from her cold, dead hands, "the rat's treasure will be ours!"

"You sick fool," shouted Clopin. "Don't you understand? There was no treasure. Lafitte was only trying to trick Master Astran!"

"Either way." Barnabas took charge. "The underground is ours to see, now. We can go anywhere. We are free!"

Astran led his dejected mother toward the restaurant that Bloodford had visited the night they encountered Chumsa. Tranah trailed a small distance behind them, hoping that perhaps Syrinx would spot her and come to join them, but this was not to be. They tucked into the alley and took shelter in the trash can.

"I say we rest here until daybreak," Astran yawned. "I don't foresee anyone else coming to bother us for another couple of hours and it's a long walk back to our side of the lake." The thought of what he'd just said tickled him privately, when he thought of how he secretly placed a spell on their party to make them all faster when they'd first set out, the night that he and Tranah and the Menudos first met Bathin. It seemed appropriate then, but now, with all the other grand and illustrious magicks he'd employed, it seemed foolish to pull that one again. Astran looked further down, and realized just how much energy he'd put into his spells when he didn't even approve of such things. It was funny how situations could temporarily change your priorities, he supposed.

The three of them got comfortable, and as Astran shed his princely robes he figured it couldn't hurt to feel philosophical just then. The family had just taken a huge gamble and lost, and it wasn't even certain that by the time they got home there would be a home to go to. Might as well try to make the best of it, he figured.

Tranah was not so optimistic. Everything she'd ever known was now either a lie or no longer true. She hated her brother and mother violently, cursing them for allowing her to get swept up in this business. She would never let go of her anger and sense of betrayal, she thought, and while it never appeared to her in words, it was right then and there that she decided that if ever came a day when she could betray them in the same fashion, she would do it.

A stone flew off the ground from seven inches away, hitting the side of the trash can. They all ran out, expecting the worst and finding it: in the early morning sunlight, his shadow cast larger than life, was Marrow, his eyes bulging and pale with insane rage, his smallish frame swelling to twice the build of normal, his posture twisted and his claws bared. He heaved and snorted like a bull staring down a pack of wolves, slashing away at his collar and sleeves, seeming more like an animal than at any other time in his existence.

"You..." He glared at the One-Eyed Witch.

Marrow-Vinjians, Chapter Twenty-Eight: The Beginning Of The End

"I'm not going to lie to you, Bloodford," Metatron says, as my eyes continue to adjust to this new place, wherever it might be. "I've taken a bit of a shine to you. Can't quite say why, but now it seems that I can't be neutral in this conflict anymore."

"Neutral?" I spit sarcastically.

"Yes, I had hopes that your enemies would be willing to play fairly, like you, but unlike you they have no sense of honor."

I finally get a hold of my senses. We're no longer in the park, we're in the alley I fought Chumsa's sewer rats in. After pausing to ensure My Queen will be fine by herself for a second, I have a look around and spy My Liege by the trash can from the other night. Something's not right here.

"Metatron, where exactly do you fit into all this?" I whisper without looking at him.

"Call me an angel, if you like." Something in his voice tells me he's not joking.

"Why have you brought me here?"

"That's why…"

Before I can ask, My Liege cries, "You!" and storms into the trash can, only to be thrown back out by two nude rats of Least-Rogonian heritage! Without another thought I unsheathe my blade and run for him…only to feel a great magnet dragging me back through the air, past Metatron and back into the haze, and through a great tunnel of darkness until I at last hit a hard surface and feel the cold sting of talons wrapping around me. Oh no.

"You know," the gasping voice of Sivad rings, "I really thought you could have taken the Strega out, I really did. Then he had to get involved."

He sets me down and I wheel about to face him. He's back in the form of a hawk-clawed hare, but withered and clutching at the sucking wound in his abdomen where Metatron had rammed my sword through him. His dripping onyx-colored blood pulses erratically and burns the dirt beneath him like acid.

"What's going on?"

"The Strega never attacked you. Well, they did, but they only did it because they weren't themselves just then, you know?"

Somehow, I just know the ferret is behind this. "Who is he?"

"He's a Valkyrie of sorts, an Angel of Death who collects heroes. He thought if he forced the paw of both sides you and the one called Astran would kill each other and he could get both of you at once. I know that now…"

I sink to my knees. This is all so much to take in at once. "Sivad, tell me everything…"

"I was only supposed to play the 'mysterious heathen god' bit to make sure you had weapons that could take the Strega out, but then he got to Reuel and everything just went all to Hell. I lost my mind completely…"

"So." I pause, my head spinning, trying to reconcile everything I know with what he's just told me. "What of the frogs? Where do they fit?"

"Nowhere. Not that I know of."

"So, I'm not really possessed?" I chirp weakly, but hopefully.

"Probably not, but does it really matter? In a very short while we're both going to die." He sits cross-legged, and summons an orb the size of a baseball between us. "It was after he buried his sword in my belly that I truly saw his plan. He doesn't realize, but any weapon from my graveyard is a part of me, and anyone who wields them shares their thoughts with me. That's how I've been able to keep abreast with the surface world all these years. I hate to tell you this, but you're not the first one to bring one back with you. When he raised it against me, I could see into his mind, and the whole perverted scheme fell right into my lap. I'm going to die today, I know that now, but I used the sword to call you back because I can't let him win. He doesn't see that if you two kill each other as he wants, the mortals will be plunged into chaos."

"But why now?" I ask dejectedly. "Why couldn't you have brought me back to you a few hours ago, when my friends were still alive?"

"I'm afraid I only just now regained consciousness," he admits. "But that doesn't matter anymore. You need to know…"

He conjures the image of My Liege fighting those naked vermin in the alley. The first one, a female, claws at him viciously, her every action framed with rage, her body vibrating even as it soars back and forth across the plain of battle. The second, a male with staff, bats at him from the side, but his posture is one of conflict. He looks as if he'll only attack defensively, but he'll do nothing to stop the female. He looks familiar…

My Liege gets under her and sinks his teeth into her leg;

she undulates in pain, howling! I get a closer look at her; it's the One-Eyed Witch herself... I wish I could say that surprises me, but I've given up that luxury. But that other rat... I know I've seen him somewhere before. Ophiuchus has her jaws around His Majesty's neck and her left foot digging into his side. He jabs repeated in her stomach but she refuses to let go. Finally he gets his legs under him and jumps, forcing her off-balance long enough to escape her grip. He lands near the male, who swings at him but misses, only to have the female attack from behind before my king can respond.

A second female, carting an ax, emerges from the trash can and darts for My Liege, but the One-Eyed Witch attacks her with a spell that destroys her weapon and hurtles her to the ground. It seems that that's whetted her appetite, for she finally uses her powers to fasten His Majesty to the ground. In slow disbelief, I watch as she advances, sadistic and mad, grabbing him by his nostrils and exposing his neck. I scream at the vision to no avail as she sinks her teeth into his neck and severs his main artery.

I fall to my knees, hitting my injury far too hard, and try to force myself to look away. I succeed, but not before, I realize to my horror that the male who stood and witnessed Marrow I enter eternity is his own son, Marrow II...

Least-Rogonians, Chapter Twenty-Nine: Marrow-Astran I, Ruler Of Greater Vinjia

It was all over. Marrow was dying in Ophiuchus' arms and the weight of what she'd done was tumbling over her. He looked in her eyes, and though she had hated him for so long, the way he gazed at her, it was as if it was the first time that they had met, when she'd snuck into Octave-Vinjia with the sole purpose of stealing him away. He'd been so beautiful then.

He, strength failing rapidly, stroked her whiskers lovingly as the soul eked out of his body. "Ophiuchus, my son… Vinjia needs a king…" They were the last words he ever uttered on Earth.

The One-Eyed Witch sobbed with his body in her arms; Astran squatted plaintively, a hundred different visions of what might come to pass attacking him simultaneously, filling him with a desperate urge to drink; and Tranah, poor thing, was about to break from the confusion of seeing her mother and brother going soft over the death of their most hated enemy.

"Ophiuchus…" Octavia finally moved toward them, making

her presence known. Seeing her, her sister automatically recoiled. The feeling of her deranged sibling attempting to violate her for the entertainment of the rat she once loved was fresh in her mind, but the expression on Octavia's face was much different now. Furtively, Ophiuchus set Marrow's body down and took her sister by the arm, leading her to her family. Tranah had never seen her, but the look of confusion and loss of innocence triggered such compatriot sympathy in Tranah that she damn near throttled Octavia embracing her. The two of them were of no good to anybody then, but to each other, sister strangers in a well of emotions that was too deep for them.

"What happens now?" Ophiuchus mused.

"You heard him." Astran sighed, the path becoming clear. "Vinjia needs a king."

"But you're a Least-Rogonian," Tranah shouted angrily, no longer able to contain her feelings of treachery toward everyone around her. "You can't be both!"

"But I am." He grimaced. "And so..." He rolled his eyes at what he was about to say, even though it was the best solution for all involved. "Prince Marrow II will return and tell all of his subjects that the Least-Rogonians have been conquered, and Astran will tell the reverse to our tribe; the two shall unite, and somewhere along the line it will work itself out."

"If it doesn't lead to civil war," said Octavia, shocking everyone. "The army will never support you as king if they find out your Least-Rogonian heritage; not so long as Lord Bloodford still has their loyalty."

"Who's he?" Astran asked, before remembering that he knew who Bloodford was.

"He was Marrow's favorite, and our greatest hero. If he learns that your mother killed him he'll kill her, then you. He'd have no honor, otherwise…"

"Then we have to convince him," Ophiuchus roared.

"No," said the ferret, "you have to kill him!"

The family turned, Astran and Tranah seeing the stranger Bathin, Ophiuchus the prophet Rommel, Octavia a monstrous vision like a hangman's tree.

"Why should we listen to you?" Ophiuchus spat. "You've been nothing but trouble!"

"I should say the same thing about you lot," he replied furiously, "but if you want this fragile peace you've suggested to survive you'll need my help!"

"I thought you said you were only interested in both sides fighting fairly…" Astran said.

"Situations change, or haven't you been here the last few minutes?"

Ophiuchus turned to her son and silently mouthed, "You know him?"

"You really think having him kill Marrow-Vinjia's greatest hero the same day its king dies will end all the fighting?" snapped Octavia, gaining more ground with reality by the second.

The ferret sighed in defeat. "You really think he'll listen to you?"

Astran stood, his new role in life fitting him better than he would have imagined. "What harm can it do?"

"Fine," the ferret sighed once more, finally breaking character and creating a portal behind himself. "I'll take you to him…"

"You're not who you say you are, are you?" a shocked Astran accused.

"Is anyone?" was all the ferret had in his defense.

Marrow-Vinjians, Final Chapter:
That Place Where The Wave Finally
Broke, And Rolled Back

||||||||||||||||||||||||||||||||||||||||||||||||||||||||||||||||||||||||||||||||||||||||||||||||||||||||||||||||||||||||||||||||||||||

I wish I could pretend I don't understand. I don't know why the Phantom Prince has allied himself with our enemies, but it doesn't matter. He has allowed the death of my king. As a soldier, I must avenge King Marrow I, but as a Marrow-Vinjian I cannot rise against his son, his rightful heir and my new Liege. It all becomes clear to me what I must do to preserve my honor and the memory of the old ruler: I must challenge my king to battle me to the death. And lose.

"Was it always going to end this way?" I put to the heathen god.

"If it's any consolation, after Astran kills you the ferret will kill me."

"Is there an afterlife?" I ask, foolishly. There must be one if there are Angels of Death.

"I hope not. Any last words?"

I think about that for a second, then laugh as I realize the only appropriate choice, "All I ever wanted was to not exist. I think I've achieved that now…"

At last, the portal opens and My Liege, followed by Metatron, emerges into the Land of the Blind. I marvel at how much he reminds me of his father just now. Metatron, happy that he's finally managed to throw us together, leans smugly against the wall, his arms crossed. My Liege carries himself toward me, worn but humble, cautiously sizing me up even as he extends his paw in friendship.

"Bloodford," he chimes, his tone peaceful. I don't reply, but raise my sword threateningly. He looks uneasy, but he spies the orb in Sivad's claws and quickly puts it all together. "It doesn't have to be this way."

"Your Majesty," I begin, "for almost two-hundred years my family has given thirty-seven members to our people's army, and twenty of them are considered to be its greatest heroes. Every moment of every day since my great-grandfather earned his place in history on the battlefield of Warren's Burrow, our only dream has been to one day be the general who leads the final charge against our enemies, the Least-Rogonians. It's been all we've ever wanted; all our lives ever had to justify themselves. Now, what are we repaid with? I, the last of my line, am forced to watch as the leader of the opposing tribe strikes the life's breath out of my king in alley with no spectators or allies to come to his aid, and now the son of that murderess is, by all rights of lineage and law, the rightful successor.

"What we are repaid with is the sight of a king whose allegiance is not to our family obsession, but to an era of unification, and peace, and other such things which no true warrior can ever accept, no matter how badly his conscience eats at him over them. I am but one of a handful of rats who knows your secret, Your Highness.

Very soon, everyone will know, and there will be confusion and outrage, but in the end all who truly give it thought will see that it is the only way, and everything you and your family spoke of will come true, even if it takes a hundred years.

"But where will that leave me? I who spent my adult life serving the rat you've just murdered, I must now, by law, lay down my sword and follow your rule. As a citizen of Marrow-Vinjia, I cannot oppose you. As a warrior, as a member of my family, and as someone who served Marrow with unquestioning loyalty even as the true horror of what he had become was laid bare, I cannot allow you to take control.

"As a rodent of honor I can neither oppose you nor support you. That leaves me with only one choice…"

I turn to the treacherous ferret. "In playing your game you've upended the entire social order, for no reason but the chance to gloat to yourself. I can only hope that your hubris should bring about your own death, someday. I hate you. God only knows just how much I hate you."

"It doesn't have to be this way!" Marrow II repeats.

"Yes it does," I mouth silently, unleashing my weapon and charging him. He throws up a mystical shield but the enchanted fire within my sword cuts through it and it's only his staff which saves him from being impaled. He pushes me back, his power propelling me much farther than it should, and he raises his weapon offensively. Knowing all that will happen next, I dutifully fling my blade at him like a javelin, which he deflects and fires a neutralizing blast of flame, which I, with my arms spread-eagled, accept readily.

The pain only lasts a second, and I have left the world of the living.

My soul lingers while I wait for Metatron to lead me into the next world, but he's frozen in anger, enraged that his wishes have been denied. While he's rooted, Sivad winks at me, grows to many times his size and transforms into what humans call a manticore, a lion with the face of a man, and poisonous barbs in the tail. He lets out a mighty roar and snaps his teeth, swallowing Metatron in a single gulp. Naturally, the Angel of Death fights back, creating from within the beast a deathly brown glow, which expands to fill the entire creature. The manticore fights back, creating its own glow of vermilion and the two shades swirl and battle each other all over his body. My Liege instinctively hurls himself back into the portal to the surface just as the colors cancel each other out and the monster explodes, with a force that I know intrinsically destroyed them both, winging them off to wherever it is gods go when they die.

My soul remains, unheralded.

As I become one with eternity, I can see what shall come. My Liege will unite both kingdoms and there will be a tenuous peace for twenty years. Thereafter, Chumsa, with the help of a dormouse named Barnabus leading an army of disenfranchised rodents, will finally seize the Citadel. The last remaining Strega, overjoyed at the prospect of its care being entrusted to a blood relation, will willingly surrender, and finally die. With the power of Hurucan at his disposal, Chumsa's rule will be unquestioned in the underground, and will, in very short order, come to threaten the rule of Marrow II, and war will loom on the horizon once more.

Perhaps if I had lived, I might have been able to stop the fall of Vinjia. But, without my death, it would not have survived at all, and now it will limp on with a half-life. I suddenly feel very cold, my sacrifice has solved nothing. I don't want to watch my life's work be destroyed. I don't want to know that the ferrets will be there, to play both sides against each other…

The End